OTHER BOOKS BY AMY M. READE

Secrets of Hallstead House

The Ghosts of Peppernell Manor

House of the Hanging Jade

The Juniper Junction Holiday Mystery Series

The Worst Noel

Dead, White, and Blue (coming soon!)

The Malice Series

The House on Candlewick Lane

Highland Peril

Murder in Thistlecr

D1197511

PRAISE FOR AMY M. READE

Secrets of Hallstead House: "Thank you, Amy, for taking me to a new place and allowing me to imagine." From Phyllis H. Moore, reviewer

The Ghosts of Peppernell Manor: "If you're a fan of ... novels by Phyllis A. Whitney, Victoria Holt, and Barbara Michaels, you're going to love *The Ghosts of Peppernell Manor* by Amy M. Reade." From Jane Reads.

House of the Hanging Jade: "House of the Hanging Jade is a suspenseful tale of murder and obsession, all taking place against a beautiful Hawaiian backdrop. Lush descriptions of both the scenery and the food prepared by the protagonist leave you wanting more." From The Book's the Thing

House of the Hanging Jade: "I definitely see more Reade books in my future." From Back Porchervations.

The House on Candlewick Lane: "As in most gothic novels, the actual house on Candlewick Lane is creepy and filled with dark passages and rooms. You feel the evil emanate from the structure and from the people who live there ... I loved the rich descriptions of Edinburgh. You definitely feel like you are walking the streets next to Greer, searching for Ellie. You can feel the rain and the cold, and a couple times, I swear I could smell the scents of the local cuisine." From Colleen Chesebro, reviewer

Highland Peril: "This is escapism at its best, as it is a compelling mystery that whisks readers away to a land as beautiful as it is rich with intrigue." From Cynthia Chow, Kings River Life

Murder in Thistlecross: "Amy Reade's series has a touch of gothic suspense, always fun, and this particular entry has the extra added attraction of the old Clue board game (later a movie that was equally delightful) wherein the various suspects move around the castle and the sleuth has to figure out who killed who, how and where." From Buried Under Books

TRUDY'S DIARY

A LIBRARIES OF THE WORLD MYSTERY: BOOK ONE

AMY M. READE

PAU HANA PUBLISHING

Pau Hana Publishing

Print ISBN: 978-1-7326907-2-1

Ebook ISBN: 978-1-7326907-3-8

Printed in the United States of America

For Rich Thompson, who always knew whodunit

ACKNOWLEDGMENTS

This book has been a long time in the making, and there are several people who were instrumental in helping me bring it to publication. As always, I'd like to thank my husband, John, who is my first reader.

My editor, Jeni Chappelle, also deserves a big thank-you for her advice and recommendations, all of which were invaluable in making this a much better book.

I would also like to thank the DiMarco Family of Ocean City, New Jersey, for their support of the Ocean City High School Drama Club. The DiMarcos won the opportunity to name a character in one of my upcoming novels. Gabriella DiMarco chose the names Gertrude ("Trudy") and Grover, both of whom have prominent roles in the book.

Finally, I owe a debt of gratitude to Amanda Zimmerman, a Rare Book librarian at the Library of Congress in Washington, DC. Amanda was very helpful in my research into the library's dime novel collection.

PROLOGUE

$\mathcal{D}$aisy Carruthers left New York City because of a murder investigation.

When her boyfriend, Dean Snyder, fell from their ninth-floor balcony to the deserted Brooklyn sidewalk below late one evening the previous year, it was Daisy who had been named the prime suspect in his death. It was Daisy who spent the better part of a year trying to clear her name, trying to get people to stop thinking of her as a ruthless criminal, trying to get everyone to understand that Dean's tragic fall had been accidental.

Trying, most of all, to grieve the loss of someone she had loved so completely.

As long as she was a suspect, she couldn't move away from the city, couldn't start fresh. She couldn't bear the thought that she might be remembered as a black widow of sorts, killing her mate so she could continue life unencumbered by a weighty relationship.

But the day came when a witness stepped forward to confirm what Daisy had been saying all along: that Dean had been alone on the balcony that night and that he had fallen over the railing trying to catch a cocktail napkin which had blown out of his hand. The witness had not realized for many months that there was an investigation surrounding Dean's death because it had so obviously been an accident.

The witness's story confirmed what Daisy had been saying all along.

Dean's death was finally ruled an accident, and Daisy was no longer a suspect.

By then, she was ready to leave the city that had been so cruel to her. She wanted to start fresh in a city she had never visited with Dean.

So she packed her bags and moved to Washington, DC.

CHAPTER 1

ONE YEAR LATER

*D*aisy stood pouring herself a much-needed cup of coffee in the galley kitchen of the Global Human Rights Journal offices. Rain from her jacket dripped onto the linoleum floor.

Jude Laughton, the senior editor, looked up from the table where she was reading the headlines on a discarded newspaper and frowned. "You're getting water all over the floor. Are you going to wipe it up?"

Though Daisy had worked for the journal in Washington, DC, for almost a year, Jude was still as cold as she had been the day Daisy interviewed with her.

"Of course I am. Just give me a minute."

"Why don't you carry an umbrella?" Jude asked.

"Because I keep forgetting to put one in my tote bag," Daisy answered, a hint of annoyance creeping into her tone.

"It's not that hard to remember. I keep one in my briefcase all the time." Daisy rolled her eyes and walked to the paper towel dispenser on the wall. She pressed the lever several times, tearing off a long sheet of the barely-absorbent paper toweling, then wadded it up and placed it on the water that had fallen from her coat. Jude's lips curled in a tight grimace, but she didn't say anything.

Daisy threw away the paper and left the kitchen without another glance at Jude. She walked into the small conference room between her office and Jude's office and took several manila folders out of her tote bag, spreading them on the table in a circular pattern. Jude walked by, steam curling from the mug of coffee she carried. "What are you doing?" she asked. Nothing escaped Jude's curiosity about Daisy and her assignments.

"Just organizing my work. My desk isn't big enough," Daisy answered with a sly peek at Jude. She started moving folders around, standing back with her arms crossed. She knew it irritated Jude that the Editor-in-Chief, Mark John Friole, had given her so many assignments, and laying everything out for Jude to see gave her a jolt of devilish glee. Jude, though higher in the pecking order at Global Human Rights Journal, wasn't as good a researcher as Daisy and she didn't hide her jealousy well. But it was only natural that Daisy, as a Master's-level anthropologist, should be the better researcher--if she weren't, it would just be embarrassing.

Daisy pulled out her laptop and sat down to wait for it to boot up.

"I have a meeting in this room today, so you won't be able to keep your stuff in here," Jude said.

"I'm not planning to. As soon as I get these folders organized, I'll work in my office." Daisy was pretty sure Jude didn't have a meeting later.

Jude was just turning away to go back to her office when Mark John came into the conference room.

"Update me, please. What are you working on?"

Jude stood up a little straighter and gave him a big smile. "I've made significant progress on the clean water story," she said brightly, batting her eyelashes.

"Good," Mark John said, nodding. "Daisy?"

"I'll be ready to submit my current story today, then I'll dig more into the story about childbirth centers."

"I have an idea I'd like to run by you, Daisy, if you would please hand off the childbirth center story to Jude."

"Sure," Daisy answered, suppressing a slight grin at Jude's scowl. "Do you want to talk about it now?"

"Yes. In my office, please." Mark John left.

"Don't be long in Mark John's office," Jude said. "I need to talk to him about something."

Daisy gathered up her notebook and sharpened pencils and left the room without another glance at Jude.

Mark John wasn't in his office when Daisy knocked on his door, which was partially ajar. "Mark John?" she asked, poking her head into the room. There was no answer. She went inside and sat down in one of the chairs in front of his desk. She idly flipped through her notebook, then cracked her neck and checked her watch. When five minutes had passed and Mark John still hadn't appeared, Daisy stood up and wandered around his office, picking up and setting down various mementos from his travels. She went to the window behind his desk and looked down onto the ground far below, at the people scurrying about with their umbrellas up, hiding their faces. She felt another surge of annoyance that she had forgotten her own umbrella that morning. As she turned away from the window, a photo of Mark John and his wife, Fiona, caught her eye. She picked up the photo and gazed at it for several moments, focusing on Fiona's wide smile. In her time at Global Human Rights, Daisy had only heard Mark John mention his wife's name a few times. Daisy wondered what she was like. She set the photo back in its spot and sat down to wait.

Mark John came into the office a minute later.

"Damn secretary can't do anything without asking me twenty questions about it," he said, settling into his chair.

Daisy didn't reply.

"This won't take long," he said. "I've been thinking--we should do a feature about women's roles in this country. You know, how they've changed since the time when the United States was an agrarian society."

"Sounds interesting, but that's going to take up more space than just one article."

"I know. I'm thinking we'll do it in three parts."

"All right."

Mark John sighed. "You're probably going to have to tell Jude about this, but take your time telling her. The last thing I need right now is listening to her complain about why I gave you the assignment instead of her."

Daisy grinned. "I'll keep it quiet as long as I can." She looked at her watch and chuckled. "I give it about two minutes. Maybe three."

Mark John ran his hand over his forehead and squeezed his eyes closed for a long moment. "Well, I don't feel like dealing with it today. I have a headache."

"If you prefer, we can talk about particulars of the assignment later," Daisy said. "In the meantime I'll get started on some preliminary research."

"Sounds good." Mark John looked around his office, puffed out his cheeks, and let out a sigh.

"You okay?" Daisy asked.

"Yeah," he said, rubbing his face with both hands. "There was a burglary in my neighborhood last night. A house just across the street and a couple doors down from us. A bit unnerving, you know?"

"I'm sure it is," Daisy replied. "That's scary. Was anyone hurt?"

"Not that I know of."

"Do you have an alarm system?"

"Yes, but so did the people whose house got hit. They had left a window open downstairs."

"Kind of defeats the purpose of having an alarm," Daisy said.

"Yeah," Mark John said curtly. He shook his head in disgust. Daisy knew the conversation was over and she left the office. She walked by Jude's office on the way to her own.

Jude smirked and pushed her chair back. "I'll go see him now. You were longer than I expected."

"He wasn't in his office so I had to wait for him," Daisy said. "He has a bad headache," she warned.

"I just want to ask him a couple quick questions. I won't bother him," Jude said.

Daisy returned to the conference room and sat down.

CHAPTER 2

*I*ndeed, it wasn't long before Jude came out of Mark John's office. She walked into the kitchen, where Daisy was pouring a second cup of coffee. Jude looked flushed-- her cheeks were red and her lips looked a bit puffy. Her hair was just the tiniest bit out of place.

"Is everything okay, Jude?" Daisy asked.

"What?" Jude looked distracted. "Oh. Yes. I'm fine. Mark John told me about your new assignment."

So much for not wanting her to know about it right away.

Daisy watched as Jude took a bottle of mineral water from the refrigerator, unscrewed the cap, and took a long drink of it. She leaned against the counter when she was done, looking into the glass bottle as if it held some fascinating secret.

Jude, tall, slim, and well-proportioned, typically wore a uniform of a dark pencil skirt, expensive white blouse, an elegant yet understated necklace, pumps with two-and-a-half inch heels, and tortoiseshell glasses. She wore her glossy chestnut hair either down in a long bob or up in a chignon. She was gorgeous. Daisy, on the other hand, was tall in a lanky way, wore her hair in a loose ponytail, preferred loafers to pumps so she wouldn't tower over everyone, and liked to wear wide-leg linen pants and peasant blouses. And whereas Jude's glasses gave her a sexy, alluring look, Daisy knew that if she didn't wear contacts, she would end up looking scholarly and geeky in those same glasses.

Daisy cocked her head and gave Jude one last glance. Jude wasn't paying any attention to her. Daisy, who normally saw a cold, aloof woman whenever she looked at the senior editor, tried to look at her as others might see her. And what she saw surprised her--this time she saw an elegant woman who exuded professionalism as well as, perhaps, a hint of vulnerability in the set of her mouth.

She wondered which Jude Mark John saw when he looked at her.

CHAPTER 3

*N*ot long after Daisy had moved into her Dupont Circle apartment in Washington, she joined a local oenophiles' club for two reasons: first, she loved wine; and second, she thought it would be a great way to meet people. Indeed, she had met her two best friends in that group.

Grover Tavistock owned a catering business, DC Haute Cuisine, and business was very good for a startup company. Grover had been fortunate enough to cater a few parties that ended up in the society pages shortly after he opened for business; his services had been in high demand ever since.

A chemical engineer by training, Helena Davies worked at a Washington think tank which studied the effects of climate change brought on by the use of fossil fuels. She had more brains than common sense and wasn't afraid to admit it.

Helena and Daisy had become fast friends when they were introduced at a tasting event held at a wine shop not far from Daisy's office. Helena, tall with blonde hair, dark brown eyes, and a willowy figure, had a knack for being the center of attention. Daisy, though pretty in her own right, usually felt plain and rather ignored next to her friend, but that was okay with her. She didn't want any romantic entanglements. Not after Dean. At least it allowed her to sit back and observe her surroundings and the people vying for Helena's attention, which the anthropologist part of her enjoyed doing. And in the almost-year since they had been friends, Daisy had saved Helena from more than one would-be disastrous date by sharing her observations with her smitten friend.

There was the man Daisy dubbed the "picked-his-nose-before-he-shook-your-hand" guy, the "he-tried-to-pick-your-pocket" guy, the "I-saw-him-arguing-with-himself" guy, and countless others. Helena had always been grateful for Daisy's keen sense of people's personalities.

Helena and Grover had already been friends for years when they saw Daisy at an Italian Reds tasting event. Helena introduced Grover to Daisy and those two had also become good friends.

Not long after Daisy received the women's history assignment from Mark John, she and Helena and Grover met for pizza one evening in Dupont Circle.

"I can't believe you have the night off," Daisy said to Grover as they sat down at a small table for three.

"I don't have anything on the calendar tonight or tomorrow night," he said, leaning back in his chair. He ordered a glass of Cabernet and perused the menu.

"I'm having the margherita pizza," said Helena, closing her menu. "Trying to watch my figure."

"You and everyone else are watching your figure," Daisy said with a laugh. Grover rolled his eyes.

"What's new at work?" Helena asked Daisy.

Daisy told her friends about her new assignment. "Tomorrow I'm heading over to the Library of Congress to start some research. I could do it online, but I love it over there and it's been a while since I visited."

"It's been years since I was there," Grover said. He proceeded to tell Daisy and Helena about a party he was catering later in the week.

"It's a retirement party. Anyone care to help out?" he asked, his eyes twinkling. "Minimum wage, but you can take home the leftovers."

"Sounds good to me," Daisy said.

"Can't. I've got a date," Helena said.

"Who's it with?" Daisy asked.

"His name is Bennett. This is our first date and we're going to see a play. He's a reporter I met at an event a few weeks ago."

"Is he normal?" Daisy asked with a grin.

"He seems to be. If I have any questions about him I'll give you a call," Helena replied, winking.

"Anyway, back to my retirement party," Grover said. "Daisy, can you get away from work a couple hours early on Thursday?"

"Sure. I'll be working on research that day, so I can leave whenever I want to."

"I'll pick you up in the van at three at your place."

CHAPTER 4

On the dot of three Thursday afternoon, Grover pulled his catering van up to the curb in front of the brownstone where Daisy lived in a third-floor apartment.

"So tell me more about this party," Daisy said, sliding into the front seat.

"Well, it's a retirement party," he began.

"That much I already know," she said.

"The guy who is hosting it is not the retiree--he's a teacher. The head of the retirement party committee or something like that. He doesn't seem to have much imagination."

"What makes you say that?" Daisy asked

"The guy who's retiring is a school administrator who's moving to Florida next week. The host has asked for desserts shaped like books and school supplies and stuff." He steered the van into traffic headed out to one of the DC suburbs in Virginia. "If you ask me, I think books and school supplies would be the last thing a retiree wants at his party. I think he'd want things related to retirement. You know, like palm trees and flamingos and sunglasses. But I'm not hired to change anyone's ideas, just carry them out."

A half hour later, they pulled into the driveway of a modest home just outside Arlington. A large white tent was already set up in the side yard. Grover hopped out first and swung open the back doors of the van. Daisy joined him as another woman approached the van. Daisy recognized her as one of Grover's employees, Tish.

"Hey, Tish," Grover said. "Thanks for getting here early. Are the tables set up in the tent?"

"Yup. I'll start getting the drink trays out." She clambered up into the back of the van and hefted two trays, then handed them to Daisy.

"Would you take these over to the long table closest to the side of the house?" she asked Daisy.

Daisy did as she was asked and was turning around to head back to the van for more instructions when a man walked into the tent.

"Hi," Daisy said cheerfully. "I'm Daisy." She held out her hand and the man shook it.

"Hi, I'm Walt Beecham."

"Are you the guest of honor?" Daisy asked with a smile. This man was obviously too young to be retiring.

"No, no, I'm the host." He looked at his watch. "Do you need me for anything around here before the party starts?"

"I don't think so, but you can ask Grover," Daisy replied. "Excuse me, I've got to get more stuff from the van." She hurried back toward the driveway.

The man followed her out to the van.

"Hi there, Mister Beecham," Grover said, extending his hand. "Are you ready for the guests to arrive?"

"Please call me Walt. Yes, I'm ready, though I need to run an errand before the party," Walt said.

"You've got plenty of time," Grover assured him. "We're just going to be setting up."

"All right. My wife has taken the kids over to her mother's house so they're not underfoot tonight. She'll be back soon. If you have any questions, just ask her."

"Will do," said Grover.

Walt left and Daisy, Tish, and Grover busied themselves putting out table settings, arranging chafing dishes on the long serving tables, and directing the florist where to put her arrangements once she arrived.

Grover was trying to juggle three containers of sherbet and a bottle of cranberry juice for the punch when the florist turned around suddenly and walked into him. The bottle of juice crashed to the ground, spilling all over the grass and sloshing onto Grover's khaki pants.

"Oh! I'm so sorry!" the florist exclaimed.

"It's no problem," Grover replied. "Daisy, can you do me a huge favor? Can you run to the closest grocery store and get some more cranberry juice? The punch isn't as good without it."

"Sure." Daisy reached her hand out for the keys. "Where's the closest store?"

"It's just a few blocks away. It's saved in the GPS."

"Be right back." Daisy jogged toward the van. She turned on the GPS and scrolled through various saved destinations before finding a grocery store in Arlington. "That must be the one," she murmured to herself. Grover always saved important addresses near his parties in case of emergency, like this one.

Grover had been right--the grocery store wasn't far at all. It was a small upscale store, located on a leafy street and tucked between a wine bar and a cupcake shop.

Daisy found a parking spot right in front of the store and jumped out of the van. As she hurried into the store she glanced around and saw Walt exiting the wine bar. He was carrying two glasses of wine and he placed them on a small wrought iron table on the sidewalk under a striped purple awning. He then sat down with his back to Daisy. Apparently he hadn't noticed the caterer's van parked out front.

Daisy hastened inside, found the juice quickly, and paid for it. She left the store and looked over toward Walt again. There was a woman with lush red hair walking toward his table. When she reached him, he stood up and kissed her lips. They sat down and he covered her hand with his. Daisy looked away and went back to the van. As she pulled away, she happened to look in her rear view mirror again to watch Walt and his wife; as she did so, she almost hit a woman who was standing in front of the van, just off the curb, looking toward the wine bar. Daisy let out a sigh of relief that she hadn't hit the woman and scolded herself for being so nosy.

"How sweet," Daisy thought. "A little date with his wife after she drops off the kids and before they have hoards of people at their house." She smiled to herself. Mrs. Beecham had an open, fresh-faced glow that lent a feeling of familiarity to her wholesome attractiveness.

She returned to the Beechams' house and found the party preparations in full swing. The catering staff met her as she pulled into the driveway and yanked open the back doors of the van. Two other part-time employees had joined Grover and Tish and everyone was eager to get the rest of the supplies out of the van and set up.

"Daisy, can you make the punch?" Grover asked. "The list of ingredients is taped on the wall inside the van."

"Got it," Daisy replied.

Daisy was gathering the ingredients to make the punch when a woman's soft voice interrupted her.

"Excuse me?" asked the woman, peering into the back of the van.

"Yes? Can I help you?" Daisy asked. She turned her attention away from counting out limes for the punch.

"I'm looking for Grover. I'm Mrs. Beecham. Melody Beecham."

Daisy dropped a lime and did an almost-imperceptible double-take. Melody's long blond hair was pulled into a pony-tail and she was thin and tired-looking. This wasn't the woman whom Daisy had seen with Walt.

It was the woman Daisy had almost hit with the van.

CHAPTER 5

*D*aisy managed to recover herself quickly. "Oh. Um, the last time I saw him he was headed toward the tent."

Who was the woman with Walt at the wine bar? Daisy turned away so her face wouldn't give away her discomfort.

"All right. I'm sure I'll find him eventually," Mrs. Beecham said, then turned and walked away toward the tent.

Daisy busied herself making the punch and pouring it into gallon containers that could be easily transported to and from the tent. Grover came to see how she was doing.

"How's it going?" Grover asked.

Daisy was having a hard time concentrating on the punch. How could she when she knew the party host was cheating on his wife? And that the wife had perhaps just found out about it, too?

"Okay."

"Only okay? I thought you loved helping me." He grinned.

"I do. It's just--"

"Wait a sec," Grover said. Someone was calling his name. "Be right back."

But he became involved in so many busy party preparations that she didn't even get another glimpse of him until guests had begun to arrive and she was set up at her pasta station.

Later on, during a lull in the serving, Daisy was surprised when someone tapped her on the shoulder. She turned around and found herself looking at a familiar face, though it took her a second to place the man.

It was Brian Comstock, Mark John's brother-in-law. He was a history teacher and had a passion for all things historical. He was constantly bringing things into the office--from books to candlesticks to old clothing--that he thought Mark John might find interesting.

"Brian!" she exclaimed. "I didn't know you were here."

"Walt is a good friend of mine from work. We both teach in the history department. I almost didn't recognize you because you're out of your element here."

"Yes, I guess I am. Nice to see you, Brian," Daisy said, then turned away.

"What are you doing here, anyway?" Brian asked.

"The caterer is a friend of mine," Daisy said, looking over her shoulder at him. "I'm just helping him out tonight."

"Oh. Well, that's interesting, I suppose. Tell Mark John I said hello," Brian said, then he moved away into the crowd.

He wasn't the most suave conversationalist. In fact, he could be downright obtuse when it came to small talk. Daisy wondered if he had fun at parties like this. He seemed too intro-verted to enjoy himself.

Daisy continued serving guests, then the final person through the line was Walt. He held out his plate for a helping of pasta, but had a pained look on his face. He didn't look at Daisy, nor did he speak to her.

Daisy felt she had to say something--it would be too awkward for her to ignore the host of the party.

"Are you enjoying yourself?" she asked.

"What? Oh. It's all right, I suppose."

"Is there anything I can do for you?"

"No." He left without another word.

After the dessert buffet was laid out and coffee had been served, the number of guests slowly began to dwindle until only Walt and Brian and a few others remained, including the guest of honor. Grover suggested that Daisy get a ride home with Tish while he waited to settle the bill with the retirement party committee. He knew from experience that it could take a while, and he didn't want her to have to wait around for him.

"Thanks for letting me help tonight," Daisy said. "It was enlightening." Grover, who had been perusing the bill, glanced up at her.

"What do you mean?"

"You coming, Daisy?" Tish asked as she approached.

"I'm ready," Daisy answered. "Talk to you later, Grover."

"Thanks a lot for helping out tonight. I owe you one. I'll call you soon," he called after her..

When he called later the next week, though, it was with bad news.

CHAPTER 6

*S*omething was nagging in the back of Daisy's mind as she prepared for bed that night. Tish had been chatty all the way back to Dupont Circle, talking about working for Grover and some of the parties she had helped him cater. Daisy was listening, but she was also thinking. Thinking about the woman Walt had kissed at the wine bar.

There was something about her...

The next day at work everyone seemed to be in a foul mood. The reason was simple: a deadline. An issue of the journal had to be completed by midnight and Mark John was projecting his stress onto everyone in the office. Daisy had finished her contributions to the issue ages ago, but Mark John was a firm believer that misery loves company. Before lunchtime, she, too, was in a bitter mood that only an escape from the office would cure.

By the time six o'clock rolled around, there was nothing more she could do to help Mark John and Jude, both of whom were buried in last-minute details. Daisy packed her tote bag, slung it over her shoulder, and left without saying a word to anyone. She picked up a sandwich on the way home, figuring the last thing she wanted to do was make dinner and wash dishes that evening. She ate the sandwich on the sofa, nursing a glass of wine and watching old movies, her coping mechanism of choice.

When she had enjoyed her fill of "Laura" and "To Catch a Thief," two of her favorite old films, Daisy felt her eyelids getting droopy. She washed out the wine glass and threw away the sandwich wrapper, all the while trying to figure out why her brain wouldn't shut itself down.

She took two melatonin, hoping they would help put her mind at rest so she could go to sleep, and crawled into bed.

As she was drifting off, she suddenly realized what her mind wouldn't let go.

She *had* recognized the woman Walt kissed--it was Fiona.

Mark John's wife.

ow Daisy couldn't sleep. How could she, when she knew such a devastating secret? Did Mark John know his wife was cheating on him? Had Melody Beecham found out the afternoon of the retirement party that her husband was cheating on her?

Should she tell someone?

Daisy's mind reeled with questions about Fiona, the woman in the picture whom she'd never met in person.

She had so many questions. She knew one thing--she didn't want to go to work on Monday morning. She couldn't face Mark John.

But Monday morning came, as it always did, and she had to go to work. She tossed and turned all Sunday night until the sun brightened the eastern sky with a gossamer ribbon of pink.

She had looked forward to spending the day ensconced in research at the Library of Congress, but she couldn't summon the energy she needed to take the Metro and fight the tourists thronging around the federal buildings.

Daisy was on her second cup of coffee when Jude came into her office. She had a bad habit of barging in without knocking--

apparently she felt it was her prerogative as the senior editor to go into anyone's office any time she felt like it.

It annoyed Daisy more than usual that morning.

"Do you ever knock?" she asked.

"Someone got up on the wrong side of the bed this morning," Jude replied.

Daisy took a deep breath and reminded herself to be polite.

"What do you need?" she asked.

"Mark John isn't here yet," she said. "I'm just letting you know so that if you need anything, come to me."

Daisy nodded tightly. "Okay." Jude left quickly, seeming to sense that Daisy wasn't in the mood to listen to her.

It was just like Jude to let everyone in the office know she was temporarily in charge, Daisy thought with disgust. Did anyone even care?

Mark John came in about an hour later. He looked like he hadn't slept much, either. He closed the door to his office a little too loudly and Daisy waited for Jude to go running to him.

She didn't have to wait long.

A minute or two later Daisy heard Mark John's voice.

"Dammit!" he yelled. There was a sound of breaking glass. Daisy winced.

A lower, softer voice responded to Mark John a moment later. Daisy guessed that Jude was trying to calm him down. Daisy wondered what was going on. She briefly considered tiptoeing to the door to listen, but she quickly discarded that idea as both nosy and stupid.

She tried to concentrate on the work in front of her, but the office felt too unsettled, too charged with emotion. She grabbed her jacket and went outside for a walk.

When she returned, the receptionist nodded silently and gave Daisy a small smile. Daisy hoped that meant everything had calmed down in the office.

She walked past Jude, who was in her own office, and noticed that everything seemed to have quieted in her absence.

As much as she didn't want to bother Mark John, Daisy had to get started on the research for the women's history articles. She took her notebook and knocked lightly on Mark John's office door.

"Yes?" he asked.

"It's Daisy. Are you interested in talking about the women's history articles right now?"

She could hear him sigh. "Might as well. Come in."

She opened the door reluctantly, expecting to see Mark John sitting behind his desk. Instead, he was pacing before the big window. There were large bags under his eyes and his hair was disheveled. A quick glance revealed to Daisy that the photo of his wife was missing from the credenza.

"Sit down," he said, gesturing toward a chair. He didn't turn around from the window.

Daisy sat down and opened her notebook. As much as she loved her computer, she couldn't give up her real paper and pencils.

"What do you have in mind?" Mark John asked, finally turning around and sitting down at his desk.

Daisy spent several minutes fleshing out some of the ideas she had jotted down for the articles. Mark John seemed to like the direction she wanted to take, and she was thrilled because her approach was going to require a lot of research. That was her favorite part of the job.

"I'm sorry about earlier," Mark John said as Daisy stood up to leave. "It's been a long morning."

Part of Daisy wanted to ask what was going on, but part of her was pretty sure she'd hear more than she wanted to know.

It wasn't long before her hunch was confirmed.

CHAPTER 8

*J*ude came into Daisy's office about mid-morning and perched on the edge of Daisy's desk.

"What are you working on?" she asked.

"An assignment," Daisy replied tersely. It was none of Jude's business, and she knew it would annoy Jude if she refused to give any information about it. "I've got a deadline, so if you don't mind telling me what you need..."

"All right. I was wondering if you'd like to go out for lunch today."

Now she had Daisy's attention. "You want to go out for lunch with *me*?" she asked, not sure she had heard Jude correctly.

"Yes. My treat. I thought we should get to know each other a little better." Strange, waiting until Daisy had worked at GHR for so long to seek to get to know her better, but Daisy agreed, curious about Jude's motives.

"We can go to lunch, but only if I'm able to get this article written," she said, hoping Jude would take the hint. She did. After telling Daisy she'd come by at one o'clock, Jude left, closing the door behind her. She didn't mention Mark John's earlier behavior, but Daisy figured she would learn more at lunch.

She was able to get right back into the paragraph she had been writing when Jude interrupted, choosing to focus solely on her work rather than the odd conversation that had just taken place.

But as lunchtime grew closer and her stomach started growling, Daisy's thought began to turn toward lunch with Jude. She put a few finishing touches on her document, hit "send," and cleaned up her desk, wondering all the while what was behind Jude's seemingly innocent invitation. It was unlike her to seek to spend any time with Daisy outside the office, and the request to have lunch together had come out of nowhere. *Come to think of it, I have no idea what Jude does for lunch every day. I don't know where she lives or what she drives or what she likes and doesn't like. I only know that she's the senior editor because she doesn't let me forget it.*

Promptly at one o'clock Jude opened Daisy's door. "Ready?" she asked brightly.

Daisy grabbed her canvas tote bag and slung it over her shoulder. Jude glanced at the bag but said nothing as she tucked her petite designer clutch under her arm. Daisy generally liked being tall because it made her feel powerful and confident, but next to Jude as they walked to lunch she felt frumpy, gangly, and underdressed.

When they reached the restaurant Jude had chosen, a doorman ushered them inside, where a cool, dark space provided a quiet, refined destination for diners who lunched on elegant entrées and sipped sparkling water or stronger libations. Daisy would have been happier with a visit to the Pita Palace and an iced tea, but this would have to do. She sat down across from Jude, wondering where the conversation would lead. Clearly Jude intended it to go somewhere.

But the niceties came first as they ordered from a small but expensive menu and the server laid napkins across their laps. Daisy couldn't help but reach for hers to do it herself as the server's hand came across her torso.

Once they had ordered, Jude gazed around at the other diners as if looking for someone she might recognize. This was definitely the type of place where one would go to see and be seen. Finally Daisy could stand it no longer.

"Jude, this lunch invitation was unexpected. Is there something you wanted to talk about?"

"Actually, yes. I was serious when I said we should get to know each other better, but it's more than that. I wanted to talk to you in private about Mark John."

Ah, now the truth comes out, Daisy thought. She hid her smile as she raised a glass of water to her lips.

"What, specifically, would you like to discuss about Mark John?"

Jude sighed. "I know I've mentioned this before, but I wanted to reiterate that you should probably look to spend less time with Mark John while you're at work. It's rather unseemly, to be honest."

"Unseemly how?"

"You don't want to be giving anyone the impression that you're, shall we say, interested in Mark John for reasons that have nothing to do with work."

"You mean like I've got romantic feelings for him?"

Jude shifted in her chair and looked around the room again. "Yes. That's exactly what I mean. Do you have romantic feelings for him?" Jude turned an intent gaze on Daisy. Daisy almost laughed out loud.

"No, I can assure you of that. I have no romantic feelings for him whatsoever." She was surprised when Jude tilted her head and gave her a confused look.

"May I ask why not? I mean, he's certainly attractive. And smart."

It was Daisy's turn to tilt her head and stare at Jude for a moment. "So now you're wondering why I don't have feelings for Mark John? I'm afraid I don't really understand where this is going."

"I just mean that in my opinion Mark John would hold a certain appeal for any woman. Don't you agree?" Daisy took her time before answering. Something was beginning to dawn on her--something she should have seen before now.

Jude had feelings for Mark John. Suddenly Daisy recalled the looks Jude gave him at work. The smiles, the flirtatious eyelash-batting, the eagerness to please him.

Now this conversation was beginning to make a little more sense. Jude was both jealous and insecure in her feelings; she was wondering if there was something about Mark John that other women didn't find attractive. She was the type, thought Daisy, who would fall for someone just because every other woman wanted him. If someone didn't want him, Jude would naturally want to know if there was something she was missing.

"Oh, he's definitely attractive," Daisy replied after several moments. "It's just that I have no interest in men whatsoever at this point."

"Are you a lesbian?" Jude asked. Daisy was glad the food hadn't come yet because she would have choked over the extremely personal nature of the question.

"No, Jude. I'm not, though I can't think how that might be any business of yours. I'm just not interested right now. I love my work and that's enough for me." Jude gave Daisy a bewildered look as Daisy sat back to allow the server to place her lunch in front of her.

When he had slipped away, Daisy picked up her fork, then put it down again. "Jude, I think it's time we come clean with each other about everything. If we're going to continue working together we should not keep workplace secrets from each other."

"What do you mean?"

"I mean I think you have feelings for Mark John. I've seen how you look at him. It's obvious that you like him, and I'm embarrassed to think I didn't realize it before now. So don't worry about me. I am completely uninterested in workplace romance, and whatever you and Mark John choose to do is your own business. But I also want you to understand that I don't appreciate being interrogated over my feelings about my boss. It makes me feel uncomfortable and it's just plain weird."

Jude's shoulders relaxed as she took a sip of her drink. "I didn't mean to make you feel uncomfortable. I'm sorry. It's just that I'm very sensitive about my feelings for Mark John."

"Well, if you're worried about me trying to compete against you for his affection, you can cross that off your list." Daisy smiled. Jude actually looked like she was beginning to relax. *Maybe she should give some thought to Mark John's marital status, though*, thought Daisy.

"Do you feel better now that everything is in the open between us? I know I do," Daisy said.

"Yes, I do feel better," Jude admitted, a sheepish look replacing her smile. "Thanks for understanding."

"You don't have to thank me. Just keep me out of it," Daisy said.

"I will, I promise."

For the next several minutes the two women ate lunch, talking only about the food and the decor of the restaurant. All the while, though, questions were swirling in Daisy's mind and finally her curiosity took over.

"How do you feel about Mark John being married?"

Jude set her fork down slowly. She didn't answer right away, though she stared at Daisy, almost inviting a challenge.

"I'm not all that concerned."

Daisy decided to change the subject. "Was Mark John okay when he came in this morning?" she asked.

Again, Jude was silent for several moments before answering. Finally, after folding her napkin and placing it in a tidy square on the table next to her, she spoke.

"He found out his wife is having an affair."

Since noticing the picture of Fiona was missing in Mark John's office and given his behavior, Daisy had harbored a hunch that he had somehow found out. Her secret about Fiona was apparently no longer a secret.

"How did he find out?" Daisy asked.

"Fiona's lover called him and told him," Jude said, toying with her spoon. Daisy raised her eyebrows, inviting further explanation, but none was forthcoming. She figured it might be wise to stop asking questions.

The meal, which had started on an uncomfortable note, had come full circle. Jude signaled for the bill and paid it, quickly scrawling her name on the credit card receipt while Daisy waited, noticing with a glance that Jude was a stingy tipper. When the elegant senior editor of Global Human Rights Journal preceded Daisy out the door, Daisy took a ten dollar bill from her tote bag and placed it on the table next to the receipt. Outside, Jude told Daisy that she had to run to the drugstore before returning to work and headed in the opposite direction. Daisy was sure Jude simply wanted to walk back to work alone.

When Jude returned to the office, she closed her door and didn't emerge before Daisy left for the evening. Daisy was not disappointed--she hoped Tuesday would be a better day.

It wasn't.

CHAPTER 9

*W*hen Daisy got to work Tuesday morning the thing she noticed first was the silence. The lights were on and she could smell coffee, but she didn't hear the *tap-tap-tap* of the receptionist's computer, she didn't hear the sound of printers or copy machines or phones. No one sat at the reception desk. Jude's office door was closed and Mark John's stood open with the lights off.

She went to her own office and turned on her computer, then went to the kitchen. The receptionist and Mark John's office assistant sat huddled together at the small table.

"What's going on?" Daisy asked. "It's so quiet in here this morning."

Both women looked up at Daisy, their faces grim. "You should probably go talk to Jude," the receptionist said.

"What's going on?" Daisy asked again, this time a hint of uncertainty creeping into her voice.

The women exchanged glances, but said nothing.

Daisy turned around and headed straight for Jude's office. When Jude called for her to come in, Daisy opened the door tentatively, as if she were afraid of what she might find on the other side.

Jude sat at her desk, the heels of her hands pressed to her eyes. When she lifted her head up, her eyes were wide and her mascara smudged. She was ashen and her hands shook.

"Jude, what's happening?"

"Mark John's wife was murdered last night," she said in a flat voice.

Daisy inhaled sharply and fell into the seat in front of Jude's desk.

"What--I mean, how did it happen?"

"Someone came into the house and slit her throat. Mark John had been in the office all evening and found her, already dead, when he got home."

"Do the police know who did it?"

Jude shook her head, letting out a shaky breath. "They don't know. They're investigating, obviously."

"Where's Mark John? How's he doing? And what was he doing here last night?"

"He's at Brian's house. You know, Fiona's brother. The one who's always coming around here with stuff for Mark John. And Mark John is not doing well, as you might expect. He was here because we were working on a new layout for the journal."

"So you were both here last night?"

Jude nodded.

"When did you find out about Fiona?" Daisy asked.

"Early this morning. He said he won't be coming in for a few days."

"Do the police know when it happened?" Daisy asked.

"I don't know."

"How late were you here last night?"

"I left before Mark John. I was here until about seven, but I think he was here until after eleven."

Daisy closed her eyes. "Have the police talked to you yet?"

"No."

"They will--just give them time."

"How do you know that?" Jude asked.

"Unfortunately, I know what it's like to be part of a murder investigation because I was the suspect in my old boyfriend's death."

Jude gasped and covered her mouth with her hand.

"You had a boyfriend?" Daisy looked at her with a mixture of disbelief and disgust.

"Yes, though that's not really the point here, is it?"

"No. I'm sorry. I mean, that's terrible. What happened?"

"I don't really want to discuss it. But it was an accident and eventually a witness came forward who could corroborate the whole thing."

"How did he die?"

"I'm not going to talk about it any more."

"Sorry. That must have been awful."

"It was. You know Mark John is going to be a suspect, right?"

Jude let out a tortured sigh and her shoulders slumped. She looked so unlike the Jude Daisy knew.

"I know." She covered her face with her hands.

"What do you think is going to happen?" she asked.

"I don't know. Hopefully they'll find who did it and Mark John will be off the hook."

"There have been those burglaries in Mark John's neighborhood lately--maybe this was a burglary that went wrong."

"Was anything stolen from the house?"

"I don't know. Mark John didn't say."

Jude's phone rang and she picked it up in a flash.

"Hello?"

She covered the mouthpiece with her hand. "It's Mark John," she whispered to Daisy.

Daisy made a hand motion asking if Jude wanted her to leave. Jude shook her head *no*.

After a few moments Jude hung up.

"How's he doing?" Daisy asked.

"He's coming into the office for a few files, then he's going back to Brian's house to stay for a few days. The police aren't letting him in his house right now. He sounds awful."

Daisy stood up to leave. "I'll be in my office if you need anything."

Before she went into the hallway, Jude spoke again.

"Daisy?"

"Yes?"

"We have to help him. Will you help me clear his name?"

"I'll do what I can, Jude. But I'm no detective."

"I know, but we can't just stand by and do nothing."

"I'll help," Daisy promised.

Jude nodded her thanks and Daisy left.

Once in her own office, she couldn't concentrate. She knew what was in store for Mark John, and she knew the coming days and weeks were going to be stressful, painful, and otherwise miserable. And as for helping find Fiona's killer, it seemed that the police were in a far better position to do that. But she had promised, so now she had to do something.

When Mark John arrived a short while later, he went straight to his office, closed the door, and didn't come out for about an hour. Jude went in to see him after a few minutes; when Daisy went to the kitchen for a bottle of water, she could hear their low voices. She couldn't make out what they were saying.

CHAPTER 10

Not much work got done around the offices of Global Human Rights that day. Daisy was glad when five o'clock came and she could go home, though she knew the evening would bring more of the same--uncertainty, confusion, and a general feeling of foreboding. She wondered what would happen at Global Human Rights if the editor-in-chief was embroiled in a murder investigation. She supposed Jude would take control, at least temporarily.

Over the next couple days Jude managed to rally somewhat and took over the day-to-day basics of Mark John's responsibilities around the office. She was in frequent contact with him with questions and issues that cropped up.

Daisy had put her Library of Congress research on hold until things calmed down at Global Human Rights. She did as much online research as she could, but spent a good deal of time helping Jude with different tasks of running the journal.

She was sitting on the sofa reading Thursday evening when the phone rang. She glanced at the caller ID, saw that it was Grover, and picked it up with a smile.

"Hello?"

"Hi. It's Grover." His voice sounded strangled and tight.

"Grover? Is everything all right?"

"No. I need your help."

Clutching the phone in a vice grip, Daisy was immediately on alert. "Sure. What's wrong?"

"Remember I stayed to get the money from Walt last Thursday night after the retirement party?"

"Yes."

"Well, he talked to his friend for so long that evening--you know, the guy you knew from your office?"

"Yes. Brian Comstock."

"Anyway, they talked for so long that Walt asked me if I could come over to his house to get the money sometime this week."

"Is that normal?" Daisy asked.

"Sometimes. If the host is too busy to pay me, I arrange a time to get the money later."

"Okay."

"I went over there around five this afternoon to get the money."

"Okay. I don't understand what's going on here. Why do you need my help?" Then Daisy had an awful thought. "Don't tell me he refused to pay you."

"I got the money. But Walt was murdered after I left. I was the last person to see him alive. The police have been here to talk to me, Daisy."

CHAPTER 11

*D*aisy had remained standing while she talked to Grover, but now she moved to the living room and collapsed into an armchair.

"I can't believe it," she murmured.

"What should I do?" Grover asked.

"Just tell the police the truth. And get yourself a lawyer, just in case."

"Do you really think I'll need one?"

"Hopefully not, but if you do need one, it can't hurt to be prepared."

"I'm completely at sea right now," Grover said. His voice had risen considerably just since Daisy picked up the phone.

"Listen, Grover. This is just procedure. Just because the police talked to you doesn't mean you're a suspect. If you were the last person to see him alive, then they're just doing their job. You have to remember that. I'm sure you're not a suspect."

"But what if I am and they're just not telling me?"

"You'd know if they thought you were a suspect, believe me. Everything changes in the way they speak to you. I know from bitter experience."

"I know. I know exactly how you must have felt."

"Well, I was *actually* a suspect and hopefully you won't be. Hopefully you won't know *exactly* how it felt."

Grover was silent for a moment.

"Grover? You still there?" Daisy asked.

"I'm here. Could I come over for a little while? I'll bring wine."

"You just said the magic words," Daisy said, attempting to lighten the mood. "See you when you get here."

Grover showed up just a little while later with a bottle of white wine. Daisy got two glasses from the kitchen and sank onto the sofa.

"So tell me everything. What happened when you went to talk to Walt? Was there anyone else there?"

Grover shook his head. "His wife was pulling out of the driveway just as I was getting there."

"So the wife wasn't home. Do you know where the kids were?"

"Walt invited me into the house. He said the kids weren't home and that his wife had just gone to pick them up."

"Okay, so neither the wife nor the kids were home, though it sounds like they were heading home once she picked them up. Go on."

"I followed him into the house and he asked me to wait in the kitchen while he went to get his checkbook. He was only gone for a minute or two. Then he wrote out the check and handed it to me and I left."

"He stayed in the house when you left?"

"Yes. He went to the door with me, but he stayed inside the house and closed the front door behind me."

"What was his mood like?" Daisy asked.

Grover shrugged. "He's not a really gregarious guy. I mean, he wasn't a gregarious guy."

"So he was quiet?"

"I would say so."

"Did he talk about anything besides the retirement party or the bill?"

Grover thought for a moment, his eyes squinting. "I don't think so."

"Are you sure?"

"Yeah. He was standing in front of the house when his wife pulled out of the driveway, though. He was shaking his head and he looked furious. But he seemed back to normal by the time I got to the front door."

"That's interesting," Daisy mused, half to herself.

"Why do you say that?"

"I meant to tell you this the night of the party, but I never got a chance and so much has happened since then. When I went to pick up the cranberry juice at the grocery store I saw him with a woman I assumed was his wife, but wasn't. And then I almost hit someone with the van. The person I almost hit turned out to be his wife. I met her at the party. She saw him with the other woman."

"Wow," Grover breathed. "I had no idea."

"There's more," Daisy said. "So much has happened in the days since I saw you last."

"What do you mean?"

"I mean, the woman I saw with Walt was Fiona, my boss's wife. And now she's dead, too. She was murdered just a few nights ago."

"Oh, my God. You're kidding," Grover said.

"I wish," Daisy replied.

"So your boss's wife was having an affair with a married man. And Walt's wife found out about it. Did your boss know?"

"He found out over the weekend, apparently. From Walt. He came into the office Monday and was in a horrible mood."

"Has anyone been charged with the wife's murder?" Grover asked.

Daisy shook her head. "I guess the investigation is still ongoing. But Mark John hasn't been arrested, so that's a good thing."

"He must have been devastated."

"I'm sure," Daisy agreed.

"So this changes things," Grover said.

"It sure does," Daisy agreed.

"It certainly puts Melody Beecham squarely at the top of the suspect list in Walt's murder," Grover said.

"That's true. That's good news for you," Daisy said, pointing at him with her fork. "His wife knows he was having an affair and suddenly he turns up dead. She's a much better choice for suspect than you are."

"You're right. Her misery is my good luck. I hate to think of it that way, though."

"In a murder investigation, you have to look out for yourself first." Daisy gave him a tired smile. "I wish I didn't know so much about being a murder suspect, but it's coming in handy," she said with a wry laugh.

Grover smiled and shook his head.

When they finished their wine Grover stood up to leave. "Thanks for letting me come over tonight," he said. "It would have been nicer under different circumstances, though."

CHAPTER 12

*D*aisy knew that Grover felt a little better when he left her apartment, but she spent that night tossing, turning, and mulling over his misfortune in her overtired mind.

The next day she was already grumpy when she got to work. She wanted nothing more than to be left alone in peace, but Jude had other ideas. She came to sit across from Daisy in Daisy's office not long after the work day started.

"What is it, Jude?" Daisy asked, running her hand across her eyes. "I feel that I should warn you--I haven't slept much and I'm a grouch today."

"I can't sleep, either," said Jude.

"Worried about Mark John?" Daisy asked.

Jude let out a long sigh. "Yeah. I have a little more information."

"Jude, I have more information, too." Daisy fixed Jude with a pointed stare.

"You go first," Jude said.

"Walt, Fiona's paramour, was murdered last night."

"Oh, my God."

"So you obviously hadn't heard that." *Does Mark John know yet?* Daisy wondered.

Jude covered her mouth with her hand as the full implication of Daisy's news struck her.

"They're going to think Mark John did it!" Jude cried. Daisy didn't answer. Jude was probably right. First the cheating wife is murdered, then her boyfriend? It looked as bad for Mark John as it did for Melody.

"Jude, what did you want to tell me?" Daisy asked. She spoke softly, albeit with an effort, knowing Jude was probably becoming more emotionally unglued by the minute.

"What?" Jude asked crossly. "Oh. Yeah. I came in to tell you that Fiona's funeral is on Saturday. You should probably plan to be there."

Daisy nodded. *I didn't even know the woman,* she thought. "Are you going?" she asked.

Jude looked down at her fingers, which were intertwined in her lap. "I would rather not. She wasn't exactly my favorite person."

"Why? Because she was Mark John's wife?"

"Yes." Jude looked away, her eyes downcast.

"I suppose I can represent both of us," Daisy said.

"Thanks."

Funerals made Daisy nervous. The last one she had attended was Dean's, and it had been horrible. Overwhelming, sad beyond any words, and emotionally draining. And that was before she knew she was a suspect in his death. She knew Fiona's funeral was unlikely to have that same effect, but still. It was a funeral.

Daisy woke up Saturday morning with a headache. A tension headache, no doubt. She was anxious about the funeral. At Dean's funeral, there had been lots of rude whisperings about his cause of death--this funeral was sure to be different since the victim had obviously been murdered. The whisperings would be about who did it. Daisy didn't care to listen to whispering or gossiping or conversation of any kind.

She had made plans to have lunch with Grover after the funeral, so at least she looked forward to that, but even the thought of Grover made her anxious. The more time that went by without an arrest in Walt's murder, the longer Grover could potentially be considered by the police as a suspect in the crime.

She rolled out of bed, took a shower, and tried to do something to hide the gray bags under her eyes. Her efforts were in vain. Eventually she pulled on a gray dress to match the bags and hailed a taxi to take her to the funeral home.

She was surprised by the number of people milling about. She wasn't surprised that she only knew two of them--Mark John and Brian.

Mark John was greeting mourners who had come to pay their last respects. He hugged the women and shook hands gravely with the men. Every so often he would take a tissue out of his pocket and blow his nose, but he managed to remain calm.

Not so with Brian, who was crying at the back of the vestibule in the funeral home. A woman Daisy assumed was his wife stood next to him, her hand on his forearm.

Daisy didn't want to approach either man, but Mark John saw her and walked over to her.

"Thank you for coming, Daisy. I appreciate it. I'm sure Brian does, too."

"It was the least I could do, Mark John. I'm so sorry for your loss. And I'm sorry I never had a chance to meet Fiona."

Mark John nodded, his eyes vacant, and let out a long breath.

"Funerals are awful, aren't they?" he asked, looking around. "They're filled with people one doesn't know very well and it's hard to be authentic."

"I know what you mean," Daisy said. "Brian doesn't seem to be doing very well."

Mark John turned around quickly to glance at his brother-in-law. "He's an emotional guy. But he'll be okay. That's his wife with him. She'll make sure he's all right. Listen, Daisy, I have to talk to the funeral director before the service starts."

"Sure. See you later."

Mark John left and Daisy stood at the back of the room where the service was to be held. It was a large room and seats were starting to fill up. She was about to find a seat when there was a tap on her shoulder.

"Hi, Daisy. Thanks for coming." It was Brian, and he had stopped crying, at least temporarily.

"Oh, Brian, I'm so sorry for your loss," Daisy said, reaching to shake his hand. His grip was weak and clammy; Daisy had to fight the urge to wipe her hand down the front of her dress.

"Thank you. So tragic. This is my wife, Stacey," he said, indicating the woman standing with him.

Daisy shook Stacey's hand and stood back to let them pass through the doorway and down into the first row of seats reserved for family. Daisy noted that only Brian and Stacey were seated in the front row. Mark John would no doubt be joining them, bringing the total number of family members to three. That in itself was very sad. At least at Dean's funeral Daisy had been surrounded by his brothers and sisters and parents. Today she sat alone in the back row of seats.

The service was short and lovely. The sounds of sniffling were all around Daisy, though she could not bring herself to shed any tears for the woman she hadn't known. Mark John, Brian, and Stacey were the first ones to leave the large room for the receiving line in the vestibule, and Daisy waited her turn, letting all the other mourners file out before her.

She was the last person to shake hands with Mark John and

Brian. While she waited in line, she had noticed they were not looking at each other. In fact, they were standing stiffly side-by-side, taking obvious care not to glance in the other's direction.

Something wasn't right.

CHAPTER 13

*D*aisy waited her turn to express her condolences once again, then the funeral director stepped up to speak to both men as soon as she stepped away from them. Stacey was outside talking to other guests. Daisy needed to use the ladies' room before she met Grover at the restaurant, so she slipped down a hallway and into the restroom.

When she came out she was startled to hear slightly raised voices coming from the vestibule. She walked slowly toward them, not knowing how else to exit the building, but not wanting to get caught in the middle of an argument.

Before she reached the corner to turn into the vestibule, she recognized the voices. Mark John and Brian.

She stopped, not wanting to interrupt them and not wanting to embarrass them by showing up in the middle of their discussion. She couldn't help but overhear what was being said.

"I told you, of course I knew about it!" Brian hissed.

"Why didn't you say anything?" Mark John asked.

"Because she was my sister, for God's sake! I couldn't betray her like that."

"Don't you think I had a right to know what my own wife was doing behind my back?"

"I don't know. You didn't have a right to find out from me, though."

"Some friend you are."

"Mark John, it wasn't like I sat by and watched it happen without trying to do anything about it," Brian said, his voice a bit lower.

"Ha! Sure," Mark John sneered. "Name one thing you did to do stop it."

"For one thing, I called Fiona at least once a week and begged her to stop seeing Walt," Brian said. "You think I'm glad to be the one who introduced them? How was I to know they'd end up falling for each other?"

Silence from Mark John.

"How did you find out, anyway?" Brian asked.

Daisy could hear the sneer in Mark John's voice when he answered. "Your good friend Walt called me. Apparently she finally took your advice and tried to break it off with him last Thursday before some party Walt was having. He called me the next day to tell me what had been going on. Did it out of spite the weekend before she died. He probably killed her."

"Did you know Fiona called Walt's wife to tell her about the affair?" Brian asked. He had apparently decided to gloss over Mark John's accusation that Walt had murdered Fiona. The two men were speaking more calmly now, their voices low.

"No. I didn't know that," Mark John answered.

"It's true. After Walt told you, Fiona was so upset she called Melody and told her what had been going on. But Melody already knew--she had seen them together somewhere."

At the wine bar on the day of the retirement party, Daisy thought. She felt a twinge of embarrassment for continuing to stand there eavesdropping, but she couldn't help it. And it would be strange to step into the vestibule now.

"I'm sorry, Brian. I didn't mean to lash out at you. Of course you were in a tight spot, knowing Fiona was cheating and not wanting to betray her confidence. I just wish things had turned out differently, that's all."

"So do I," Brian replied. There was a brief silence, then Daisy could hear the funeral director's voice again.

"Gentlemen, if you could come with me, we're leaving for the cemetery now." A moment later the door closed and the funeral home was silent. Daisy waited another moment before stepping into the vestibule, her mind racing with the things she had heard. Brian had known about the affair! He had begged Fiona to stop. *He* had introduced the two lovers. *His conscience must be sinking under all the pressure*, Daisy thought.

This was all good news for Grover, though. The more people who knew about the relationship between Fiona and Walt, the less likely it was that the police would decide the caterer was the culprit.

The very thought of it was preposterous.

Daisy left the funeral home through the front door and watched the cars pulling away from the curb for the drive to the cemetery. One car was left behind on the quiet street. It didn't move to follow the other cars. A woman sat behind the steering wheel, also watching the funeral procession. She didn't seem to notice Daisy.

It was Melody Beecham.

CHAPTER 14

Grover was already at the restaurant when Daisy arrived. He stood up when she walked in, as though she might have missed him if he remained seated. He was six and a half feet tall with a shock of blond hair and a lopsided smile that could turn even the grumpiest person's day around.

"How was it?" he asked as they both sat down.

She shrugged. "It was a funeral. They're always awful. But I did learn something interesting." She leaned forward and was about to tell him about the conversation she had heard between Mark John and Brian when their server appeared.

Daisy ordered a glass of white wine and Grover ordered red. When the server had brought their wine and taken their food orders, Daisy leaned forward again.

"It seems Brian, Fiona's brother, knew she was having an affair. Walt works with him and Brian introduced the two of them."

"I don't get it. Why is this news?" Grover asked.

Daisy stared at him for a moment. "Don't you see? The more people who knew about the affair between Fiona and Walt, the better it is for you. Brian not only introduced Fiona and Walt, but he felt terrible about what happened between them. He *begged*--his own words--Fiona to stop seeing Walt."

"How do you know this?" Grover asked, taking a sip of wine and looking over the top of his glass at her.

"How else? I was eavesdropping."

Grover stared at her, his eyes wide. "You shouldn't have done that. What if one of them killed Fiona--and Walt--and got mad that you were listening? You could be next," he said in a low, urgent voice.

"Oh, please. That's not the point. The point is that Brian felt very strongly about the affair and wanted it to stop."

Grover set his glass down slowly.

"You know what else?" Daisy asked.

"There's more?"

"Remember I told you I saw Fiona and Walt at the wine bar the afternoon of the retirement party? She was there to break up with him. He was so upset he called Mark John the next day and told him everything. And then Fiona was so angry about what Walt did that she called Melody and told her. Of course, Melody had seen them together, so she already knew about it."

"So where does that leave the whole investigation?" Grover asked.

"The only thing we know for sure is that Fiona didn't kill Walt. She was already dead," Daisy said. She looked around to make sure no one was listening. She didn't mind eavesdropping now and then, but she didn't want to be the target of someone else doing the same thing.

"There were a lot of people who were angry with Fiona," Daisy said, lowering her voice even more. She started to tick names off on her fingers. "Mark John, obviously. Walt, because Fiona broke off their relationship. Melody, because she was the spurned wife. And even Brian, because he was fiercely against any romantic relationship between Fiona and Walt. Not to mention the burglars who have been in Mark John's neighborhood recently."

Suddenly Daisy stopped.

"What's the matter? You're turning white," Grover said in alarm.

"I just thought of something," Daisy whispered. "What if Jude killed Fiona because she wanted Mark John to herself?"

"I don't know, Daisy," Grover said. "Do you think she's capable of doing something like that?"

"I don't know Jude very well," Daisy conceded. "I really don't know anything about her except that she has feelings for Mark John. Suppose she killed Fiona to get her out of the way so she could have a future with Mark John?" Daisy shivered as she thought of all the time she'd spent in the office with Jude the past week.

"Okay, so the list of people who could have killed Fiona is long. What about Walt?" Grover asked. "We know Fiona didn't do it. But anyone else on that list could have killed him, too. Mark John, Brian, Melody; even Jude, though I'm not sure what her motive would have been. But probably not the burglars."

"You're right--probably not the burglars. And as much as I hate to say it, we have to remember that as far as the police are concerned, you're on that list, too."

CHAPTER 15

*W*ith that, lunch took a decidedly depressing turn.

"Don't remind me," Grover said.

"Have the police been back to ask you any questions?"

"I had to go into the police station to give a formal statement," Grover said.

"Did you take a lawyer with you?"

"No," Grover answered, a sheepish look coming over his face.

"Why not?" Daisy asked, putting her fork down and staring at her friend.

"Because it makes me look guilty, don't you think?" Grover asked.

"No. It makes you look smart. Grover, you have to take this thing seriously."

"I am," Grover said in a beseeching voice. He made a pleading gesture with his hands. "I just think that the minute I take a lawyer in with me, they're going to think I have something to hide."

"I just don't want to see you get in deeper," Daisy said, her gaze softening. "I can't stand the thought of you being arrested. It would ruin your career, your life, everything."

"I know. Believe me, I've thought of that," Grover replied. He put his elbow on the table and set his chin miserably in his hand.

"I'm sure the police are going to investigate all the links between the two victims, if they haven't already," Daisy said in an effort to cheer him up. "That'll take any focus away from you, I would think.

"And there's something I didn't tell you yet," Daisy continued. "Melody was in the parking lot of the funeral home after the funeral. Just watching. She didn't go into the funeral home, as far as I know."

Grover's eyes widened. "Why do you suppose she was there?"

Daisy shrugged. "I don't know. Morbid curiosity, maybe. Or maybe she just wanted to assure herself that Fiona was dead."

"They say murderers sometimes do stuff like that--like visiting the cemetery or showing up at the funeral home or even revisiting the scene of the crime. I'll bet she killed both of them, Daisy."

"You might be right," Daisy said. They sat in silence for a couple minutes.

"Speaking of leaving things out, there's also something I didn't tell you," Grover finally said.

Daisy didn't like the way that sounded. "What do you talking about?" she asked, drawing her words out slowly.

"I should have said something sooner, but Walt disagreed about the amount of the catering bill," Grover explained.

"Tell me that's not true, Grover."

"It is true."

"Why didn't you tell me?" Daisy asked.

"I didn't think it was important at first," Grover said, shaking his head.

"You definitely should have said something sooner. Do the police know?"

"Yes. Brian told them." Daisy closed her eyes and shook her head.

"How did Brian know that Walt disputed the catering bill?"

"I guess Brian is on that retirement committee with Walt, or was, and Walt mentioned it to him. When the police talked to Brian, apparently he told them about his conversation with Walt."

"Did Walt talk to you about the bill, or just Brian?"

"He mentioned it to me."

Daisy closed her eyes and shook her head. "Grover, this looks bad. What did you say when he brought up the amount of the bill?"

"I told him that was the amount I had quoted before the party and that he had an obligation to pay it."

"Did you have the conversation at his house?"

"No--over the phone before I got there."

"And how was it resolved?"

"I knocked three hundred dollars off the bill just to collect the money and be done with him."

"That's probably not a good thing for you." A cold worry was beginning to gnaw the inside of Daisy's stomach.

"Why not?"

"Because he refused to pay the whole bill and now he's dead."

"Who would kill someone over three hundred dollars?" Grover asked.

"Don't you read the news?" Daisy asked, exasperated. "It happens more often than you'd think."

Grover took a deep breath in an effort to calm himself. "Daisy, what am I going to do?"

"If the police ask any follow-up questions about it, just tell the truth. There are enough people who could have killed Walt that hopefully they'll be investigating other suspects. In the meantime, maybe I can find out more about...I don't know, about anything."

"Okay. You'll keep me posted?"

"Of course. It helps that I work with Jude and Mark John, so maybe I can glean some information at the office. Mark John should be returning to work before long."

"I have a party tonight," Grover said, signaling for the checks. "I've got to run."

"Need any help?" Daisy asked.

"This is a small one," he said. "Tish and I can handle it."

"Maybe I should come along anyway, just to make sure you don't do or say anything stupid," Daisy said with a grin. Her attempt to lighten the mood fell flat, though.

"You're probably right," Grover said with a grimace. "Maybe I should just wear a muzzle."

He paid his bill and gave Daisy a sad smile before leaving. Daisy knew she was going to have to work fast if she was going to clear Grover's name.

CHAPTER 16

On Monday Daisy was relieved to see that Mark John was back in the office. She knocked on his door and he called for her to come in.

"Hi, Mark John. How are you doing?"

"About as well as can be expected, I guess," he answered. "They finally let me back in my house and I just couldn't stay alone there any longer. I had to come in to work."

"I don't blame you," Daisy replied. "I'm going to head over to the Library of Congress today to get started on the women's history research, okay?"

"All right," he said tersely. "Please call in and let me know how it goes."

"Will do." Daisy left his office and returned to her own, where Jude was waiting for her.

"I heard the funeral was well-attended," Jude said when Daisy sat down.

"Yes. How did you hear that?"

"Mark John called me Saturday afternoon." So they were talking outside the office. That wouldn't look good to investigators.

"It's probably a good thing you didn't go," Daisy said pointedly.

Jude sighed, showing no signs of leaving.

"Listen, I need to get to the library. We can talk about this later," Daisy said She stood up and Jude finally left.

She took the Metro to the Capitol South stop and when she emerged from underground it was raining. She hoisted her tote bag over her shoulder as she made her way up the long block toward the Madison Building, one of the three main buildings of the Library of Congress.

Once inside, she went straight to the reader registration room to renew her library card, noting along the labyrinthine corridors that there were several people milling around who looked decidedly lost. She tried to help them as best she could, and was glad when it turned out some of them were looking for the reader registration room. She arrived in the large office space leading a parade of bedraggled researchers, all of whom were overwhelmed by the size and scope of the Madison Building. Since Daisy only had to renew her reader identification card, it was a quick in-and-out of the office. She smiled as she left the room, grateful that she didn't have to sit and wait for her identification card. It wouldn't have been a long wait, but she was eager to get started in the Main Reading Room of the Jefferson Building.

She traversed the distance to the Jefferson Building in the underground tunnel connecting the two library buildings. Its light-colored walls, security cameras, and exposed pipes had always reminded Daisy vaguely of the tunnel leading to the S train in Times Square.

After a walk that saved her from having to go out in the drizzling rain, Daisy arrived at the elevator to the main floor of the Jefferson Building. A quick elevator ride, another long walk through a maze of hallways, and she found herself at the information desk and coat check where she emptied her tote bag and placed all her belongings, as per Library of Congress rules, in a clear plastic bag provided by the coat check attendant. She lugged the plastic bag containing her laptop, pencils, and personal items down another twisting hallway until she found the opulent elevators that would take her to her final destination, the Main Reading Room.

When she exited the elevator she made her way to the security station, where she had to sign in and present her reader identification card. From there she walked toward the Main Reading Room. She passed through a much smaller room filled with desks and reference librarians—she might need their help eventually, but she was excited to get to the Main Room. And when she walked under the marble arch into the soaring space, she stopped short for a moment, as she had always done, simply to gaze in awe at the magnificence around her.

The Main Reading Room was adorned with dark red walls, marble columns, stained glass, and gleaming wood. Desks were arranged in concentric circles around the massive reference desk in the middle of the immense room. Looking skyward, Daisy admired the statues keeping watch over the room far below the domed ceilings.

Daisy decided to sit at a desk facing the entrance of the room. That way she would be practically invisible to the people far above who could look down into the reading room via the visitors' gallery off the main atrium of the Jefferson Building. Only researchers were allowed in the reading room, so that kept tourists who might disturb them to a minimum.

Daisy pulled her laptop out of the plastic bag and plugged it in under the desk. She brought up the Library of Congress website. After a few carefully-worded searches, Daisy found a trove of articles paying homage to the history of American women from the days of the Jamestown settlement to the present. She spent the next several hours jotting down notes and making lists of items she would request from the reference librarians the next day. As five o'clock approached and the library staff shuffled around, clearly getting ready for the work day to end, Daisy saved her work, closed her laptop, and made her way back to the cloak room to retrieve her belongings.

As much as she tried to focus on other things, her mind turned to the murders of Fiona and Walt as she rode the Metro to her Dupont Circle stop. A full day of work, and she had learned nothing except that Mark John and Jude had spoken after the funeral, outside the office.

The whole thing was so confounding.

She called Helena when she got home.

"Want to grab dinner?" she asked.

"Sure. Where?"

"You choose," Daisy said.

"What's the matter? Are you all right?" Helena asked.

"I'm just going crazy at work," Daisy said. "I'll tell you more about it when I see you."

They met an hour later at a small cafe not far from Daisy's apartment.

"So what's going on?" Helena asked as she slid into a booth across from Daisy. Daisy let out a long sigh and told her friend everything that had happened since the retirement party. Helena stared at Daisy, mouth agape, as Daisy told her the grisly story.

"I can't believe this," she said. "Why didn't anyone tell me? Grover is a suspect in a murder investigation and no one tells me?" Her eyes flashed.

"He's not technically a suspect, and don't take it personally," Daisy said in her best soothing voice. She wasn't surprised at Helena's reaction to the news--just disappointed. Rather than focusing on her friend's plight, she seemed to be concentrating on having been left out of the loop.

"And why shouldn't I take it personally?" Helena demanded.

"Because I've been a murder suspect, that's why. Grover

knows that. I'm probably the best person to talk to in this situation because I've been there and I know what he's going through." Daisy spoke in tight tones that she hoped would jolt Helena out of being sorry for herself.

It worked.

"You're right. I'm sorry. I don't mean to sound like a baby."

"That's better. Let's concentrate on helping Grover out of this mess, shall we?" Daisy smiled at her friend.

Though the two women talked for over an hour while they ate dinner, they couldn't come up with anything that might help Grover out of his predicament.

"My money is on Walt's wife," Helena said.

"Melody? It's definitely possible," Daisy said. "She had a good reason to kill both Fiona and Walt."

"It's too bad we don't know her," Helena said, twirling her hair around her finger. "If we could just talk to her, we might be able to get a lot of information."

Helena's musings were beginning to take root in Daisy's mind. There was one person she could talk to about Melody...Brian.

"You know, you've given me a good idea," Daisy said, pointing her dessert spoon at Helena.

"Great. What was it?" Helena asked, grinning.

"I'm going to talk to Brian. He knows everyone involved very well. His sister, Mark John, Walt, Walt's wife, and even Jude. He sees her in the office quite often. He might know something and not even realize it. It's odd if he doesn't come into the office at least once a week, so I'm sure I'll see him soon."

"That was a great idea I had," Helena said. "You know, I've been thinking about something."

"What?" Daisy asked, returning her attention to a scoop of ice cream in front of her.

"Once this is all over, I think you and Grover should start seeing each other."

All at once Daisy's ice cream lost its appeal.

"Don't," she said.

"Don't what?" Helena asked.

"Don't start anything," Daisy warned. "I am not interested in a relationship right now. And certainly not with Grover. I know him too well."

"But that's perfect--don't you see?" Helena asked. Her pretty eyes twinkled. "You two were practically made for each other!"

"No. End of discussion," Daisy said firmly. "I'm already married. To my job. Remember?"

Helena rolled her eyes. "Whatever you say. But you can't stop me from thinking it's another one of my great ideas."

"I've got to get home," Daisy said. "And you should go home and take a long, hot bath. Get these silly ideas out of your head."

"Whatever you say," Helena repeated. She was grinning.

CHAPTER 17

*D*aisy had been right to assume Brian would pay a visit to the offices of Global Human Rights before the week was out, but she was at the library when he arrived. She returned late that afternoon to find that he had been in to see Mark John right after school and that he hadn't stayed long.

Mark John was in his office when she returned from the library. She knocked on his door just as Jude opened it and came out, smiling coyly.

"Don't be long, Daisy," she said. Daisy rolled her eyes. Had the woman no shame?

"Mark John, I just wanted to let you know that I will probably go straight to the library tomorrow and spend the day there," Daisy said, walking into his office with a backward glance at Jude's form disappearing down the hallway.

"All right. Call in so I know how the research is going, please," he said.

"Okay. I'll be able to start coming up with an outline for the three articles in a couple days."

"Good." He puffed out his cheeks and idly reached for an item on top of a stack of books on his desk.

"Daisy, I'd like you to do me a favor," he said.

"Sure. What is it?"

"Brian dropped this off earlier this afternoon. He wants me to read it and tell him what I think of it. I just can't. Not right now. But I didn't have the nerve to tell him no."

"And you want me to read it?" Daisy asked.

"Would you mind?" Mark John asked.

"First, what is it?" Daisy countered.

"It's an old diary. At least, I think it's a diary. Brian didn't give me too much information. You're the expert at looking at old things."

"All right, I'll take a look. I assume it's written in English?"

Mark John shrugged. "Probably. Brian wouldn't have asked me to look at it otherwise."

"Why does Brian want you to read it?" Daisy asked.

"Why does Brian do anything? Because he's weird. He thinks I'm fascinated by all these things he finds."

Daisy felt a twinge of sadness for Brian. He probably missed his sister. He was probably just reaching out to Mark John in the spirit of friendship and Mark John was spurning him.

"Okay, I'll take a crack at it," she said. Mark John held out the diary to her. She could tell from a cursory visual examination that the diary was old and fragile.

"Wait," she said. "Let me get a pair of gloves from my office. I don't want the oils on my skin to degrade the paper." She hurried to her office, grabbed a pair of white cotton gloves which she kept in a desk drawer, and returned to Mark John's office. She accepted the book carefully.

"I'll start looking at this tonight," she promised.

Before finishing up some paperwork and leaving for the day, Daisy pulled the white gloves on again and placed the diary on her desk for a closer examination.

It was tattered and brown; it looked like it was made of some kind of animal hide. She picked it up and leafed carefully through the pages, which were yellowed and brittle. A quick glance at the faded and wispy writing revealed to her trained eye that the book was probably a diary, likely written by a woman, almost certainly in the nineteenth century.

She opened the front cover; it was, indeed, a diary. There was a name scrawled on the frontispiece: Trudy Hauchfen. German, Daisy surmised. Under the name was written "Nebraska Territory." A familiar thrill passed through her, that same feeling she got whenever she held something that had belonged to someone else many years before. She had been privileged in her work to have held many such items, and she never tired of looking at old books, old clothing, old household goods, old tools, old anything. She turned the pages carefully, looking for a date. The first entry was dated 1865.

She looked up when Jude passed her office on the way to Mark John's office, and Daisy sighed. She didn't want to be around when Jude finally emerged from his office, so she decided to head home for the day.

Just a few minutes later Daisy was on the Metro headed to her apartment. Sitting down with her tote bag on her lap, she debated whether to take the diary out and read it on the ride home, but she decided against it because the diary was simply too fragile to handle in such a crush of people. She couldn't wait to get home to start reading it.

She passed her favorite wine shop on the way home from the Metro station and bought a bottle of pinot gris. Her apartment was located on a leafy street of brownstones, the colors of their façades being the only difference among the houses. Her building was a bright, melon-coral color with white trim. The color of the building was the thing that had sold Daisy on renting in that building—she knew she would love coming home every day to such a cheerful place.

Once inside, she ran lightly up the three flights of stairs to her apartment and kicked off her shoes as soon as she was through the front door. Placing her tote bag on the table next to the door, she hung up her jacket and went straight to the kitchen carrying the bottle of wine. After pouring herself a small glass, she retrieved the tote bag, curled her legs up on the couch in the living room, and gingerly pulled the diary out of its protective sleeve. She reached for a pair of white gloves she always kept on the end table and slipped them on. She opened the diary carefully and traced her finger lightly across the ink on the frontispiece, wondering about the identity of Trudy. The entries began on the page facing the frontispiece. Paper would have been hard to come by in the American west during that time, Daisy knew, and people wasted no space when they wrote. She squinted and began to read.

CHAPTER 18

OCTOBER 19, 1865- THURSDAY

We were up long before sunrise this morning because it was the first day of the corn harvest. I love the corn harvest because Uncle Rupert and Uncle Theo come to help Papa and the boys, and Aunt Greta and Aunt Verna help us in the kitchen. My cousins help, too. Everyone stays the night and it is like a party. The women and girls were busy preparing food all day long. We only saw the men and boys long enough to feed them. We could hardly keep their plates full, they were so hungry.

During the afternoon there was a knock at the door. We do not like it when strangers come to the door because you never know who is going to be there. It could be Indians. Mama made us all stand across the room while she opened the door. I was standing behind Margaret, but I could stand on my toes and see who was there. It can be very aggravating to be shorter than one's younger sister.

There was a man standing there. He was lost. Mama gave him directions to the place where he said he was going and then he left. Mama locked the door behind him and told us that you can never be too careful when you open the door to a stranger.

We were still serving the food long after sundown. Even so, I wasn't tired because I enjoy having my cousins visit. Tonight we will all sleep in the room Margaret and I share with our brothers and it will be just like Christmas.

T

The writing in the diary was small and faded. It took Daisy several long minutes to read the passage and when she finished she put the diary aside and squeezed her eyes closed to give them a rest. The rest turned into a full-fledged doze and Daisy was startled when the phone rang.

"Hello?" She looked around, wondering how long she had slept. It was already dark outside.

"Hey, it's me." It was Grover.

"What's up?" Daisy asked. "What time is it, anyway?"

"About eight thirty. Want to grab something for dinner?"

Daisy stifled a yawn and looked at her watch. "I must have fallen asleep. I was reading. Um, sure, we can get something for dinner. Want me to meet you somewhere?"

"What do you feel like eating?"

"Pizza," Daisy responded without hesitation.

"I figured you'd say that," Grover said. "Why don't we meet at Giuseppe's in about fifteen minutes?"

"See you then." Daisy hung up and looked in the mirror hanging over her couch. She fluffed her hair with one hand with a quick, nonchalant gesture and grabbed her keys from where they hung next to the front door.

A few minutes later she was waiting outside Guiseppe's Trattoria. She saw Grover before he could see her over the heads of the people milling about on the street in front of the bar next door.

He finally caught sight of Daisy and raised his hand in greeting. "I'm starving," he said as he walked up to her on the sidewalk. "I hope there isn't a wait."

"It doesn't look like it," Daisy replied. She opened the door and he followed her into the darkened interior of the trattoria. They found a table in the front window and a server brought them menus right away.

Once they had ordered Grover sat back in his chair with a sigh.

"Everything okay?" Daisy asked. "Any new developments?"

"I guess everything is okay," Grover replied. "I mean, I'm not in jail yet, right?"

"Don't talk like that," she scolded him.

"All I do is worry. I've got to get out of my own head," Grover said, and he ran his hands through his hair as if to emphasize the point. "Tell me something interesting."

Daisy told him about the diary she was reading for Mark John. "I think it's going to be an interesting project," she said. "Brian brought it into the office today. I was reading that before you called. It was written by a young woman named Gertrude— she calls herself Trudy—in the eighteen-sixties. I actually think I might be able to incorporate it into the research I'm doing for a women's history project."

"How so?"

"It's a first-person account of what women did in the region that was the American west over a century and a half ago. It's totally relevant to the topic of women's history. I've only read one entry and already the division of labor is obvious. And women's distrust of strangers."

"That does sound interesting," Grover said. And he meant it. His capacity for curiosity was one of the things Daisy liked best about him—he was always up for an adventure or learning something new.

"How are you doing?" Daisy asked when she had told him more about the diary entry she had read.

"Okay, I suppose, all things considered," he answered. "I've got a big wedding this weekend, so we were busy getting things ready for that. In fact, I have to go back in tonight. At least it's helping to keep my mind off my problems. We're doing the reception on Saturday night and the brunch the next morning."

"Need help?" Daisy asked.

"Nah," he answered. "We've got things pretty well under control."

As they ate Grover told Daisy the dishes he was making for the wedding festivities. "Sounds complicated," Daisy said, looking pensively at her pizza crust. "But everything sounds delicious."

She was happy to listen to him talk. He was visibly more relaxed when he talked about work and the food he was going to prepare, and she was thankful he had that outlet to keep some of his stress at bay.

They parted ways out front of the restaurant, promising to talk on Monday, after Grover had had a chance to decompress from the wedding events.

Daisy walked home deep in thought. The diary had captured her imagination, as historical objects tended to do, and she was eager to get back to it. She wanted to read one more entry before turning in for the night. Once back in her apartment, she curled up on the couch and opened the diary again.

CHAPTER 20

OCTOBER 26, 1865- THURSDAY

We have been working from before dawn until after dark every day except Sundays, trying to get the corn in. It has rained a few times, but Papa and the boys have to work even in the rain. The aunts and uncles and cousins left after the first two days of harvest, but they have returned once to help.

The man who came to our door on the first day of the harvest was in church on Sunday and he brought his two children with him. I recognized him right away, even though I only saw him for a moment the day he came to our house needing directions. I was surprised to see him at church. Mama decided he can't be all bad if he goes to church and Papa invited the three of them to supper afterward.

His name is Thomas Sheridan and he hails from the east, from Washington. He is tall and stocky with dark brown hair and a beard. He reminds me a bit of Papa, though of course Papa is much older. He doesn't say much, but he has a lovely smile and his children are well behaved. There is a girl and a boy. The girl is Adelaide, but Jesse, her brother, calls her Lady. They are very sweet.

Mama has asked them to return next Sunday for supper after church. I confess I'm looking forward to their visit.

T

Trudy writes remarkably well for a farmer's daughter in the American west at that time, Daisy thought. She withdrew a notebook from her tote bag and began jotting down some notes about the diary entries. They would be good fodder for her women's history articles. She also made a note to herself, though she was sure she would remember, to look for other diaries in the Library of Congress written by other women—surely there would be more information to mine in those.

And when she returned to the Library of Congress the next day, she did just that. In addition to looking for the sources she had already researched, she found diaries written by women who worked in New York City sweatshops at the turn of the twentieth century, women in towns where railroads were being built, and women of African descent who worked as household servants in the mid-twentieth century. The women who authored all the diaries had certain things in common--hard work, low wages, and despicable working conditions.

Daisy found an absorbing account of one woman's days spent at the Triangle Shirtwaist Factory. The journal chronicled the woman's miserable existence in the famous New York City sweatshop before it burned to the ground, trapping scores of women inside. As the writer of the journal perished in the fire along with almost one hundred fifty others, Daisy made a note to find other first-hand accounts of the fire for more information.

When her phone buzzed, it startled her. She looked around, hoping it hadn't disturbed anyone in the reading room. Phones were supposed to be on silent or off, but the vibration of the phone still made a noise against the wooden desk. One or two patrons looked in her direction, frowning, and she answered the phone quickly.

"Hello?" she whispered. More disapproving looks. Daisy stood up quickly and walked out of the Main Reading Room into the hallway where the elevators were located.

"It's Mark John."

"Oh. What do you need?" Daisy was annoyed. *Why is he bothering me right now? He knows I'm busy.*

"Just checking in to see how you're doing."

Daisy sighed. "Fine. I'm getting some good background information."

"When do you think you'll be back in the office?"

Daisy rolled her eyes. It was common for Mark John to make these calls, which he didn't seem to realize did nothing but waste everyone's time. "I thought I told you I would be here all day. I was just going to go home from here tonight and then come in first thing Monday. Does that work for you?"

"Yeah, sure. I'll see you Monday, then."

Daisy turned off her phone after she hung up with Mark John. She didn't want to give him the chance to bother her again. Then she returned to the reading room, where she quickly lost herself again in the Triangle Shirtwaist diary. It was horrifying to think that women had suffered under such treacherous conditions only to die tragically, not living to see the strides made in worker safety after the event. She took copious notes as she read, always being careful to note the source of quotes and other information. When she could identify a primary source with library catalog information, it made keeping track of her research much easier.

On the train back to Dupont Circle that evening after the library closed, her thoughts turned to the provenance of the diary Mark John had given her. She had taken to calling it "Trudy's diary." At the top of her to-do list when she arrived at work Monday morning would be to contact Brian to ask where the diary had come from and how it came to be in his possession.

With Grover busy with the wedding event preparations, Daisy decided to spend Friday evening with Trudy's diary.

She fixed a cup of herbal tea and sat on the couch in her pajamas, eager to open the book and delve back into the world of early Nebraska life.

CHAPTER 22

OCTOBER 29, 1865- SUNDAY

Thomas, Lady, and Jesse came for supper after church today. I helped prepare part of the meal last night. Mama and Margaret are very quiet around Thomas and his children, I think because they don't want to overwhelm them. But I like to talk to them, even though I know Papa does not approve. It's so interesting to have other people in our house!

Papa and Thomas talked for a long time about farming. Thomas has farmed before, in Ohio (after leaving Washington), but Nebraska is different, he says. The weather is harsher, the land less forgiving. He says that by next spring he will be able to plant crops, but until then he will be preparing the land and building a wooden house for himself and his children.

Lady and Jesse are quite young, about five years old, twins. They speak to each other in words I do not know—it is as if they have a language only they can understand.

Thomas and Papa will attend a meeting at the church together this week, once the corn is in. I wish I could go. I asked Papa if I could go with them, but he said the meeting is no place for a girl.

T

*D*aisy was up early the next morning to run errands and clean her apartment. She had just finished a load of laundry when she remembered she had left a flash drive at the office. The drive contained research materials she would need over the weekend. After starting another load of clothes, she grabbed her coat and the office keys she kept in her tote bag and headed over to K Street. When she reached her office building, she took the elevator up to the Global Human Rights offices and let herself in. She immediately noticed that the lights were on in the rear of the suite.

She was a bit relieved to find she wasn't alone--she didn't like to be the only one in the office, especially on the weekend, because the entire building was practically deserted. The only people around were the facilities people who worked in the building lobby and in the basement offices. Having watched one too many horror movies as a teenager, Daisy harbored a fear of the dark and of being alone in an otherwise empty space. She hurried toward her office and closed the door behind her.

A moment later she had the flash drive in her hand. Slipping it into her pocket, she opened her office door and stepped into the hallway just as a shuffling noise came from the direction of Mark John's office. Or perhaps it was the other direction, from Jude's office. Daisy couldn't tell. She glanced over her shoulder and walked straight into the water cooler in the hallway. It teetered in its base, making loud gurgling noises as large bubbles rose to the surface of the water inside. She reached for the water container to steady it, then heard a voice behind her.

"Hello, Daisy." She jumped in surprise, not recognizing the voice immediately, and whirled around to see Brian standing in the hallway outside Mark John's office.

"Brian! What are you doing here?" she asked breathlessly, tapping the cooler to make sure it was in place.

"I was just leaving some books for Mark John in his office."

"How did you get in?" Daisy asked. She had recovered from her surprise quickly, but was curious about Brian's unexpected appearance.

"One of the guys who works in the lobby let me in. He's seen me here plenty of times. He must think I work here," Brian said with a chuckle.

"Heh," Daisy gave a half-hearted chuckle. "On Monday I'll let Mark John know you were here."

"Oh, no need for that," Brian replied. "I just texted him. He knows I'm here."

Daisy nodded and glanced toward the door. "Well, I've got to go. I have a load of laundry that has to go in the dryer. See you later, Brian."

"I'll go with you. I mean, down in the elevator. Not back to your apartment," he said with a laugh. Daisy smiled thinly and followed him to the front door of the suite. She trusted Brian. Didn't she? She didn't know him well, but her interactions with him had been harmless and his geeky reputation in the office was legendary. *He is just a sweet man who misses his sister and wants to connect with his brother-in-law,* Daisy thought to herself. But still, she felt better walking behind him so she could see him. He stepped out into the elevator bank and she locked the Global Human Rights door behind her, rattling the door handle to make sure it was locked. She hoped Brian was catching on to her subtle hint—that the employees of GHR cared about their security and didn't want guests entering uninvited when the office was closed.

They stepped into the elevator. Daisy inched toward the back corner while Brian pushed the button for the lobby. Thankfully, only the service elevators in the rear of the building weren't monitored via video feed, so Daisy wasn't really worried about being in one of the main elevators with Brian. The guards in the lobby could see her, so that eased her anxiety. She considered asking Brian about the chain of ownership of Trudy's diary, but seeing him in the office had so unnerved her that she decided not to. She just wanted to get off the elevator. She glanced at Brian, who happened to look at her at the same moment. He smiled at her and whistled a nameless tune through his teeth as they descended. She was relieved when the elevator reached the main floor and *dinged* softly as the doors slid open. She made a motion with her hand inviting Brian to exit the elevator ahead of her, but he responded saying "Ladies first."

She nodded and stepped out in front of him, then pretended she was searching for something in her coat pocket while she waited for him to leave the building. She briefly considered speaking to the doorman about Brian and asking that he not be let in again while the office was closed, but then she reconsidered. If he really did have Mark John's permission to be in the office on the weekend, it would be inappropriate of her to ask that he be barred from entering.

Brian left the building and Daisy watched him turn left and disappear into a coffee shop up the street. She was headed in that direction, too, but something told her to go the other way. She headed to the right once she was outside the building and walked around the block. When she had walked most of the way around the block and returned to K Street, she was dismayed, but not really surprised, to see Brian standing across the street leaning against the front window of the coffee shop, his arms folded in front of him. Too late, she realized he had seen her. She picked up her pace in the direction of her apartment, trying to be discreet as she checked over her shoulder to see if he had followed her.

He hadn't. He was watching her walk away, but he stayed where he was in front of the shop. Daisy shuddered. *Why does he make me uncomfortable all of a sudden?* she wondered. *He's a nice person. A harmless history buff.*

She slowed her pace as she began to relax, scolding herself for being so timid. Back at home, she finished the laundry, fixed herself a quick lunch, and decided she deserved a reward for all she had accomplished during the morning. She sat down on the couch and opened Trudy's diary.

CHAPTER 24

NOVEMBER 5, 1865- SUNDAY

Mama invited Thomas and the children for supper again after church today. I noticed Thomas watching me as Mama and I prepared the food. His gaze unsettled me so, I suppose because there are rarely men in our house, except for family.

They stayed longer than they have the other times they have come for a meal. Margaret and I watched Lady and Jesse play in the yard while Mama read the Bible to the boys inside the house and Papa talked to Thomas. I think they share many conversations about farming, but I cannot be sure because I am not invited to participate.

It was late in the afternoon when Thomas and the children left. They live in town right now, while Thomas is building a small house on a homestead about five miles from here. I would like to see the house when it is finished. I would think it will take Thomas a long time to build it himself. When Papa built our house my uncles and brothers helped. It is a small house and it was built quickly. With winter coming, I don't know if Thomas will be able to finish the house before the snow begins to fall. It will be starting soon.

Just before he left, Thomas asked me if I would like to accompany him and the children to a gathering at the church next Saturday afternoon. Papa and Mama had both given their consent already, so I told him I would like to go with him. I am very much looking forward to our outing.

T

*D*aisy smiled as she finished the entry in Trudy's diary. She was enormously pleased that a romance seemed to be budding between Trudy and Thomas and she couldn't wait to read the next entry. She resisted the urge to flip to the back of the diary to see how it ended. It was just like reading a novel.

While she worked that afternoon on the research materials she had obtained from the flash drive, the thought of seeing Brian at the office was never far from her mind. Again she debated with herself whether to call Mark John and tell him about the incident, but she decided not to call. After all, Brian and Mark John were family and it was not Daisy's place to be tattling on Brian.

Her mind wandered while she was trying to work. Why had Brian been waiting across the street from the office, watching her? Why did he watch her as she walked away from the building? Why didn't he follow her if he was so interested in her and where she was going?

This is silly, she chided herself. *He was probably there getting a cup of coffee and he simply happened to see me walking around the block.* Daisy shook her head as if to rid herself of such thoughts and continued working.

The weekend sped by with all the housework and writing Daisy had to do. On Monday morning she was in the office, putting the finishing touches on the story she had been working on. She waited until Jude was in her office with the door closed before going into Mark John's office to tell him of her progress on the women's history.

She gave a peremptory knock on his office door. "Mark John, I just wanted to let you know how my research is coming along," she said, ducking her head into his office.

"Good," he said, looking up from his computer. "Sit and we'll talk."

She sat down in the chair opposite him and told him what direction she was planning to take for the articles on women's history. She wanted to start with American women, as Mark John had requested, then branch out to other regions and cultures for comparison. Mark John had a list of questions that he wanted answered in her articles and it was clear she would need to do far more research.

She told him she'd go back to the Library of Congress to take a look at their collection of old diaries, then she stood up to leave. Keeping her voice light, she said casually, "I was surprised to see Brian in here over the weekend."

"Brian was here?" Mark John's head snapped up. "What was he doing?"

Daisy shrugged. "Just dropping off some things for you to see, I guess. He said he had texted you about it."

"He probably thought he did," Mark John said. "He can be a little absent-minded." He paused. "I didn't see anything on the conference table that he might have dropped off. Where did he leave it?"

"I don't know. I assumed he left it in here. He was in here when I got here."

Where were the books Brian had dropped off, if they weren't in Mark John's office?

"What the hell did he come into my office for?" he thundered, then smacked his hand on the top of his desk. "I've told him if he comes into the office on the weekends to drop things off, just leave them on the table in the conference room," he fumed. "I'll have to remind him. My office is not public property."

Though his reaction was a little over the top, Daisy understood how Mark John felt. It would alarm her if she knew someone had been in her office while no one else was around. She hesitated a moment before leaving Mark John's office, wondering if she should tell him about seeing Brian across the street several minutes after they left the building. She decided against it and returned to her office, then left for the Library of Congress a little while later.

After doing some preliminary research in the Main Reading Room, Daisy was excited to find more diaries to read in the Rare Book reading room. The librarian brought one diary at a time so Daisy could read and take notes. The old leather-bound volumes were beautiful objects in their own right--the handwriting was old and faded, the script fancy and slanted, the animal hide covers supple and soft. No one wrote like that anymore—cursive was barely even taught in schools nowadays. Daisy was dismayed by the thought that diaries like the ones she had the privilege of reading were no longer being written. *All the more reason to take care of the ones we have and to let the world know what these women from other centuries had to say about their own lives.*

The research was going well and Daisy was almost ready to start putting ideas down in outline form. She made her way back to the Main Reading Room and opened her laptop at one of the wooden desks. She was just opening a blank document to start typing when something made her look up at the gallery above, to the Plexiglass-walled alcove where tourists could gaze into the Main Reading Room without disturbing the researchers below. She was shocked by what she saw.

Mark John was standing in the gallery with the rest of the tourists, watching Daisy work. She held his gaze for a moment, then whipped out her cell phone and texted him.

What are you doing up there?

She looked up again and watched as Mark John realized he had a text and pulled his phone from his pocket.

I was in the neighborhood for a meeting and thought I'd check in.

She grimaced. You could have just texted me.

Mark John replied, I know, but I haven't been to this library in a while and I wanted to have a look.

Daisy didn't believe him. Are you sure you weren't just checking up on me?

Of course.

With that, Mark John frowned at her and stepped aside, out of her sight, so that other people could crowd into the alcove to get a look at the world-famous reading room. She put her phone down and tried to concentrate on the outline in front of her, but she found that her fingers wouldn't type. She was convinced Mark John had come to the library specifically to check up on her. This was becoming a worrisome habit of his, and one she found invasive and upsetting. She was a professional and intended to be treated as such. She didn't need him babysitting her—she was capable of doing her job well without supervision. She wondered briefly if he behaved the same way with Jude. It would be hard to tell, because Jude was normally in the office and he could easily check up on her in the normal course of his day. Daisy vowed to discuss the issue with him first thing the next morning.

But the next morning Mark John wasn't in the office. Jude was perturbed, asking the receptionist at least every fifteen minutes if she had heard from him. She tried calling his cell, his house, and even Brian, to no avail. He finally came into the office around noon, looking bedraggled and wan. Daisy was in her office when he arrived, but she knew he was there because of the commotion Jude caused over his appearance.

"Mark John! Are you all right? What on earth happened to you? We've been so worried."

Daisy rolled her eyes. She hadn't been at all worried about Mark John and felt Jude's concern was overblown. Mark John passed her office followed closely by Jude, and they both ignored Daisy. When they were in his office they shut the door and though Daisy strained her ears to hear what they were talking about, she couldn't hear anything. She had an idea that Mark John was listening to a litany of complaints from Jude about his unexcused absence from her sight.

They were holed up in his office for almost an hour. When Jude emerged, she heaved a deep breath and stalked past Daisy's office without a word. Daisy didn't know what was going on with Mark John, but she still intended to speak to him about his suspicious appearance yesterday at the Library of Congress. She knocked on his office door.

"Mark John, I'd like to speak to you if you have a minute," she said when he called for her to come in.

"What is it, Daisy?" he asked, running both hands over his face.

"If you'd rather wait..." she offered, feeling suddenly that he might actually be having a personal crisis. Maybe the police had learned something new about Fiona's murder...

"No, I don't want to wait." *I see he's just as pleasant as always,* thought Daisy.

"I was wondering if there was any particular reason you were at the library yesterday when I was working. I suppose I just want to make sure that you think I'm doing a good job and that you don't feel the need to be checking up on my work habits."

He glared at her for a moment, then his face softened. "I'm sorry if you felt that way. I was in the neighborhood for lunch and I thought I'd go have a look at the library." *So was it a meeting or lunch?* Daisy wondered. Maybe both. Maybe she had seized upon a trivial discrepancy in his stories and there was nothing to it.

"That's fine. I just don't want you to think I can't be trusted to get my assignments done."

"Of course I believe you can get your assignments done, Daisy," he replied in a tired voice. "Now if you don't mind, I have some phone calls I need to make." Daisy took the hint and left.

She was fuming when she got back to her desk. She didn't believe for a minute that he trusted her to get her work done. The Library of Congress was a time-consuming detour even if he had had a meeting—or lunch—in the area, and she had a feeling he was there solely to make sure she was working.

Then a thought occurred to her. Had Jude been putting ideas into his ear, suggesting that Daisy couldn't be relied upon to do her work like a professional? That sounded like the sort of thing Jude might do. But then again, why would Jude do such a thing? She had asked Daisy for help finding the person who killed Fiona--surely she wouldn't be attempting to sabotage Daisy's job. Besides that, Jude had already proven herself the jealous type, and she wasn't likely to suggest to Mark John that he spend more time keeping an eye on Daisy.

Daisy was developing a tension headache by the time she left work. She called Grover and asked him to come over to her apartment for dinner. He accepted, so she stopped at the grocery store on the way home to pick up the things she needed to make a quick meal for the two of them. She felt the need to vent about work, but she also wanted to know if the police had contacted him again about Walt.

He arrived a little while later with a box containing two pieces of cheesecake. "I hope whatever we're having pairs well with this," he said with a grin. "It was left over from the party Saturday night."

"Perfect. We're having BLTs and tomato soup," she replied.

Grover sprawled out on the couch while he waited for her. He had picked up Trudy's diary on the end table when she walked into the living room.

"Don't touch that!" she yelled.

He gave a start and dropped the diary where it had been and put his hands up. "What did I do?"

"You can't touch that without gloves," she scolded. "That's the diary I was telling you about. It's very old and it doesn't belong to me and if something happens to it I'm in big trouble. My boss already thinks I can't be trusted."

"What?" Grover exclaimed. "Why not?"

"Who knows?" Daisy answered with a sigh. "He showed up at the library where I was working yesterday and I saw him watching me in the reading room."

"Sounds like a creep," Grover offered.

"I don't think he's a creep. I just think he doesn't believe I can do the job."

"Is there anything wrong with that? I mean, if he's really checking up on you, then he's obviously finding out that you're capable of doing the work. Now maybe he'll leave you alone."

"But he calls me when I'm out of the office, too, to see what I'm doing."

"Maybe he's just a control freak."

"Maybe," Daisy said doubtfully.

Over dinner Grover regaled her with tales from the wedding over the weekend. Apparently the bride had a hangover on Saturday and threw up right before the wedding. The groom got lost on the way to the church. Grover had Daisy in stitches before the end of the meal.

"Stop!" she cried, holding her sides from laughing. "You have way more fun at work than most people." Grover grinned. It was nice to see him smiling, and the worry lines had lifted from his forehead since arriving at her apartment.

"So let's get down to business," Daisy said. "I haven't talked to you in a few days. What do you hear from the police?"

Grover sobered immediately. "I've been trying not to think about it. But two officers came to my apartment to see me Saturday morning. They wanted to know more about Walt's refusal to pay the entire bill."

"I wonder why they wanted to know that," Daisy mused.

"I'll tell you why. Because Melody reported that Walt's wallet had been stolen. So now they think I took his wallet after I killed him because I wanted the three hundred bucks."

"You're kidding," Daisy said, her mouth hanging open in dismay.

"I'm not. Do you think it's possible that he was killed in a robbery that went south?"

"I don't know what to think. I want to believe Melody did it, but a robbery is certainly a possibility. Was anything else stolen?"

"Not that I know of," Grover replied.

"Did the police ask to search your apartment?"

"No. Do you think they will?"

"I don't know," Daisy said. "I'm sure they got a good look around while they were there, but obviously they couldn't have looked in drawers or anything like that. They might come back with a search warrant."

"So what do I do then?" Grover asked.

"Call a lawyer."

"And if I don't?"

"Then let them search. Hopefully it won't come to that,"

Daisy said with a sigh. "What did you tell them about the dispute over the bill?"

"The same thing I told them before. Walt complained, I disagreed, and then I ended up giving him a three-hundred-dollar discount."

"Did things get heated between you and Walt?" Daisy asked.

"I wouldn't say so. He was just being a jerk, Daisy. He didn't want to pay the price he agreed to, and he was trying to put something over on me."

"So why did you take the three hundred dollars off the bill?"

"Because I didn't want him to bad-mouth DC Haute Cuisine. My reputation is worth the three hundred bucks."

"And that's what you told the police?"

"Yes. Almost word-for-word."

"We need to find out Melody's story," Daisy said. "Let me work on Brian and see what I can learn from him."

"Okay. Thanks for your help. I should get going. Want help with the dishes?"

"No. You probably spent half the weekend doing dishes," Daisy replied. "I'll see you later."

After Grover left and the dishes were done, Daisy settled down to read more of Trudy's diary. She was finding that a stillness came over her each time she opened the diary and she was eager to follow Trudy's days in the early American west.

CHAPTER 26

NOVEMBER 15, 1865- WEDNESDAY

Thomas and I and the children had such fun on Saturday at church. I haven't even had time since then to sit down and write about it because we got snow on Sunday and we've been busy making sure everything on the farm is ready for winter.

Thomas and I attended a meeting in town last night. It was held to discuss the building of another store on Main Street. Thomas is interested in finding out as much as he can about the town since he is a new resident. He didn't say anything during the meeting, but discussed it with me on the way home. He does not agree that the town needs another building, and especially not another store. He thinks the town is growing too big, too quickly. I'm not sure I agree with him and I told him so. He seems to like discussing things with me. He says I'm smart.

When we got home Mama asked him to come to supper again on Sunday after church and to bring Lady and Jesse, of course. He said they'd all come, and I'm happy that I'll be seeing him again.

T

NOVEMBER 30, 1865- THURSDAY

I have not been seeing much of Thomas and the children because the snow has come to stay for the winter. He has been working on the inside of their house. He has invited me to come see it when it is done, but he fears that won't be until the springtime.

Papa has spent a lot of his time with my brothers in the stable making all the repairs he did not have time to make during the autumn. Mama and Margaret and I have been putting up the last of the harvest for the winter. We have a lot of food. Sometimes it seems like we'll never be able to eat all the food we have stored, but I know we will be running low by the time spring comes.

The snow is about a foot deep right now. I like to walk outside when it's snowing, but it makes Mama nervous so I don't do it very often.

I miss seeing Thomas and Lady and Jesse. I was getting used to seeing them at least one or two times a week. I'm afraid that won't be possible again until the weather gets better.

T

DECEMBER 24, 1865- SUNDAY

I can't believe what just happened. Thomas and the children couldn't come for supper today because Lady is sick. But Thomas came into church as the service was ending and gave me a package wrapped in newspaper. A Christmas gift! I haven't opened it yet because he said to wait until tomorrow. I'm so excited!

T

*D*aisy was dying to know what Thomas gave Trudy that Christmas back in 1865, but before she could read any further the phone rang. Annoyed, Daisy picked up the receiver.

"Hello?"

"Hello, Daisy? This is Brian. Brian Comstock. How are you?"

"Oh," Daisy said, surprised. "I'm fine, Brian. Can I help you with something?" She was wary, given the circumstances of her last encounter with Brian.

"I'm wondering if you know whether Mark John has read the diary I sent him last week. The one from the mid-eighteen hundreds Nebraska. I was thinking about it tonight and I can't seem to get in touch with him."

Daisy knew Mark John was supposed to be reading the diary, but she couldn't lie to Brian. "Actually, I'm reading it myself right now. I asked Mark John if I could read it first and he said that would be okay. Is it all right with you?"

"Oh, yes. Of course it's all right. Are you enjoying it?"

"Yes, very much. I read a little of it each night before bed. Do you mind if I ask where you got it? I'd like to include some of the material in an article I'm writing for the journal, but before I can use it I need to know where it came from."

"Uh, well, I don't know exactly. I found it."

"Can you tell me where you found it?"

"In a box."

"Where was the box?"

"In my garage."

"Where was it before you found it in the garage?"

"Um, I'm not precisely sure."

This was getting ridiculous. Was there some reason Brian couldn't divulge where the diary had come from?

Daisy suppressed a sigh of frustration. "Tell you what, Brian. If you're able to remember where the diary came from, could you let me know? I'd appreciate it."

"Yes. Sure thing."

"While I have you on the phone, I was wondering if you could tell me a little bit about Melody Beecham."

There was silence on the other end of the line.

"Brian?" Daisy thought maybe they had been disconnected.

"I'm here. Why do you want to know about Melody?"

"I'm just wondering. She's lost a husband, you know, and I was wondering how she's been handling it."

"I'm sure you know that Walt and my sister were having an affair before they died," Brian said.

"Yes."

"I begged Fiona not to do it," Brian said. His voice sounded anguished. "Our parents are deceased, but they would have been so disappointed." This wasn't about Melody, but Daisy figured she should listen carefully. It sounded like Walt needed to talk and besides, she might learn something interesting.

"Did you ask her why she was drawn to Walt?" Daisy asked.

"Of course. She always said the same thing--Mark John never paid any attention to her."

"And Walt did?"

"Walt was completely besotted. He told me he had found his soulmate." Brian sneered the last word.

"Wow," Daisy said, unsure of what to say next.

"Marriage is sacred," Brian continued, a touch of scorn creeping into his voice. "You can't just pretend your marriage vows don't exist because you're not receiving enough attention."

"Did you ever mention this to Mark John?"

"No. I didn't want to embarrass the man. I'm sure he didn't want me knowing about all his marital troubles. But I did try to hint around to him sometimes, you know. For example, I would tell him about things going on in the community and suggest that he and Fiona go. Things like that."

"He didn't follow up on your suggestions?"

"Not that I know of."

"So, getting back to Melody," Daisy said, "how is she doing?"

"She's a mess. First she finds out her husband is sleeping with another woman, then he's murdered. The poor woman doesn't know how she's going to explain this to her children when they get older."

"I'm sure she's devastated," Daisy murmured.

"And the police won't leave her alone," Brian added.

"Why not?"

"Because she looks guilty, of course. The jilted wife, couldn't take it, that sort of thing."

"Do you think there could be any truth to that?"

"If you're suggesting what I think you're suggesting, Daisy, it's highly inappropriate of either of us to make any such accusation."

Uh-oh. The last thing I want to do is antagonize Brian, thought Daisy. *He's one of the few people who can help figure out this mess.*

"Oh, no, no. I wasn't making an accusation. What I meant was, do you think Melody could have been so upset she didn't know what she was doing?" Daisy asked.

"Oh, I doubt that. Anything is possible, I suppose, but Melody has a wiser head on her shoulders than that."

"I'm sure you're right," Daisy said in a soothing voice. "What a relief."

"I've got to get going, Daisy."

"Sure. Oh, one more thing, Brian. Where did you get my number?"

"I found it online. It was surprisingly easy."

In the days that followed Daisy was busy with assignments for Global Human Rights. She went to work every morning still tired from the day before, and she went to bed each night exhausted from a long day. She didn't even have a chance to pick up Trudy's diary. She didn't see Grover or Helena again until two weekends later, when the three of them gathered for an early lunch before Grover had to get to work for an evening garden party. Daisy finally had a day to herself without any deadline hanging over her head.

Helena was telling them a story about her new boyfriend, Bennett, when Daisy's phone rang. It was Mark John. Daisy excused herself from the table and took the call on the sidewalk outside the restaurant.

"What's up?" she asked.

"What are you doing right now?"

"Having lunch with some friends. Why?"

"I just talked to Brian and he's obsessed about that diary he gave me. He says you have it. Do you?"

"Yes. You asked me to read it and you told me to let you know if there's anything interesting in it so you could discuss it with him if he asked about it."

She could tell Mark John was thinking back, trying to recall the incident. Finally he said, "So you're still reading it?"

"I've been too busy for over a week now to even look at it. Do you want it back?"

He sighed. "Not really. Is there anything in it I should know about?"

"I don't think so. It's just a young woman from Nebraska and what seems like a courtship between her and a man with two children. I haven't read enough to know for sure. Nothing you'd be interested in."

"All right. Keep it for now. I may have to ask for it if he doesn't get off my case."

"No problem. Is that all you wanted?"

"I suppose. Which friends are these that you're having lunch with?"

"Helena and Grover. You've probably heard me talk about them."

"Ah, yes. I guess I have. Well, enjoy."

Daisy shook her head as she ended the call. *He's so nosy*, she thought.

She returned to the table just as Helena was telling Grover about a man she had met recently. Daisy sat down and Helena turned to her excitedly. "I was just telling Grover about Dave, a guy I met last week. He's not my type, but I think he would be perfect for you, Daisy."

Daisy replied without hesitation. "Not interested."

"Why not?" Helena whined. "We could double-date. Come on, it would be fun!"

"Nope," Daisy said. "I'm not looking for a date or a boyfriend or anything like that. I'm too busy."

"I'll get a picture of him. You'll change your mind."

"Want to bet?" Daisy asked with a smirk. Grover watched the exchange with interest.

"Why don't you want to, Daisy?" he asked.

"I just explained why. I'm not looking for anyone. I don't have time."

He looked at her thoughtfully. "You work too hard."

"Stop it. Now who wants to go to the Natural History

Museum? My treat." Daisy grinned. None of the Smithsonian museums charged an admission fee.

"I'll go," said Helena.

"Can't," Grover said, signaling the waiter. "Got to get to work."

Back at the office on Monday morning, Daisy decided to return to the Library of Congress to do more research for the articles she was working on for Mark John. She went straight to the Rare Book Reading Room and found the librarian who had helped her on her last visit. The librarian remembered Daisy and offered to get her the books she needed. Daisy spent the day doing the things she loved most—reading and writing. She took notes, worked on her outline for the articles, and pored over old documents and primary sources. She was tired when she went home that evening, but in a good way. She wished she could spend more time trying to help Grover and Jude, but if she was honest with herself, she didn't know where to look for answers. What could she learn that the police couldn't find out? And her job had to come first--without it, she'd be no help to anyone.

That night she ate a quick dinner and sat down to read Trudy's diary. She had been looking forward to it for a couple weeks, since the last time she set it aside. As she recalled, it had been Christmas Eve, 1865, and Trudy had received a Christmas gift from Thomas.

CHAPTER 28

DECEMBER 25, 1865- CHRISTMAS DAY, MONDAY

It was all I could do this morning to finish my chores in the house and the barn before I opened the gift from Thomas. And what a gift it is! It is a beautiful brooch with a white enamel figure against a background the color of a robin's egg. Mama protested that I couldn't possibly accept such a gift from a man, but Papa just smiled and said I should pin it to my dress to see how it looked.

I looked just like one of the ladies in the magazines I see in the shop in town. I love it! I am very eager to see Thomas to thank him for such a beautiful and generous gift. I'm keeping it, no matter what Mama says.

I wonder when I'll see him again. And Lady and Jesse too, of course. But mostly Thomas.

T

JANUARY 10, 1866- WEDNESDAY

What a surprise it was when Thomas visited this evening! He brought the children with him and Mama insisted that they stay for the evening meal. Lady and Jesse seem tired. I think they're bored because they haven't been able to spend much time outdoors—the weather has been stormy and wild. I don't know how Thomas was able to get here over the drifts of snow between our house and the town, but I'm glad he did.

I thanked him for the brooch while Mama looked on disapprovingly. Papa just smiled again. It was as if he knew Thomas was going to give me that brooch.

Thomas had good news—the inside of his house is completed, so as soon as the weather gets better he'll be able to get back to complete the smaller details on the outside. The house should be ready for him and the children to move into by spring.

I hope he hasn't forgotten that he said he would show me the house after he finished it.

T

I knew it! Daisy thought when she closed the diary for the night. *I knew he would give her something feminine and personal! Definitely a romance brewing.*

Jude was in a funk the next morning at work. Daisy hesitated to ask what the problem was, but the more often Jude walked past her office and let out a labored sigh, the more obvious it became that Daisy wasn't going to get any work done if she didn't find out what was troubling the senior editor.

"Jude, is everything okay?" she asked when Jude had walked by for the umpteenth time.

"Is it that obvious?" asked Jude, stopping short in the doorway.

Daisy didn't answer.

"It's just that the police aren't making any progress in finding out who killed Fiona," she said, flopping uncharacteristically into the chair opposite Daisy.

"It's a murder investigation," Daisy reminded her dryly. "They can't hurry stuff like that. They don't want to get it wrong."

"But I'm worried about Mark John. He can't move on with such uncertainty hanging over his head."

"And by 'moving on,' what do you mean, exactly?" Daisy asked.

"Well, obviously, I mean getting on with the rest of his life."

"And the police haven't come up with any promising leads?" Daisy asked.

"Not that they've shared with Mark John," Jude replied. "Have you found out anything that could help Mark John? Anything at all?"

"I wish I had good news, but I don't. I talked to Brian about Melody, Walt's wife, to see if he could shed any light on her state of mind, but he seemed rather protective of her. He seemed angry when I hinted that Melody might have been capable of murder. He's the only person involved who knows Melody, so any information about her has to come from him."

"I wonder how he's so sure she didn't do it," Jude mused.

Daisy shrugged. "I don't know. Listen, I've got a lot of work to do. If I find out anything else, I'll let you know."

"Sorry to keep you for so long. It's just that you can be more objective than the rest of us," Jude said, smiling at Daisy. "I believe that you'll be able to figure this whole thing out and get Mark John off the hook."

Daisy smiled as Jude left. But her smile turned to a frown as soon as Jude was out of sight. It was unlike the senior editor to praise Daisy like that. Was it possible she was just trying to throw Daisy off the scent of the real killer--or killers? Was it possible that Jude had killed *both* Fiona and Walt, and orchestrated the whole thing to make it look like Melody did it, all to pave her way to a relationship with Mark John?

Or was she protecting Mark John?

Or had Melody become unhinged when she found out about her husband's affair?

Any one of them could be the killer.

CHAPTER 30

FEBRUARY 1, 1866- THURSDAY

Today was unusually warm and Thomas came to our house to ask me to go for a ride in his sled. The children were in the sled and they seemed happy to see me. We had a lovely ride. I try to talk to Lady and Jesse so I can get to know them better, but they are still very quiet around me. I think they must talk more when they are at home with their father. I've noticed they have continued to talk to each other in their special language. It is quite sweet, and very intriguing.

I want to ask Thomas about the children's mother, but he had not said much about her. She must have been lovely, since Lady and Jesse are both fair-haired and delicate, unlike their father, who has dark brown hair and is strong and tall.

Margaret teases me that Thomas and I will be getting married before the end of the summer, but Mama tells her to be quiet. Margaret doesn't seem to like Thomas, but I think she's jealous. I like him very much.

T

CHAPTER 31

a fter reading just one entry in Trudy's diary after work, Daisy fell asleep on the couch that night. She was startled awake after midnight when the phone rang, jarring her from a lovely dream about Prague.

"Hello?" she answered with a yawn.

"Daisy, this is Brian. I'm sorry to wake you."

"Brian?" Daisy shook her head to wake up, not remembering for a moment who Brian was. "Oh, Brian. Hi."

"Did you talk to Mark John today? I can't seem to get in touch with him."

"He was still at work when I left. As far as I know he was there all day. I don't know where he went after I came home, though."

Daisy suspected her words had upset Brian. There was an edge of anger in his voice when he replied. "He must be ignoring my calls. I need to talk to him about something." Daisy didn't ask what that something was, but it had to be important, she presumed, or Brian wouldn't have called her at home and so late at night.

"I'm sorry, Brian. I wish I could help." She didn't know what else to say.

"That's all right. I'll swing by his house to talk to him."

Daisy didn't reply except to say good-bye. She couldn't imagine what could be so important that Brian would need to leave his own house to go in search of Mark John at such an hour. The man was obviously anxious about something. She was too tired to give it any more thought, though, and tumbled into bed.

The next day Daisy didn't go into the office. She had enough work on her laptop to stay occupied at home, and she loved to work remotely on occasion. And as a bonus, she was able to eat lunch at her own kitchen table in peace and quiet.

It wasn't until after lunch that she received the call from Jude. "Daisy," she began breathlessly, "Brian was here and he was upset about something. He says he talked to you in the middle of the night about Mark John. What did he say?"

Daisy was startled. "I just told him Mark John was in the office all day yesterday and I didn't know where he went after I left work. That's it. What's the matter?"

"Mark John doesn't want to talk to him. He says Brian is losing his mind and he wants nothing to do with him."

"So have they spoken?"

"No. As soon as the receptionist called Mark John to tell him Brian was in the Global Human Rights vestibule, Mark John left through the emergency exit in the back and I haven't seen him since."

"What did Brian say?"

"It's not what he said, it's what he did. He ran into the suite even though the receptionist told him to stay in the vestibule, and he went running through the office, slamming doors when he couldn't find Mark John. Then he left. He was crying, Daisy. I've met Brian a hundred times and he doesn't seem like the type of man who cries in public. I'm afraid of him. The receptionist wanted to call the police, but I know Mark John feels sorry for Brian, so I told her not to."

"It sounds like Brian's behavior is escalating, though I guess we should let Mark John decide what to do about him."

Jude's voice had a tentative note to it when she spoke. "You haven't heard from Mark John in the last half hour, have you?"

"No. I'm sure he'll call you before he would think to call me." Daisy felt both amusement and a twinge of pity for Jude, who still seemed insecure about Mark John.

"If you hear from him, let me know, will you?" Jude asked. "Like you said, I'm sure he'll call me first, but you know, just in case I don't hear the phone or something and he can't get in touch with me."

"I will," Daisy assured her. "But don't forget, Mark John is a big guy. He can take care of himself. He probably wants some time alone to figure out what to do about Brian."

Daisy hung up and just a few seconds later Helena called. "Pretty please, won't you go out with that guy I told you about? Dave—remember? He's a friend of Bennett and I told him all about you. He's recently been through a breakup and Bennett's trying to get him out and interested in women again. We can make it a double date on Friday."

Daisy sighed. "Helena, I really don't want to go out with anyone, and especially not someone on the rebound."

"For me? Please? Bennett and I would really appreciate it. I'll be forever in your debt."

Daisy laughed. "All right, I'll do it. But only as a favor to you and Bennett, not because I'm interested in Dave at all. Please make that clear to him before we meet on Friday."

She could hear from Helena's voice that she wore a wide smile. "Thank you! I'll give you a call tomorrow and let you know what the plan is."

Daisy shook her head as she hung up the phone. She hadn't been on a date in a long time. Not since Dean. But she forced her mind away from thoughts of New York and turned her attention back to the diary. She found, however, that she couldn't concentrate on Trudy's words. She was already nervous about Friday and was regretting her decision to agree to go on a double date. *But Helena will be there and she'll talk to Dave first. It'll be fine.* Daisy eventually convinced herself that Dave was going to be completely harmless and was able to get back to work on her research and writing assignments.

That night she sat at her kitchen table leafing through a magazine and eating a grilled cheese sandwich when the phone rang. It was Grover.

"My party for Friday night just cancelled because of Walt's murder." Daisy could hear the pain in his voice.

"Oh, Grover. I'm really sorry to hear that."

"Not much I can do about it," he replied with a sigh.

"Have the police said anything to you?"

"They came over to tell me not to leave the DC-Virginia-Maryland area. Sounds like I'm getting closer to being named the prime suspect." Another sigh. This was devastating.

"Maybe not," Daisy tried to reassure him. "Maybe they have more questions and just want you to stay close by."

"We're both smarter than that, Daisy."

"I'm trying to figure it out, Grover. I just don't know where to look for answers."

"I don't want to talk about it," Grover said. "Are you busy Friday? I thought we could go to a lecture at George Washington University. There's a guy talking about his experiences in Tibet. I can't just sit around doing nothing. I need to do something. That's assuming I won't be in the lockup."

Daisy groaned inwardly. She had always wanted to visit Tibet.

"I can't. I'm sorry. I wish I could go."

"What do you have going on?"

"Ugh. I agreed to go on a double date with Helena. Against my better judgment, I might add."

"So you're going out with that guy she was talking about at dinner the other night?"

"Yeah."

"Oh. I thought you said you weren't interested in anyone."

"I'm not. I'm doing this strictly as a favor to her."

"Well, there'll be other lectures. Or not. Whatever."

"Oh, I'm sure there will be other lectures," she hastened to assure her friend. "We can go to a different one sometime. Are you busy Saturday afternoon? We could do something then."

"I have a graduation party. Again, as long as I'm not in jail."

"You won't be in jail, Grover. Keep your attitude positive. What are you doing for dinner tomorrow? Want to meet somewhere?"

Grover hesitated before answering. "Actually, I have to get some paperwork done in the shop and tomorrow night is the only time I have to do it."

"All right, then. I'll see you next week."

"See you later," Grover said, then hung up.

Daisy was a little worried about Grover. It seemed clear his nerves were stretched taut.

She took the diary with her when she went to bed that evening. She pulled on her white gloves, which were by now getting brownish-gray from the dust on the diary, and settled back against her pillow to read. It was a good thing it was so interesting, because she was worried about Grover.

CHAPTER 32

MARCH 1, 1866 - THURSDAY

I can't believe I'm writing this, but Thomas has asked me to marry him! I am going to be Mrs. Thomas Sheridan.

Mrs. Thomas Sheridan

Gertrude Sheridan

Trudy Sheridan

In all my nineteen years, I have never been so excited.

Thomas came to visit today and asked if I would like to take a ride in the wagon. I told him I would, but he asked if I would mind waiting for a little while so he could speak with Papa, who was in the barn. I told Thomas I would be waiting for him when he finished talking to Papa.

While he was gone Margaret said, "You know what he's doing, don't you? He's asking Papa for your hand."

I scolded Margaret for saying such a silly thing, but it turned out that Margaret knew exactly what she was talking about. Before long Thomas came back to the house to fetch me. Papa accompanied him,

and he was talking to Mama in the corner of the kitchen as I left with
Thomas. They were looking at me in a funny way. It made me
nervous because I thought I had done something wrong.

Thomas and I drove for a while. We went through town, then he
told me he had a surprise to show me. He took me down the road that
led out of town to the west and after quite a long time I could see a
homestead in the distance. I could tell it was new because of the color
of the wood, and I knew somehow that it was the house he had built.
He drove right up to the front of the house, which is lovely. It has glass
windows (I don't know how he was able to afford them, but they are
beautiful) and a wooden front door with a brass doorknob. There were
curtains in the windows.

He reached for my hand to help me out of the wagon and he didn't
let go of my hand as we walked up the front steps. I have almost never
seen a house with front steps out here in Nebraska. People simply do
not use them. But since Thomas is from back east, he is used to such
things.

I marveled at the inside of the house. Each room is painted a
different color! We don't even have paint on our walls at home. Mama
says paint is expensive and extravagant, but it certainly is beautiful.
And if Thomas has the money to buy paint, then why shouldn't he
paint the inside of his new house? I smile as I write this because soon it
will be our house.

The children each have a room of their own. That is very rare.
Most homes are too small for children to have their own bedrooms.
The children's rooms are quite small, but they each get some space to
call their own! Lady's room is yellow and Jesse's is green. The bedroom
where Thomas sleeps is white.

Once Thomas had given me a tour of all the rooms in the house, he
stood me in front of the fireplace and told me to close my eyes. I was
confused about his request, but I did as he asked. When he told me to
open them, he was standing in front of me holding a beautiful ring! I
must have looked very surprised, because Thomas started laughing

and asked me to wear the ring because he wanted me to marry him. I said yes immediately!

We went back home and told Papa and Mama and Margaret and the boys the good news. Papa and Mama already knew, of course. Papa smiled, but while Mama and Margaret looked happy, I could tell they were a bit worried, too. I suppose they are concerned that I will not be around the house any longer to help them with chores and cooking once Thomas and I are wed. The boys simply wanted to know all about Thomas' new house.

There are many things to do before the wedding, which will be in the spring. Mama and Margaret and I will begin sewing the things I'll need to set up the new house: linens, a wedding quilt, and my personal things.

Thomas said he would tell Lady and Jesse about our marriage. I wish I could be there when he tells them, but I think they will be happy and excited. It has been a long time since they have had a woman in their home.

T

CHAPTER 33

*D*aisy let out a happy squeal as she closed the diary for the night and crawled beneath her covers. She could only imagine the excitement and happiness Trudy must have felt on her engagement to Thomas. She was eager to read about the family's preparations for the wedding, but she savored the time she spent reading the diary and wanted to space out the entries, just as Trudy had so many years ago.

The next morning when Daisy went into work she was surprised to see that Mark John was leaving already.

"Where are you off to so early?" she asked.

He looked at her absent-mindedly, as if he didn't understand what she had said, then gave his head a little shake and answered.

"I have to run an errand."

Daisy got the feeling it was something private, so she wished him a good day and went back to her office. Only a moment later Jude knocked on the door, opening it at the same time. .

"Hi, Jude. How are you this morning?"

"I've been better," Jude said, sitting down and crossing her long legs.

Daisy waited, watching Jude, knowing she would explain herself any moment.

"I found out why Brian was here looking for Mark John yesterday," Jude began, sitting up a bit straighter.

"Is everything all right?

"He lost his job."

Daisy gasped. "His teaching job?"

"That's the only job he had, as far as I know."

Snarky, thought Daisy.

"Why? What happened?" Daisy asked.

"We don't know. Mark John's gone to talk him off a ledge."

"Not really," Daisy said, covering her mouth with her hands. The very thought of it was horrifying.

"Of course not, Daisy." Jude looked at Daisy as if she had two heads.

"Then don't say stuff like that, Jude. It's heartless."

Jude had the decency to murmur an apology.

"I'm sure Mark John will call you as soon as he finds out what happened," Daisy said. "Let me know what he says." It wasn't subtle, but it worked. Jude stood up and walked out.

Brian fired? And on the heels of the death of his sister and his good friend? What was this going to do to him?

Mark John returned to Global Human Rights a couple hours later and Jude immediately disappeared behind his office door. They were in there for longer than Daisy expected.

When Jude left Mark John she came into Daisy's office. "Want to go for a drink after work?" she asked.

Daisy stopped typing and looked up, not bothering to conceal her surprise.

"You and me?" she asked.

"Sure." Jude tilted her head toward Mark John's office and raised her eyebrows.

"Um, okay. I can go for a little while," Daisy said.

"Great." Jude turned and left. Daisy didn't see much of her

the rest of the day, but when five o'clock rolled around Jude came to Daisy's office.

"Ready?" she asked.

"Sure. Give me a minute." Daisy turned off her computer and grabbed her tote bag from the back of her door.

"You know, you're a big girl now," Jude said, glancing at the tote bag. "Maybe you could think about getting an actual briefcase."

"Really? Is this why you asked me for a drink?" Daisy asked in exasperation.

"No, of course not. I was just thinking a briefcase might be more professional."

Daisy rolled her eyes and didn't answer. She followed Jude to the elevator bank.

"Where do you want to go?" Jude asked.

"Somewhere quiet," Daisy replied. She didn't feel like talking over a hundred other voices.

"I agree," Jude said. She led the way out of the building and down the street to a small bar.

When Jude had ordered a gin and tonic and Daisy had a glass of white wine, Jude sat back in her seat. "Do you want to know why I invited you out?" she asked.

"I assume it's to tell me what Mark John had to say when he got back to the office today," Daisy said.

"You're right." Jude sounded deflated.

"So what did he say?" Daisy asked.

"You're not going to believe it," Jude said. She leaned forward. "Brian lost his job because he helped his honors students cheat on a state test."

"You're kidding," Daisy breathed.

Jude gave a smug nod, obviously pleased that she knew something Daisy didn't.

"How did the school find out? Did all his kids get the same grade?" Daisy asked.

"Walt told the administration." Jude sat back with a satisfied smirk.

"*Walt* told them?" Daisy asked. Her eyes were wide and her mouth hung open.

"It's true," Jude said. "I guess Walt has known about it for a while, but his conscience got the best of him after Fiona died. He spilled the beans to the school administrators two days before he was killed. Apparently he had also told Fiona. You know, pillow talk? Loose lips sink ships?" She arched her eyebrows and gave Daisy a significant look.

Jude was being incredibly callous about the entire thing.

This news changed everything. If Walt and Fiona had been the only ones who knew about Brian's indiscretion, would Brian be worried about their ability to expose him? Would he be worried enough to kill?

She couldn't wait to tell Grover the news.

As soon as she left the bar she pulled out her cell phone and dialed Grover's number.

"Hello?" he answered.

"Hi. It's me. You'll never guess what I just learned!" Daisy blurted out breathlessly.

"What?" He sounded uninterested, almost to the point of listlessness.

"What's the matter? Have you talked to the police again?" she asked. She couldn't wait for this ordeal to be over, and she knew that Grover was even more anxious about it.

"No. What did you learn?"

"Brian just lost his job at the high school. Apparently he was helping his students cheat on a state test."

"So?" Grover asked.

"You didn't let me finish," Daisy said, taking a deep breath to let her rising annoyance dissipate.

"Sorry."

"Anyway, apparently Walt knew about it and so did Fiona.

Walt told the administration about it a short while before he died. This is huge, Grover," she said.

"So you mean Brian could have been so mad at Walt for telling his secret that he killed him?" Grover asked.

"That's exactly what I mean. And since Walt and Fiona were the only ones who knew, what if Brian killed Fiona to keep her from saying anything? Then what if he killed Walt because he was angry that Walt told the school what he had done? I mean, he would have had to be pretty unstable to do kill his own sister, but you never know."

"I thought Brian was a good guy, just a little weird. That's what you've always said," Grover pointed out.

"Because that's what I've always thought," Daisy said. "But I don't know him well at all. I may have misjudged him."

"I hope so, for my sake. Thanks, Daisy. I should get going, though."

"Um, all right. If you want to talk, give me a call," Daisy said. Grover hung up. She had expected him to be as excited about this news as he had been.

CHAPTER 34

The following day seemed to fly by. Daisy had to work hard to concentrate on the article she was writing because Brian's possible involvement in the murders of both Fiona and Walt was uppermost in her mind. She had to rush to finish an assignment, and as the appointed hour for the double date approached, Daisy was becoming more and more nervous. She would catch herself twirling her hair or twisting one of her rings or jiggling her legs up and down furiously while she worked. She called Helena late in the afternoon.

"I don't know if I want to go through with this," she told her friend.

"What?! You can't back out," Helena whined. "You'll have fun, I know you will. Don't be nervous about a thing. Dave is a perfect gentleman."

"All right, I'll go. But you owe me one."

Helena laughed. "I already knew that—anything you want!"

"There's nothing I want right now, but I'm keeping it in the back of my mind." Daisy managed a smile at the thought of her friend's happiness. "I'll see you tonight."

An hour later Daisy closed her laptop and headed for home

on the crowded Metro. She showered and changed her clothes and gave herself a quick once-over in the mirror before heading out the door to the restaurant she and Helena had chosen to meet Dave and his friend.

Helena was already at the restaurant, seated at an outdoor table with two handsome men, one of whom would be Daisy's date for the rest of the evening. Daisy hesitated before joining them, giving fleeting thought to going back home, phoning Helena, and feigning illness or even death. But common sense took control. Daisy squared her shoulders and pushed the gate open.

Helena saw her immediately and she waved Daisy over. Both men stood up as Daisy approached. Helena pointed to the man on her left and introduced him as Bennett. The man on her right was Dave. Daisy shook hands with both men and they all sat down together. Helena looked around the group brightly, a wide smile on her flushed, pretty face.

Daisy ordered a glass of wine to calm her nerves, then the foursome engaged in small talk while the tables filled up around them. As the patio became noisier over the course of dinner, they had to raise their voices to hear each other. Dave was attentive and moved his chair slightly closer to Daisy as they talked. Daisy moved her chair farther away with every attempt made by Dave to get closer until she was touching Bennett's seat.

"Oh, sorry about that," she mumbled. She glanced at Helena, who rolled her eyes and shook her head, laughing. Daisy inched her chair a bit closer to Dave and listened to what he was saying, something about his job. She had already forgotten what he did for a living.

Oh, yes, he was an urban planner in one of the Virginia suburbs. A rewarding job, no doubt, but Daisy wondered whether she really needed to know about every variety of tree being used to populate the downtown area of the city where he worked, or whether the reservoir outside town could be kept secure from people trying to go for a swim at night. She nodded and smiled in all the appropriate places as Dave spoke, asking questions now and then to keep him talking even though she wasn't really listening. The truth was, she wanted to encourage him to talk so she wouldn't have to say anything. The last thing she wanted to do was open up to this total stranger about her job, her likes and dislikes, and her background. And if there was a chance her job bored others as much as Dave's job was boring her, then she wanted to keep her mouth shut. It amazed her how intensely Bennett and Helena seemed to be talking to each other. Their heads were almost touching, and Helena's eyes would widen every so often and she would gasp, or she would toss her head back with raucous laughter. Bennett seemed to be enjoying himself, too. Daisy felt almost sorry for Dave. He was trying so hard to keep up a conversation—it wasn't his fault that she didn't feel like talking. Sure, he was good-looking, but that wasn't what counted, was it? She wished he would change topics to almost anything, but she feared if she changed the topic he might expect her to talk.

What's wrong with me? she asked herself more than once. *This great-looking guy is sitting close enough to me for me to smell his cologne, he's obviously got a job that he finds fulfilling and fascinating, he's clearly interested in me, so what's the matter? Why can't I reciprocate the feeling?*

Deep down, Daisy knew why. Her relationship with Dean, and the way it had ended so spectacularly, still haunted her. She simply couldn't bring herself—couldn't allow herself—to become interested in anyone else. It was sweet of Helena to try to set her up, but the thought of going out again with this man, who looked like he might be gearing up to ask her on another date, was terrifying. Not only that, but who had time for a relationship when her job kept her so busy?

She blinked and looked at Dave, who was smiling at her

expectantly. "What do you say?" he asked. "Would you like to go to the movies tomorrow?"

"Oh, Dave, I'd love to, but I really am committed to my job," she said. "I'm afraid another date is just not in my future right now." She could see Helena's crestfallen look out of the corner of her eye. She so badly wanted to please Helena, even to please Dave, but she couldn't do it. She had known the hermit side of her would come out sooner or later, and she had to be true to herself. She just couldn't lead him on.

Dave gave a small sigh and smiled at her. "That's all right. Helena told me you might not be interested in dating, but I hoped once I turned on the charm you wouldn't be able to resist." Daisy let out a laugh. She felt a momentary pang of regret for guarding herself so closely—Dave seemed like a genuinely nice guy who wanted nothing more than to go to the movies—but she didn't give in to the temptation of changing her mind. She smiled her thanks and the group finished their meal in relative quiet.

Daisy was miserable.

Helena called her later that night. "What happened? I thought you and Dave were getting along so well."

"We were, and he seems very nice. But I told you before, I'm just not interested in dating right now." She tried to change the subject. "Did you have fun with Bennett?"

"Oh, no you don't," Helena chided. "You're not getting away with this so fast. You're going to tell me why a gorgeous woman like you doesn't want anything to do with men."

"You know the reason. It's because of Dean."

"Daisy, that was a long time ago," Helena said softly. "Isn't it time to start opening yourself up again?"

"When I open myself up, I get hurt." This conversation was digging more deeply than Daisy preferred.

"But if you don't open yourself up, you won't know how much happiness is out there waiting for you," Helena replied.

"I can't. I'm sorry." Daisy closed her eyes. She just wanted the conversation to end.

There was a silence on the phone. "Okay. I'm sorry I made you go out tonight. I just wanted you to have a nice evening."

Daisy was miserable. "I did have a nice evening, Helena. It's not you, it's me. I'm just not ready for men."

"All right."

Daisy had a hard time getting to sleep that night. She tossed in bed until she finally got up, made herself a cup of herbal tea, and sat down in the living room with Trudy's diary.

CHAPTER 35

MARCH 24, 1866-SATURDAY

Mama and Margaret and I have been sewing whenever we don't have other chores to do. All three of us, plus some ladies from church, are working on my wedding quilt right now and it's coming along slowly.

Now that the weather is getting nicer and the snow is melting, Thomas comes to the house frequently and we take long walks together. Sometimes he brings Lady and Jesse and sometimes he leaves them in town in the care of the woman who works at the general store. I have spoken to the children once since becoming engaged to Thomas and they seem very happy that I am going to marry their father and move into the new homestead with them.

Only one thing has happened to mar the happiness I've felt over the past several weeks. Yesterday Thomas came to visit and we went walking, as we usually do. I asked him about his first wife and he became sullen and withdrawn. He said he didn't like to talk about her. I think it's only normal for me to want to know about her, but Thomas disagrees. He says the less we say about her, the better it will be for everyone. Come to think of it, I have never heard the children mention her name and it makes me wonder if he allows them to discuss her at home. If they don't talk about her in front of him, perhaps they talk about her between themselves. I hope they do. It would seem very important for children to be able to talk about their own mother after her death.

As soon as I mentioned his first wife to him, Thomas turned around and started walking back to my house. He didn't even help me over the snow banks that still dot the fields. I'm glad I'm learning more about the likes and dislikes of my husband-to-be.

T

CHAPTER 36

*A*fter the disastrous ending to the date on Friday, Daisy spent most of the weekend feeling sorry for herself. Helena called on Saturday to apologize again for making her go out the night before, but they ended up talking about how much she liked Bennett. Helena and Bennett were going out again the following weekend and Helena knew better than to ask Daisy on another double date.

Grover didn't call on Sunday; she had hoped he would. She didn't want to call him because he had acted so strangely the last time they talked—she figured it would be better to wait for him to call her. She had other friends, of course, but Helena and Grover were the ones she cared about the most.

That left work. She had plenty of work to do--she had articles to work on besides the women's history series--and normally enjoyed working, but her heart wasn't in it on Sunday. Around mid-afternoon she closed her laptop and went out for a walk. She had no particular destination in mind; she wanted only to get out of her apartment and clear her head.

It was a perfect day. The sky was a brilliant blue, the few clouds were high and puffy. The temperature was just right and a slight breeze rustled the leaves that were growing in the late spring sunshine. It was a good day to leaves one's cares behind, but Daisy couldn't seem to shake the feeling that she was missing something. Missing out on something in life that she should have.

She was meandering along a path in Rock Creek Park when her cell phone rang. Looking at the caller ID, she wondered why Mark John was calling her on the weekend.

"Hi, Mark John," she answered.

"Hi, Daisy. What's wrong?" *Was it that obvious?*

"Nothing, I'm fine."

"I'm wondering if I can drop by your apartment and pick up that diary you've been reading."

"Uh, sure," Daisy stammered. She had wanted to finish reading it before returning it to Mark John.

It was as if he could read her mind. "Aren't you done with it?" he asked.

"No, but that's all right. It's your diary. I can bring it into the office tomorrow morning if you'd like, then you don't have to make a special trip to pick it up."

"Nah, I don't mind coming to get it. Brian's on my case about it, as if he doesn't have enough to keep him occupied. I guess I need to read it, that is, unless you can tell me what it says," he added.

Daisy gave him a brief summary of the entries she had read so far. "Doesn't sound like anything Brian would find particularly fascinating. I don't know what his problem is," he scoffed. "I swear, he won't leave me alone."

"Don't be so hard on him," Daisy said. "I think he misses his sister and you're the only connection he has to her. Not to mention the death of his friend and losing his job." Daisy didn't add that Brian might also be suffering from the guilt that comes of killing two people.

Mark John was silent for a long moment, then he spoke.

"That's all true, but he has to move on. Just as I'm trying to do." He cleared his throat. "I'll be by in about an hour."

Daisy turned around and hurried back to her apartment. She wanted to read as much as she could of Trudy's diary before Mark John came to pick it up. Trudy had somehow wriggled her way into Daisy's heart and mind and Daisy wanted to assure herself that Trudy and Thomas lived happily ever after.

She pulled on the gloves, snatched up the diary, and started to read even before she was seated on the couch.

CHAPTER 37

APRIL 10, 1866- TUESDAY

I have found myself with less and less time to write in my diary since my engagement. It seems there is always so much to be done! The wedding will be early in May, since Mama and Margaret and I should be able to finish all the preparations before then. Mostly we have sewing to complete, but there are a few other things that must be attended to before I can move into Thomas' house.

He brought the children with him the last time he visited and it was a joy for me to see them. I do not like when he leaves them at his house or in town to come and see me because I don't like to think of them alone and I do not want them to think I don't like them or want to spend time with them.

Lady and Jesse are growing a bit more talkative and I think they are getting used to the idea of me moving into their home with them. Of course I would not presume to take the place of their mother, but I hope in time they can love me as I am sure I will love them.

While Thomas talked with Papa in the stable, I took the children for a walk. I dearly wanted to ask them about their mother, but I fear I do not know them well enough to say anything yet. I hope the time comes when they are able to speak to me about her. I don't know why I am so interested in her, but perhaps it is just my natural curiosity.

I have not dared to ask Thomas about her again because he does not seem to like to talk about her, but his mood is much improved over the last time I saw him.

    T

APRIL 30, 1866- MONDAY

The wedding is only twelve days away and we are working furiously to get all the clothing and linens made. Papa has made me a beautiful chest in which to put all my new things and the few things from home that I will be taking with me to my new home. I am getting quite excited.

    Thomas has been visiting more and more often. I think he is excited about the wedding, too. He says he will paint the main bedroom in his house any color I want once I move in. I think that is very thoughtful of him. I have learned more and more about him, such as his favorite things to eat and the books he likes best. He loves to read and he says my most important job when we are married will be to teach Lady and Jesse to read and write. He does not want them to go to school just yet, but I am hoping I can convince him to change his mind. There are some children their age who go to school in town, and I cannot understand why someone who values reading and writing so much does not want his own children to attend school. I think they would love it. It is something I will have to work on.

    T

MAY 5, 1866- SATURDAY

The wedding is just a few days away, and suddenly I am feeling a little nervous about moving to Thomas' house. I have never been anywhere overnight except my aunts' and uncles' houses. Mama had a talk with me about the things Thomas will expect of me when we are married and I confess to being afraid. She says not to worry, that Thomas will understand.

The chest Papa made for me is packed and ready to go to Thomas' house and my wedding dress is ready and beautiful. I did the lace work myself while Mama and Margaret worked on the rest of the dress. I love it. I hope the weather is nice the day of the wedding.

T

MAY 12, 1866- SATURDAY

Our wedding was yesterday, and we were lucky that the rain did not start falling until after we had taken our vows.

I am now living in Thomas' house. The things I brought with me to the house are unpacked and I have put everything where it belongs. It is strange to get accustomed suddenly to living in a new place.

I can't tell Thomas that I cried when I said good-bye to Mama and Papa. He would be disappointed in me and perhaps worry that I don't want to live in his house with him and the children. But that is not true at all—I simply feel sad at not being able to see my parents every day from now on. I must face my womanhood with courage and strength and I don't want to cry again. But I do miss Mama and Papa and Margaret and even the boys.

Thomas says it is not a good idea for me to visit them very often because it will cause me pain and homesickness. I'm sure he is right, but I wish I could see my family every day.

T

MAY 30, 1866- WEDNESDAY

I have been the woman of the house for over two weeks now. Lady and Jesse seem to accept my presence here in the house, but they still do not talk to me very much. I long for them to sit with me and have a conversation the way they talk to each other, but they are not ready for that yet. They regard me with looks that remind me of fear and it makes me sad that they feel afraid of me. I am not going to hurt them —I merely want to love them.

Thomas told me today that he has to take a short trip farther west. He will be leaving in a few days. He does not dote on me quite the way he did while we were courting, but I suspect that happens in all marriages.

I still miss my family and have not seen them yet, but perhaps I can go visit them while Thomas is traveling.

T

*D*aisy was so engrossed in Trudy's diary that she jumped when the buzzer rang from the vestibule downstairs. Mark John had arrived.

"Darn it," Daisy said. She closed the book, took off the gloves, and pushed the button to admit Mark John to her apartment. A minute later there was a knock at her front door. She opened it and Mark John stood outside. Jude was standing behind him.

"Mind if we come in?" Mark John asked, indicating Jude with a wave of his hand. "Jude and I were both at the office, so I didn't think it would be a big deal if we both came for the diary."

"Not at all," Daisy assured him, stepping back and motioning them to come in. "Can I get you something to drink?"

"No, thanks." Mark John looked around the apartment, not bothering to hide his nosiness.

"So Brian wants to talk about the diary?" Daisy asked, at a loss for anything else to talk about.

"Yeah, he asked if we can meet to talk about it this week. Probably for dinner. I'd love to know what is so special about that diary that he can't just let me read it at my leisure--or not at all—*and* he has to discuss it with me." Mark John's voice was rising.

Jude laid a hand on his arm. "Mark John, why don't you tell Brian you can't meet with him this week? It seems to be stressing you out."

Mark John rolled his eyes so only Daisy could see, then smiled thinly at Jude. "I'll think about it."

"I have enjoyed reading it," Daisy offered. "It's just one young woman's story from the mid-eighteen hundreds. I've gleaned a lot of information about women's roles in society from her diary and I'm going to be using it as a source for my women's history articles."

"That's great," Mark John said, looking out Daisy's living room window. "My God, is that Brian down there?" Daisy and Jude went to stand beside Mark John and looked at the sidewalk below. Sure enough, Brian was standing on the corner, looking lost. He looked up and down each street from the intersection and glanced at a piece of paper he was holding. Then he looked up and down the streets again.

"I'm not going out there while he's standing there," Mark John said through clenched teeth. "He's driving me nuts."

"Mark John, I think you should call the police," Jude said.

"And tell them what? That my brother-in-law is standing on the corner?" he asked with a snarl.

Jude pouted. "I only mean that he's harassing you. You could tell them that."

"I'm not calling the police." The tone of his voice brooked no disagreement.

Jude shrugged and turned away from the window. "So what do we do now? Just sit here until he leaves? I have things to do today." Daisy hoped they wouldn't stay, but she had a sinking feeling that they would do just that while they waited for Brian to leave his post on the corner. What was he doing out there?

"What I want to know is, why is he out there? Did he follow

me here? Dammit!" Mark John seethed. He seemed not to have heard Jude's question.

"Who knows?" Jude answered with an exaggerated shrug. "He's a kook." To Daisy's dismay she sat down on Daisy's sofa and asked, "Daisy, could I have a glass of water?"

"Sure," Daisy replied, walking to the kitchen. She called over her shoulder, "Mark John, do you want a glass?"

"Yes, please," came the reply. Daisy sighed. This was not how she wanted to spend her Sunday afternoon. *Then again,* she thought, *I don't have anything better to do.*

She put three glasses of ice water on a tray and took them into the living room, where Mark John had made himself comfortable on the couch next to Jude. As she rounded the corner from the kitchen to the living room, Daisy saw Mark John take his hand off Jude's knee.

So Jude wasn't the only one with romantic feelings.

Daisy set the tray on the coffee table in front of them, trying to avoid looking at either one of them.

"You saw that, didn't you?" Mark John asked.

She nodded.

"Don't tell anyone, okay? We're not ready for our relationship to be public knowledge," Mark John said. Daisy nodded again. She searched her mind frantically for something to say.

"So," she began. "Is Brian still there?" Jude stood up and walked over to the window and nodded. Mark John made a scoffing noise with his throat. Daisy didn't know what to say to these two. She was still reeling from the knowledge that they were dating so soon after Fiona's death.

"Any plans tonight, Daisy?" Mark John finally asked.

"Nope. Just the usual Sunday night stuff," she answered. The silence grew long. Finally Jude started talking about the weather, then talk turned to politics, then sports. Daisy hated talking about sports and she suspected Jude was only joining in to get Mark John to talk.

Finally Daisy looked at Mark John and said pointedly, "I wonder if Brian is still there. If he is, should you just ask him to come up?" She knew what Mark John's answer would be, but she hoped her remark would compel one of them to check the window to see if Brian was still down on the corner. Besides, Brian was probably the last person she wanted in her apartment just then.

Jude took the hint and walked over to the window. "I don't see him," she said, and making a point of looking up and down the streets visible from the window, she turned to Mark John. "He must have given up. He's not out there." Mark John joined Jude at the window and scanned the streets.

"Good. We should get out of here before he comes back," he said. He held the diary in one hand and Jude's elbow with the other. Daisy wanted to remind him to be careful with the diary, but she figured he knew how to handle an antique artifact without damaging it. She followed them to the door and watched them hurry down the stairs to the ground floor. She went back into her apartment and heaved a sigh of relief.

Mark John and Jude were romantically involved. It was almost too unbelievable to contemplate. But she should have seen it coming--there was all the time Jude had been spending in Mark John's office, the time they were spending together after hours.

Her thoughts switched back to Trudy. She wished she had read the entire diary. The last couple entries had sounded like Trudy was a bit disenchanted with her new life as Thomas Sheridan's wife and Daisy wanted to know what happened next. She wondered if Trudy ever had children of her own and if she and Thomas reached an agreement about letting her visit her family more often. She hoped Mark John would finish reading the diary quickly and let her borrow it again so she could find the answers to all her questions.

And what of Brian's odd visit to her neighborhood? He had

to be there because he had followed Mark John. He must not have seen Mark John come into the building, or he wouldn't have looked so confused down on the sidewalk. Daisy hoped Brian's presence in her neighborhood had nothing to do with her and everything to do with Mark John.

But, then again, Brian knew she was friends with Grover...and that Grover was a person of interest in Walt's murder. How was all this connected? Was it possible Brian had been in the neighborhood looking for Daisy? Was it was merely a coincidence that he had been nearby at the same time as Mark John?

The next morning Daisy was surprised when she walked into her office and found the diary on her desk. She smiled and went down the hall to Mark John's office and knocked on the door.

"Come in," Mark John said.

She stepped inside. "Mark John, I can't believe how quickly you read that diary. Thanks for lending it to me again. Wasn't it interesting?"

He waved his hand dismissively. "I couldn't get into it and I've decided to tell Brian the truth. I don't understand the appeal it obviously holds for him. You can finish reading it and tell me about the rest of it if you want to, but for once I'm going to be straight with Brian and tell him to quit bothering me about the damned thing."

"If you wait until I finish it, I can tell you all about it and you can discuss it with him and keep the peace," Daisy said pointedly. Mark John ran his hands through his hair.

"Maybe you're right. Maybe I shouldn't tell him off. How soon can you get through it, do you think?"

"Give me a couple days and I can have it done for you," she promised.

"All right," he said with a sigh. "I guess I can put him off a little longer. God, he drives me crazy." Daisy thanked Mark John and went back to her office.

She decided to take Monday afternoon for herself to read more of the diary at home. She turned off her cell phone and settled comfortably on the couch to read. She wanted to get through as much of the diary as possible before anyone could think of another assignment to give her.

And once she started reading what came next, she couldn't put the diary down.

CHAPTER 39

JUNE 6, 1866- WEDNESDAY

Thomas left this morning for his trip. He asked me to spend a good deal of time while he is away teaching Lady and Jesse to read. I taught my brothers to read and I don't think Thomas realizes that it is a long process. I hope he doesn't expect the children to be reading by the time he comes home. If he does, he will be disappointed in both them and me.

I was surprised at the lightness that I felt once Thomas left. I suppose I have been working very hard to try and please him. The children seem to feel it, too. They have been more talkative since he departed and I have seen them smile more. Thomas dislikes the noise they make when he is home, so they try to be quiet when he is around, which is quite often. They are bored and I feel sorry for them. But I do not mind noise—in fact, I welcome it! I have told them they may play until I am done with the morning chores and then we will sit down and I will begin to teach them their letters.

I am planning a visit to my home to see Mama and Papa while Thomas is away. I suggested it to the children this morning and they seem thrilled with the idea of a short trip. Isn't it funny—I still refer to Mama and Papa's house as "my home" even though my home is really now with Thomas and the children.

T

JUNE 9, 1866- SATURDAY

The children and I took the horse and the wagon today and went to see Mama and Papa. It has been almost a month since I saw them and I cried when they came out of the house to greet me. Mama cried, too, but Papa just laughed. He said he taught me well if I was brave enough to leave my new home and bring two children over the miles to visit. I don't think of it as being brave—I would do practically anything to see my family again.

Lady and Jesse and I are staying overnight at my house. It is quite an adventure for them. Margaret and the boys played with them after supper tonight and my little charges are exhausted. They practically fell into bed even before it was completely dark outside. They slept in my old bed and I will sleep with Margaret. It is soothing to me to sit by the candlelight and write in my diary as I used to before my marriage to Thomas.

Mama and Margaret have asked me many questions about Thomas but I cannot answer most of them because I don't know the answers. They want to know what his job was before coming west, but other than the time he spent farming in Ohio, I have never asked him and he has never spoken about it. I had to tell them I don't know. They also asked about his family, but I had to admit I don't know anything about his family besides Lady and Jesse. I don't know if his parents are living or whether he has sisters or brothers. Margaret seems scornful of my marriage to Thomas, but Mama tells her to hush and mind her tongue.

I will have to ask Thomas those questions when he returns from his trip. I would like to know the answers, too.

T

JUNE 16, 1866- SATURDAY

Thomas came home today. He was very happy to see all of us. He hugged me and told me he missed me, and I felt a warm happiness when he said that. He told the children he missed them, too. He wasn't home for long before he left again to go into town for some supplies, then he came back in time for dinner.

I was nervous about him asking the children to read for him, and my fears came true. He asked them after dinner to show him that they could read, and all they could do was recite some of the letters of the alphabet. He didn't smile or tell them they did a good job, but instead told them to get ready for bed. After they left the room he was angry and told me he was disappointed in my inability to teach them more than just a few letters. I was stung by his words, but I told him that perhaps it was time to think about sending the children to school. He was angry at my suggestion and yelled that teaching them is now my job since I am the woman of the house.

I didn't want Thomas to see me cry, so I spent the evening in the parlor while he remained in the kitchen. I am waiting until he is asleep to go into the bedroom. I checked myself in the looking glass and I can see that my eyes are red and puffy from crying.

Papa has never made Mama cry, not that I know of.

T

JUNE 20, 1866- WEDNESDAY

I have been working with Lady and Jesse on their letters and numbers while Thomas works in our fields. They are making good progress, though Thomas doesn't think they are learning fast enough.

Jesse said something today that startled me. He said he misses his mother and he wishes she could see where they live in Nebraska. I had mixed feelings about what he said. I was glad that he could talk about his mother, but I felt a little sorry for myself when he said he wished she could be here. I feel like I am not good enough and that even at their young ages, Jesse and Lady realize I don't measure up to her or to their memory of her.

I am growing more curious about her. Lady said she was beautiful, with long blond hair (Lady called it "yellow") and lovely clothes. Jesse said he remembers his mother's voice. He says it sounded like a song. I wonder what else they miss about her. Did she read stories to them? Did she try to teach them things? I don't even know how old they were when she died. They were clearly old enough to have memories of her.

I think I must again ask Thomas about her one of these days.

T

JUNE 24, 1866- SUNDAY

I am shocked by something that happened today. I found a picture of a beautiful woman in Thomas' bureau. It was under several handkerchiefs and I was putting his socks in the drawer and moved the hankies.

It must be his first wife because both Lady and Jesse look just like her, but I am afraid to ask him. I don't even know her name. I have almost never seen a photograph before, so I know Thomas and his wife must have been wealthy when they lived back east.

I am realizing there is so much I don't know about my husband.

I hope that the picture is his first wife and not another woman.

T

JUNE 29, 1866- FRIDAY

I couldn't stand my curiosity any longer and I asked Thomas about the picture I found in his bureau. When he found out I had seen the picture, he was angrier than I have ever seen him. He hit me across the face. He hit me so hard I fell. My cheek is swollen and the bone around my eye is very painful.

I don't know what to do. My father has never hit my mother and I know my uncles don't hit my aunts. I cannot tell my parents because I don't know what Papa would do to Thomas. And I am embarrassed to tell them because I don't want them to think I have made a mistake in marrying Thomas. Perhaps it is good that I do not live very close to them because they will not see the bruise on my face.

T

JUNE 30, 1866- SATURDAY

When I went to bed last night Thomas apologized for hitting me. I purposely waited to go into the bedroom until I thought he was asleep, but he was waiting for me. He put his hand lightly on my cheek in the way he did before we were married and insisted that I have relations with him so he could prove how sorry he was. I could barely endure it.

This morning when Lady and Jesse saw my face Lady gave me a hug. I could tell Jesse wanted to, but something held him back. They didn't say anything during breakfast, but they hurried outside while I cleaned the kitchen and did my morning chores. I watched them out the window and they keep looking back toward the house. Their heads are together and they are talking. I don't know where Thomas is.

When I was finished with my housework I called the children inside so we could work on their letters. They work so hard. Jesse seems to be grasping the concept of reading and writing a bit faster than Lady, but she will catch up to him, I am sure.

When they came inside I knew they were bursting to ask about the bruise on my face. I checked it in the glass and it is deep purple and my eye is partly swollen shut. I can't very well hide it from them. They didn't say anything, though. They were even more assiduous than usual in their recitations. I think they wanted to please me.

When Thomas came inside for the noon meal, he was grim-faced and angry. He didn't say anything except to announce that he would be home late in the evening and to have supper without him. He didn't say good-bye when he left and he scarcely spared the children a glance. They looked down at their food during the meal, as if they knew not to bother him in such a mood. They seemed almost relieved to hear that he will not be home until late this evening. I am getting the feeling they have seen this behavior from him before.

T

JULY 2, 1866- MONDAY

This morning when I was doing my housework I turned around and was startled to find Thomas watching me in the doorway to the parlor. He was being totally silent and when I saw him I asked him if he needed something. Instead of answering, he stared at me for a moment then turned around and left the house. I cannot fathom why he was watching me clean. Maybe he doesn't think I'm doing a good job. But he would say something if he didn't like how I was doing it. He has shown himself to be very forthright about my housework and cooking. If there is something he doesn't like, he does not waste any time in telling me so.

I miss my parents dearly. The bruise on my face is fading and is becoming green-yellow in color, but it is still obvious that I have met with an accident. The children are continuing to work on their numbers and letters. I have noticed that they never talk about their father and they only speak to him if he speaks to them first. I find it a sad way for them to live. When I was growing up I always talked to my father about anything and everything.

I do not know why I never noticed this behavior from them before I married Thomas.

T

JULY 7, 1866- SATURDAY

Thomas has been behaving more and more strangely. He watches me clean and I pretend to not know he is there. I think if I said something, if I showed him that I know he watches me, it would not matter. He would stay there, saying nothing and looking at me with disapproving eyes. The children do everything they can to avoid being near him. My heart goes out to them because no child should have to live in fear like that, but the truth is that I am afraid to broach the subject with my husband.

He has been especially critical of my cooking. I can't seem to do anything right. The bruise on my face is almost healed. If I wear my hair down around my face, my parents might not notice the discoloration if I go see them. But I fear that Thomas will not allow it and I certainly can't leave without telling him where I am going.

I am in a quandary.

T

JULY 10, 1866- TUESDAY

Thomas hasn't talked to me in three days. I cannot think what I have done to make him so angry. The children spend as little time as possible in his presence when he is in the house and their eyes are wide and afraid when they are in the same room with him.

I am afraid of him. I am afraid for both myself and the children. I want to go to my parents' house but he will either forbid me to go or he will come after me and find me if I go without telling him.

I have to do something.

T

JULY 13, 1866- FRIDAY

I am writing this quickly because I can see Thomas approaching the house from a distance. He still has not spoken to me.

Lady has told me something very disturbing. She told me she is afraid because her father was like this in the days before her mother died. When I asked if her mother had been sick, she shook her head, her eyes wide and full of terror. She told me she is worried that I am going to disappear, too. This is the most personal thing Lady has ever said to me and there is a voice inside me saying she is right.

T

JULY 15, 1866- SUNDAY

Thomas locked me and the children inside the house today. I can see him outside pacing, but we are trapped.

I don't know what to do. He hit me again this morning and a large bruise is developing on my stomach. It hurts ferociously and I am having a hard time standing up straight. I fear Thomas is going to do serious harm to me one of these days.

I just watched him ride away in the wagon. Thank the Lord the children are safe with me. I have no idea where he is going or when he will return. I hope and pray we all remain safe.

T

JULY 15, 1866- SUNDAY

Thomas has returned home. He instructed the children to accompany him outside. When they left, he told me I was to remain behind and he locked me in again. I watched the three of them from the window, but they disappeared behind the barn. I can see him walking slowly back toward the house now. The children are nowhere to be seen. I am terrified for the children and for me.

I should have tried to escape.

T

CHAPTER 40

*D*aisy turned the page, realizing as she did so that she had been holding her breath. The next page was blank. She flipped through the rest of the pages in Trudy's diary, but there were no more entries. She should have been more careful with the diary and turned the pages with deliberate slowness, but she couldn't rid herself of the feeling of dread that had slipped over her like a shroud. She was desperate to find more words, some kind of confirmation that Trudy and the children were all right.

But there were no more words, no such confirmation. Had she just read the last words Trudy ever wrote?

Daisy sat in silence for a long time, she didn't know how long, lost in thought and unspeakably worried about Trudy's fate. She finally reached for a pad of paper and a pencil she kept on the coffee table, then made a list of the places she could look to learn what happened to Trudy.

Genealogy records
Census records
Newspapers

Brian- any more diaries?

She would start tomorrow morning, first thing. She had to find out what happened to Trudy.

* * *

She was in Mark John's office the next morning before anyone else was at work. Even Jude wasn't around.

"I finished the diary last night," she said, sitting down across from him.

He wasn't paying much attention. "Oh, really?" he asked, his eyes scanning the computer screen in front of him.

"I came to tell you how it ends."

"Mm? How does it end?"

"With a cliffhanger."

He looked at her, his attention finally drawn away from the computer. "Cliffhanger how?"

"It just ends with Trudy being afraid of her husband. He's coming toward the house and it just ends."

"That's it? Kind of boring."

"Don't you want to know what happened?"

"I don't really care," he answered, looking back at the computer and pushing a few buttons.

Daisy let out an annoyed sigh. "Well, I do. I'm going to do some research to see if I can find out whatever happened to her."

"Knock yourself out," he said.

"What?" she asked. She was surprised to hear him speak so flippantly.

He closed his eyes. It looked like he was counting silently to ten. Then turned his full attention to her. "I'm sorry, Daisy. I have a lot on my mind this morning. I shouldn't have been so thoughtless about the diary. You know, it might make a great story if you could find out what happened to her. If it's that interesting, maybe you could do a separate story about it for the journal. Separate from the women's history articles, I mean."

Daisy nodded. "Maybe. Let me see what I can find before we go planning any more stories about it."

CHAPTER 41

That afternoon Daisy returned to the Library of Congress, where she immersed herself in census records from Nebraska in the eighteen sixties and eighteen seventies. She was able to find Trudy's name in the Nebraska Territory Census of Eighteen Sixty as a member of the Hauchfen household. She was also able to find the Hauchfen family in the Census of Eighteen Seventy, but there was no mention of Trudy. There was no Sheridan household listed in either the Census of Eighteen sixty or the Census of Eighteen Seventy.

Next she looked at the records of births, deaths, and marriages in the Nebraska Territory. After a tedious search, she found Trudy's birth record and the marriage record of Trudy and Thomas. But as hard as she looked, she wasn't able to find a death record for Trudy. She looked under every name she could think of: Gertrude Sheridan, Trudy Sheridan, Mrs. Thomas Sheridan, and even Trudy Hauchfen and Gertrude Hauchfen. There was no mention of her at all.

It was like Trudy had disappeared. Daisy had come to a dead end.

The Sheridan household had obviously existed in the mid-eighteen sixties, but Thomas and his children, if they were still alive, had moved away from the Nebraska Territory. But where had they gone? And was it possible Trudy had lived and gone with them?

Daisy had spent the entire afternoon searching for the long-ago whereabouts of Trudy and Thomas and the children, and the announcement that the library was closing startled her. Lost in thought, she packed up her belongings and returned to the coat check station to retrieve her tote bag.

On the way home Daisy called Grover, against her better judgment. She wasn't sure he would want to talk to her, but she figured she could offer some kind of olive branch if he was angry with her for some reason.

He answered on the second ring.

"Hey--want to go somewhere for dinner? I have to get out of my own head for a while," Daisy said in greeting.

"Sorry, but I have plans tonight. Maybe some other time," Grover replied. He didn't elaborate. Daisy could feel the heat rise on her face. She couldn't pinpoint the reason for her embarrassment, but she couldn't shake the feeling that she had just been summarily brushed off. Maybe he had a date and didn't want to jinx it, she thought. Maybe he was lying and didn't have plans at all. Maybe he hadn't gotten over whatever made him upset with her in the first place.

She was faced with the prospect of spending the evening alone, so she picked up a sandwich at a shop near her apartment and set up her laptop on the kitchen table as soon as she got home. *Might as well work if there's nothing else to do*, she thought.

She pulled up a genealogy website and typed Trudy's name into the search bar. Immediately there were some leads, and for the next three hours Daisy followed the clues where they led. She learned that Trudy's father had been born in Germany and that her mother was from the state of Ohio. Daisy wondered how they had met. If they were like so many other young couples in the territories in the nineteenth century, they had met while the man made his way west looking for greater economic opportunity or more space to farm. From what Daisy could gather on the website, both of Trudy's parents had passed away while living in Nebraska.

As hard as she looked, Daisy could not find a record of Trudy's death on the website. There were death records for both her parents, so it wasn't a question of there being insufficient record-keeping at the time.

Having reached a place in her research where she couldn't find any more information about Trudy, Daisy turned her attention to Thomas. What she found surprised her: the only records of Thomas Sheridan existed in the Nebraska Territory. There were no records of his birth, his death, or his first marriage. There were no records of any marriage he may have had after his marriage to Trudy. Daisy sat back in her chair, staring at the computer. It wasn't until then that she realized how sore she was from sitting hunched over at the computer— her shoulders hurt, her neck hurt, her back hurt. She stood up and stretched to get the kinks out, then turned off the computer.

As much as she loved this research, it had taken the entire day. She vowed to get work done on her women's history articles the next day.

She had just crawled into bed when the phone rang. Glancing at the caller ID, she was surprised to see Grover's name.

"Hey. What's up?" she answered.

"Nothing. Did I wake you?"

"No, I was just getting into bed. Another five minutes and I would have been sound asleep. Everything all right? Any news?"

"Everything is okay, I guess. No news." She could picture him shrugging. "Work is slowing down a bit because of the thing with Walt." *It's more than just a 'thing,'* Daisy thought. But she knew he didn't like to talk about it.

"When's your next party?"

"Thursday night."

"Need help?"

"Sure. You can help if you want."

"I know you didn't call to talk about the party on Thursday night. What's going on?"

"I had a date tonight. It was awful."

"Oh. I wondered what you were doing tonight. Why didn't you want to tell me earlier that you had a date?"

"I dunno. I just didn't."

"What was so bad about it?"

"It's a woman I met at one of my parties a few weeks ago. She called me at the office and asked me out."

"Where'd you go?"

"Just dinner. She was so boring. Didn't talk about anything but herself all night long."

"I'm sorry. Too bad you had to spend your evening that way."

"Daisy, I…" Grover stopped talking.

"What?"

"Nothing. I forgot what I was going to say."

"Why don't we talk tomorrow? I've got to get some sleep."

"Sure. Talk to you then." There seemed to be a tinge of sadness in Grover's voice, but Daisy couldn't be sure. It was an uncommon emotion for him, so she didn't hear it in his voice very often.

$\mathcal{T}$he next day Daisy redoubled her research efforts for the women's history articles. She was amassing ideas for expanding her outlines, but she needed to make sure she had the research to back them up. She spent most of the day in her office doing online research. Jude only interrupted her once, coming into her office to ask if she had any aspirin.

"Sorry, Jude. I don't have any with me. Got a headache?"

"No, I'm achy all over. I hope I'm not getting the flu."

"Probably not- it isn't flu season. Sounds like you're coming down with a virus, though. You should probably rest and get lots of fluids."

"Yeah. I went to the doctor. He told me to rest."

"So why are you here today? I can handle anything that comes up."

"I'd rather try to work than lie around and do nothing at home. I would go berserk."

"Okay, but don't stay if you start to feel worse. The best thing for you would be to lie down and get better." *And*, Daisy didn't add aloud, *you're less likely to infect people around here if you just go home.*

Jude turned around and left, her gait slower than usual. Daisy heard her go into Mark John's office next; she hoped Mark John would send her home until she felt better. It was only a moment later, though, that Jude returned to her office and shut the door. Daisy heaved a sigh and pulled a canister of disinfectant wipes from the bottom drawer of her desk. She was wiping down her door handle to remove Jude's germs from it when Mark John came in.

"What are you doing?" he asked as Daisy stepped back from the door in surprise.

"Just a little cleaning."

He smirked. "Are you wiping down anything Jude has touched? She doesn't have the plague, you know."

"I know that," Daisy replied hotly, embarrassed to be caught in a frenzy of germ-killing. "I just like it to smell fresh in here, that's all."

"Sure," Mark John said, a knowing grin on his face. "I tried to tell her to go home, but she doesn't want to."

"So she'd rather stay here and spread disease to the rest of us?"

"Apparently so. But I didn't come in here to argue about whether Jude should be at work today. I came in to ask you to do me a favor."

"What is it?"

"Brian is coming in later today. Can you talk to him? Tell him I've read the diary but I had to run out for some reason. Um, tell him I had to interview someone for a story."

"You don't write stories. I'll come up with something better. Why don't you just talk to him? I told you how the diary ends."

"I don't even know if that's why he's coming in. I just don't want to talk to him right now." He looked over his shoulder and crossed to the door, closing it softly. "I'm afraid he's going to ask questions about me and Jude. I think he knows we're seeing each other. I'm not ready for that. I don't know how he feels about me dating after Fiona's death—we've never discussed it. But this isn't the time or place, so it's easier if I just avoid him."

"I can understand that," Daisy replied. "Why don't you just call him and tell him you're not going to be here?"

"Because I don't want him to ask about rescheduling. Besides, his phone is off and the voicemail is full." Daisy smiled.

"I'll take care of it, don't worry," Daisy said. Mark John turned to leave.

"Find anything of interest when you researched the diary lady yesterday?"

"Her name is Trudy—was Trudy—and not really. I didn't find what I went looking for, which was how and when she died."

"It's got to be there somewhere," Mark John said. "Keep looking."

"I intend to, believe me."

Later that afternoon the receptionist buzzed to tell Daisy that Brian had arrived. Daisy went to greet him, then showed him to a conference room.

"Mark John isn't in the office, so he asked me to discuss the diary with you. I've had an opportunity to read all of it."

"He's not coming?" Brian asked, his face showing his disappointment.

"No, but I've read the diary, so--" Daisy began.

Brian held up his hand. "I don't know why he refuses to see me, but he's the one I want to talk to. No offense, Daisy. But he's my brother-in-law. We have family ties."

"I get that. I just--"

Brian held up his hand again. "Listen. I'll give him another chance. If I can't discuss it with him after that, I'll discuss it with you. Okay?"

"Okay."

Brian pushed back his chair and stood to leave.

"Does he ever talk about Fiona?" he asked.

Daisy had a strong hunch he didn't mean talking about her in the context of Mark John dating another woman after her death.

"No," she said quietly. Brian left without another word.

Daisy spent the rest of the day doing research for her other projects, then went home.

She flipped on the light next to her front door and stood in the hallway for a moment listening to the silence. She kicked off her shoes and threw her keys into the basket on her foyer table. There were times when she walked into her apartment and wished there was someone to talk to, someone waiting for her. But she always tried to shake off those thoughts. This was the life she had chosen for herself. She was happy doing her job and spending time alone. She had friends she could call if she felt like going out, and there was always the option of getting a dog or a cat for company.

But on the nights she felt like staying in, it might be nice to have another human to talk to.

She shook her head as if she could physically dispel thoughts like those from her head, then turned on the television. She idly flipped channels for a while, but there was never anything good on television. She shut it off with a grunt. She got up and rummaged through the refrigerator for something to eat and found cheese and some week-old grapes that didn't look too bad. She also found some crackers in the cupboard and took the box into the living room.

She flipped through an anthropology journal and didn't find any articles that particularly interested her. Next she tried reading a mystery she had borrowed from Helena, but it didn't hold her interest. She eventually laid it aside, blowing a long breath out through puffed cheeks.

She was bored. And if she was honest with herself, she was lonely, too. She wanted to call Grover, but their last couple conversations had been so weird that she didn't think it would be a good idea. She thought about calling Helena, but Helena wasn't a talk-on-the-phone person. She preferred to be out doing something, going somewhere, talking face-to-face. Daisy didn't feel like going anywhere. For just a fleeting moment Daisy thought about calling Jude to see how she was feeling, but she quickly banished that thought from her head with a rueful chuckle. *I must be pretty desperate to consider calling Jude.*

She ended up remembering she had some bills to pay, so she spent the rest of the evening paying bills online, checking her email, and surfing the internet. She went to bed early, slept fitfully, and woke up grumpy.

CHAPTER 43

ude was at work when Daisy got there. Daisy gave her a quick wave as she walked to her office and Jude groaned in reply. *Oh, no,* thought Daisy. *Don't tell me she's sicker than yesterday. I can't be in the office with her.*

Daisy shut her door behind her and sat at the desk, intending only to stay in the office for a short time. She would spend the rest of the day working somewhere else—coffee shop, home, a library, it didn't matter as long as she wasn't near Jude. There was a knock on her door and it opened before she could say anything. She knew without looking up from her screen that Jude was standing in the doorway.

"Yes?" Daisy asked, a hint of impatience creeping into her voice.

"Mark John isn't in," Jude said, sounding dull and tired. "He's sick."

"Okay, thanks for letting me know," Daisy replied. Then she looked up at Jude. The senior editor was slumped against the door frame, looking like something the cat dragged in. "Jude, why are you here?" Daisy asked crossly. "You're going to get everyone sick."

Jude pouted. "I didn't want to stay home alone. I figured I'm going to be miserable no matter where I am, so I might as well try to get some work done."

"Pardon me for saying so, but that's pretty selfish," Daisy said. Her words and her tone surprised even her. Jude looked at Daisy through narrowed, puffy eyes and her shoulders slumped down further.

"I'm sorry. I just thought if I kept the door shut I wouldn't get anyone else sick."

"And that would be fine, but you're in my office right now. You know what? Never mind. I'm heading out. When you talk to Mark John, tell him I'm working remotely today."

Jude turned away slowly and closed the door behind her with a soft *click*. Daisy was suddenly ashamed of herself for speaking to Jude the way she did. Part of her wanted to apologize and the other part just wanted to disappear for the day until her mood improved. She hoisted her tote bag over her shoulder and walked past Jude's open office door without a glance.

She spent the day in a coffee shop near her office, where she was surprisingly able to concentrate on her work even with the din of customers talking and cash registers dinging and coffee machines whirring in the background. It always amazed her when she was able to get work done in a noisy place—it wasn't too long ago that she had required total quiet to work or study. That had all changed when she met Dean. He had been an ornithologist. When he worked from home he was always on conference calls or listening to bird sounds or tapping away on his computer, and Daisy, who had been a graduate student at the time, had learned quickly to adapt to whatever noise was in the background as she worked. It had been a valuable skill to acquire.

Daisy was taking a break from working and ordering an iced coffee when her phone rang. It was Grover.

"Whatcha doin'?" he asked.

"Working. What are you doing?"

"I'm on my way into the office. I'm going to be scheduling the staff for the party on Thursday. Can you still help me out?"

"Sure. What time?"

They agreed that Daisy would meet the rest of Grover's staff at the site of the party late Thursday afternoon to help set up. As they hung up Grover said with a laugh, "I'm going to have to start paying you more than minimum wage if you keep helping."

"I think it's fun," Daisy said. "I love to help out, so don't worry about that." She smiled to herself as she hung up the phone. That call hadn't been weird at all--maybe he wasn't upset with her anymore.

Helena called late in the afternoon and asked Daisy to go to dinner. Helena had to be in Dupont Circle for a meeting until early evening, so she would be in the neighborhood when Daisy finished work. Daisy agreed and then got back to her writing, her mood improved now that she had something to look forward to. She hated to admit to herself that having plans with other people gave her a boost and that she had been feeling sorry for herself. She was self-sufficient, so why should it be so important to her that she spent her downtime with other people?

CHAPTER 44

The party on Thursday night was a big success, and Grover managed to stay upbeat throughout the evening, despite being approached by the host and interrogated about his knowledge of Walt's murder. Though there had been nothing in the newspapers or online to suggest that Grover was a person of interest, word had gotten around and several of Grover's clients had cancelled parties and events. This host, though willing to allow the party to go ahead with catering by DC Haute Cuisine, was determined to conduct an investigation of his own to ensure he hadn't hired a cold-blooded murderer.

Daisy had been arranging cups and saucers for tea and coffee on a long table when the host first approached Grover.

"I hear you might be in a little bit of trouble with the police," he began.

Grover turned around from where he had been arranging an artful display area for the food.

"Uh, I have been questioned about a murder because I was one of the last people to see the victim alive," Grover answered, giving a long glance around the area to see who might be eavesdropping. Daisy knew he didn't want a lot of people to know about his "trouble," as the host phrased it.

"So what did you see?" the host asked. It seemed a potentially gruesome question and Grover straightened up to his full height.

"I didn't see anything," he articulated. "Nothing at all."

"Did you have an argument with the man?" the host asked.

"Yes."

"What about?"

Grover's eyes cast about, looking for anyone who could extricate him from the conversation. Daisy sensed his discomfort and hurried over to where he was standing.

"Sir," she addressed the host, "I'm setting up the beverage table and I have a few questions. Would you mind coming over to take a look?" The host, after giving Grover a long look, followed Daisy to the table. She walked slowly to give herself enough time to think up questions to ask him. She looked once over her shoulder and Grover was leaning heavily on the heels of his hands, his head bowed over the table where he had been working.

After Daisy had steered the host and his probing questions away from Grover, guests started to arrive and the catering staff was busy for the rest of the evening. The party ran quite late.

When everyone had finished packing up the van at the end of the evening, Grover walked up to Daisy.

"Thanks for coming to my rescue earlier," he said. "I don't know how I would have handled it if he had kept asking all those questions."

"No problem," Daisy answered breezily with a wave of her hand.

"Why don't I give you a ride home?" he asked. "I don't think you should be on the Metro this late at night."

"That would be great. Thank you," Daisy replied.

"Thanks again for helping tonight. Are you tired?" he asked.

"Uh-huh," Daisy replied, her voice slow. Grover chuckled.

"I forget how tired I used to be when I started in this business. Now it seems like second nature, but in the beginning I was exhausted all the time," Grover said.

"I can see why."

"Make sure you drink lots of coffee. And lots of water," he suggested. "That'll help."

"I don't know how you do it," she said, suppressing a yawn.

"Like I said, I've been doing it for years. I'll just unpack the van at the office and head home."

"Is someone going to help you?" Daisy asked.

"Yeah, Tish is meeting me there."

Daisy nodded and closed her eyes for the rest of the ride home. When Grover pulled up to the curb in front of her apartment building, she yawned and turned to look at him. He didn't look quite right. She could tell even from the little light that shone above the rear-view mirror that he looked wan and pasty.

"Grover, you look a little pale. Is everything okay?"

He turned to look at her.

"I'm really nervous, Daisy. That guy tonight has me worried about my business. What if I get arrested? What if word gets out that I've been interviewed because one of my clients was killed and I was the last one to see him alive? What if it gets out that I argued with him about the bill?"

"What if you stop worrying about the what ifs and just concentrate on your work and doing what you do best?" Daisy asked. "You can't control what the police do or what party hosts do. All you can do is control what *you* do. I know it's a tall order to stop thinking about this murder investigation, but you can't let it control your life. You have a business to run, so go run it. I'm still trying to figure out exactly what was going on between Brian and Walt and Fiona and the whole test-cheating scandal. I'll do what I can on my end--you just keep throwing good parties."

Grover's gaze softened as he looked at Daisy. "Thanks, Daisy. I'm sorry for being a jerk lately."

"That's okay." She could have insisted that he hadn't been a jerk, but he had. He was right. She couldn't discuss it or she'd fall asleep, though, so she got out of the car, went inside, and dropped into bed.

CHAPTER 45

The next day was Friday. Mark John usually urged everyone in the office to start the weekend a few hours early on Fridays. Daisy suspected it was because he wanted to start his own weekend early and felt awkward leaving before everyone else. She walked home so she could enjoy the warm weather and so she could stop at her favorite market. They always sold whatever remained of the day's fresh bread at half price on Friday afternoons. She had just picked out a loaf of asiago cheese bread and a couple chocolate croissants for the weekend when a familiar voice made her turn her head.

Grover and Tish had just come into the market. Instinct told Daisy not to let them know she was there. She moved around the end of the nearest aisle and stood facing away from them while they perused the bread on sale.

"I'll pick out a loaf of bread and you get some sandwich fixings," Tish suggested.

"All right," Grover answered. "What do you want?"

"How about Brie, fig jam, and arugula?" she asked.

"Sounds good." He strolled over to the fresh cheese case and Daisy figured that was a good time to pay for her bread and scram. She didn't know what Grover and Tish were doing and, for a reason she couldn't explain, she didn't care to find out.

The young man at the counter put her bread in a paper bag and she grabbed it off the counter, intending to beat a hasty escape. Something in the back of her mind wondered why she was running away from one of her best friends, but she couldn't concentrate on those feelings right now. She wanted to get home. In her haste, though, she dropped the bag on the floor and a croissant fell out.

"Oops, let me get you another one," the man at the counter offered.

"Oh, no. It was totally my fault," Daisy said, her words tumbling out in a rush. "I'll just go."

"But you paid for two croissants and I want you to have two croissants. It was my fault for not closing the top of the bag."

While Daisy fumed at the counter the man went back to the breads and picked out another croissant for her. He wrapped it in waxed paper and held it out to her as he approached the counter, but he wasn't fast enough. Grover and Tish were coming up to the counter right behind him.

"Daisy!" Grover exclaimed. "What are you doing in here?"

"Oh, just picking up some provisions for the weekend. How about you two?" she asked, indicating Tish with a wave of her hand.

"Getting some stuff to make sandwiches."

"Got a party tonight?" Daisy asked.

"Unfortunately, no," Grover answered. Daisy wondered for a brief moment why he hadn't called her to do something, but then she mentally pinched herself. *Duh. Obviously he already has plans.*

"Well, have fun," Daisy said with a half-smile, accepting the replacement croissant from the man and tucking it inside the sack. "See you later."

"See you," Grover said.

"See you," Tish echoed.

Daisy walked toward home, wishing she had taken the Metro. She didn't want the bread anymore. Though she couldn't explain why, she suddenly felt completely empty. *Not this again,* she told herself. *Get a grip. You aren't Grover's only friend. He's allowed to do stuff with other people, too.* But the farther she walked, the more dejected she became. By the time she got to her apartment, she didn't even want dinner. She sat down at the kitchen table and set up her laptop, doing the only thing that came to mind—work.

She spent the next several hours writing a bibliography for one of the articles that was due the following week. She checked and double-checked the sources, making sure the bibliography was perfect.

Her thoughts eventually turned to Mark John and Jude. How was it the two of them had managed to find love in the office? Part of her was fascinated and part of her was repulsed. She didn't like to think of what they might be doing in Mark John's office with the door closed. She pushed that thought out of her head with an effort.

It didn't seem fair. Neither one of them was a particularly nice person—maybe they deserved each other. Maybe their relationship was God's way of keeping them from dating other, nicer, people.

Who was she kidding? She was jealous- jealous that they had found each other, jealous of the time they spent together doing something other than work.

The phone rang, jarring Daisy out of her unpleasant thoughts. It was Helena.

"What are you up to tomorrow?" she asked.

"Nothing. Just work," Daisy replied, her voice dull.

"What's the matter?"

"Nothing," Daisy said again. "Why? Do you have plans?"

"I thought we could rent a car and go visit a couple wineries in Virginia. Unless you have too much work to do."

"Aren't you going to be busy with Bennett?" As soon as she asked the question Daisy knew she sounded snarky and petty. But she couldn't put the words back in her mouth.

"What's the matter with you?" Helena asked again. "You sound miserable."

"I'm sorry. It's just been a rotten day. And I'm a little grumpy because I was up late last night."

"Oh. Well, to answer your question, Bennett has to work this weekend. And I haven't been to a winery since you and I went last summer and it's one of my favorite ways to spend a Saturday. You interested?"

"Yeah. That sounds fun."

Daisy went to bed early that night, feeling a little more hopeful about her weekend.

CHAPTER 46

The next morning dawned sunny and dry, a good omen for the day ahead. Helena drove. They cranked up the volume on the radio and opened the car windows. Daisy navigated from a winery map Helena had brought. Their first stop was at a winery outside Alexandria. They were among the first customers of the day and the winery had hired a jazz band that was setting up on the hilly lawn next to the tasting room.

Helena and Daisy each paid for a flight and sat at a table on the tasting room's patio overlooking the valley nearby. Daisy took a sip from the first glass and settled back into her chair with a contented sigh. "I love this," she said.

"It sounded to me like you needed a break this weekend," Helena said, taking a sip from her first glass. "Work not going well?"

Daisy let out a sigh. "It's not so much work as all the extra drama that comes from knowing the people at work. If I had never met any of them I wouldn't be so worried about who killed Mark John's wife or her lover."

"You'd still be trying to help Grover, though," Helena pointed out.

"That's true," Daisy conceded.

"And if you didn't know the people at work, you wouldn't be in such a great position to help him," Helena continued.

"Also true, though I don't know how I'm supposed to help him. Then there's the whole relationship between Mark John and Jude. That complicates everything," Daisy said.

"Are they kissing and stuff in front of people?"

"No, nothing like that."

"Then what are they doing?"

Daisy should have known Helena would press for details. "I can't really explain it," she said, talking into her wine glass. "Let's talk about something more pleasant."

Helena told Daisy all about the project she was working on —she thought she might get a trip to Colorado out of it.

"I would love to go there," Daisy said wistfully. "Do you need a traveling companion?"

"I suppose so," Helena said. She suddenly found the jazz band set-up enthralling and stared at it for several long moments.

"I get it. Bennett's going, isn't he?"

"Well, we talked about it. I'm not even sure I'm going. But yes, if I go he's planning to go with me."

Daisy nodded and took another, rather large, sip of her drink.

"You're supposed to sip wine, not gulp it," Helena said, pointing to Daisy's glass. Daisy looked. It was almost empty.

"The samples are small."

"You know, why don't I just tell Bennett we can go to Colorado anytime? I'd like you to go with me," Helena said. Daisy felt a twinge of guilt and knew it would grow into a crippling sensation if she didn't nip it in the bud.

"No, you go with Bennett. You and I can go some other time. Like you said, you don't even know if you're going yet. I'm just feeling sorry for myself. I don't mean to ruin your day."

Helena put her glass down and leaned forward. "You want to tell me anything else?" she asked in a quiet voice.

Daisy sat back and watched the puffy clouds drift by as she gathered her thoughts. "There's nothing besides everything I just told you."

"Well, as far as Mark John and Jude go, I wouldn't worry about it. They both sound like pretty nasty people," Helena said.

"That's just the point—how can two people who aren't very nice find each other when it's so hard for nice people to find someone?" Daisy asked, her hands gesticulating.

"I don't know. It doesn't seem fair. But the good news is that when the mean people find each other, the rest of us don't have to worry about them. Sounds like that's the silver lining in the whole Mark John-dating-Jude thing."

"You're right."

"Come on. The band is starting. Let's take the rest of the wine and go down closer where we can hear them better." Helena picked up her tray of three glasses and Daisy followed suit, then they went and found a place to sit on the grass. Couples and families were starting to arrive with beach towels, blankets, picnic baskets, and lawn chairs. Some people went up to the tasting room and returned with bottles of wine and the good cheer started flowing. Helena and Daisy enjoyed the music and the atmosphere while they finished their wine, then just as it was getting a little too crowded they got in the car and drove to the next stop on their itinerary.

Daisy was glad Helena was driving because she was enjoying the scenery of the northern Virginia countryside. She was also enjoying her fair share of the wine, so at the second winery Helena decided she would be the designated driver. She only had small sips of wine after that, whereas Daisy had decided it was her duty as an oenophile to sample as many kinds of wine as possible.

After the second winery Daisy's tongue loosened just a bit.

The third winery was farther along the Virginia backroads, so the women had plenty of time to talk in the car.

"I haven't talked to Grover in a while. How's he holding up?" Helena asked.

"As well as could be expected, I guess," Daisy replied. "I know he's worried, and I'm worried about him."

"Me, too," Helena said.

"I helped him out at a party Thursday night and the host was asking all kinds of questions about Walt's murder. Word is getting around that Grover was questioned by police."

"Being questioned isn't the same as being arrested," Helena said.

"Right, but people always have a morbid curiosity when it comes to murder. They don't seem to realize that asking questions is very nerve-wracking."

Daisy was starting to feel the effects of the alcohol.

"I got that host out of Grover's hair and he seemed to be glad. At least he finally apologized for being such a jerk lately."

"I'm sure Grover appreciates your help."

Daisy smirked. "Yeah. He appreciated it so much that he and one of his employees had dinner together the next night."

Helena turned away from watching the road to stare at Daisy for just a moment. "You're jealous! Is that why you're so grouchy today?"

"I'm not grouchy," Daisy said with a scowl. "I'm just tired. And I'm not jealous, either, so stop saying dumb things."

"You are, too, jealous," Helena said, laughing and shaking her head. "I didn't know you like Grover that way, though I think I may have suggested it once or twice before."

"What way? I don't like him any way except as my friend!" Daisy protested loudly.

"Okay, okay," Helena said, lifting her fingers from the wheel in surrender. "My mistake. So how do you know Grover went out to dinner with some woman who works for him?

And is he out of his mind, dating a woman who works for him?"

"I ran into them at a bakery I stop at on Friday afternoons. They have half-price bread and it's really good. They were in there acting all lovey-dovey over sandwich fixings."

"That doesn't sound like something Grover would do," Helena said. "He should know better than to date an employee. Plenty of men have learned that the hard way."

"It's *really* dumb," Daisy said, leaning her head against the passenger window. "I'm just going to close my eyes for a few minutes."

Helena knew the conversation was over and that Daisy wouldn't wake up until she stopped the car at the next winery. Daisy started to snore and Helena smiled. She drove in silence for almost an hour, then pulled into the small parking lot at the next tasting room. She shook Daisy's shoulder gently. "Daisy, we're here."

Daisy blinked twice and sat up, her hair matted on one side of her head and a small bit of drool on her cheek. She wiped her face with the sleeve of her shirt. "Did I fall asleep?"

"Snored the whole way here," Helena said with a laugh.

"You lie," Daisy said, but she knew Helena was telling the truth. It wasn't the first time she'd been told she snored. She joined Helena's laughter. "Sorry about that. All you had to do was push me and I would have stopped."

"Then I wouldn't be able to tease you," Helena pointed out.

They went indoors, where it was dark and cool. Daisy ordered a flight of white wines and Helena ordered a glass of seltzer water. "You're so nice to be the driver today. And it was your idea to come here," Daisy said apologetically. "Next time I'll drive and you can do the drinking. I promise."

"I'll be taking you up on that offer, believe me," Helena said. "As long as I'm the designated driver you should enjoy yourself. Seems like you could use it."

"I sure could."

CHAPTER 47

"So seriously. Now that you've had a chance to sleep off the effects of our last tasting room visit, tell me about Grover and this woman. Who is she?"

"Her name is Tish. You may have met her when you've helped Grover at one of his parties. She's a really nice person and pretty, too. Medium height with blond hair and huge brown eyes. It's no wonder Grover likes her."

Helena narrowed her eyes, something she did when she was trying to remember something. "I think I've met her. She was a nice person. She's been with Grover longer than any of his other employees, hasn't she?"

"I think so."

"What were they doing that was lovey-dovey?"

"Oh, you know. They were all like, 'What do you think we should get?' and 'You get the sandwich stuff, I'll stay here and pick out the bread.'"

Helena raised her eyebrows and screwed up her mouth. "That doesn't sound lovey-dovey to me. That sounds like two people who want dinner."

"It was the stuff they chose. You know, French bread, Brie.

Fig jam, for God's sake. It was like something you'd see in a Viagra ad."

Helena laughed. "People don't just eat those things when they want to sleep together, you know. They eat that stuff because it tastes good. And don't forget, Grover loves gourmet stuff. It wouldn't surprise me if Tish does, too. A caterer who's also a foodie isn't the weirdest thing in the world. What *would* be weird is if Grover was dating an employee. I just don't see him doing that."

"Maybe you're right. That makes sense," Daisy said. "I was tired and surprised to see them. I may have seen what I thought was there, not reality."

"So my next question should be obvious: Why did you assume they were on a date? And more importantly, why does that upset you?"

Helena had gone straight to the point with ruthless speed.

"Is that why you don't want to go out with Dave? Is it because you have a thing for Grover?" Helena asked, her eyes widening.

"No," Daisy said, looking beyond Helena toward the winery's gift shop. "I didn't want to go out with Dave because I don't want to date right now. I like my job."

"Plenty of people who date also like their jobs. The two activities are not mutually exclusive," Helena pointed out wryly. "And don't think I didn't notice that you didn't answer my second question. Do you have a thing for Grover?"

"The thing about Grover is, he's one of my best friends. I just feel a little bit of jealousy when I see him hanging out with other people. That's all. Really."

"You sound like you're trying to convince yourself."

"I am not!" Daisy took a long sip of her wine. She wrinkled her nose. "Too dry."

"What if Grover had been out with another guy looking for sandwich ingredients? Would that have made you jealous?"

Again, there was that uncanny ability to cut right to the chase.

"Probably," Daisy said, avoiding Helena's steady gaze.

"Now you're lying."

"Can we just change the subject? I'm not ready for a relationship yet. Not after Dean."

"Don't you think Dean would want you to carry on with your life?"

Daisy nodded. "It seems disrespectful to his memory, though."

"I'm sure he wouldn't see it that way," Helena replied.

"Plus there's my job..." Daisy's voice trailed off.

"We've talked about that. Not a consideration," Helena said with a smile, waving her hand as if she were flicking away an annoying insect.

"Can we change the subject?" Daisy asked again. She sounded like a petulant child, but she didn't care. Helena was talking about things that cut too deeply and made Daisy think too much.

For the rest of the day the women enjoyed the weather, the live music that several of the wineries offered, and conversation about everything. Everything except Grover, Tish, and Dean.

CHAPTER 48

$\mathcal{L}$ ate on Monday morning Daisy was in her office working on an outline to submit to Mark John about a proposed article when he poked his head around the door. His mouth was set in a thin line and his eyes flashed.

"What's wrong?" Daisy asked. She didn't feel like dealing with one of Mark John's moods just then.

"Brian's here," he hissed. "I don't want to see him."

"So what do you want me to do about it?" she asked. She was pretty sure she knew what he wanted.

"The receptionist buzzed me to let me know even before he was fully in the vestibule. She didn't even wait to see what he wants. Would you talk to him?"

"We've tried that, Mark John. You do this all the time. He wants to talk to you, not me."

"Please, Daisy. Just this one last time. If he doesn't give up, I'll talk to him the next time. I promise."

"All right," Daisy said with a sigh.

"Thanks." Mark John disappeared before Daisy had a chance to change her mind. She pressed the button on her intercom to talk to the receptionist.

"Can you send Brian Comstock back here to talk to me?" she asked. She didn't know whether to hope Brian would talk to her or wouldn't talk to her.

"I'm sending him back," the receptionist replied a moment later.

There was a knock on her open door and Brian stood in the doorway. He had a package in his hand. Daisy invited him into her office and he sat across her desk from her.

"What brings you here, Brian? I'm sorry Mark John isn't available to talk to you right now."

Brian crossed his legs and fixed Daisy with a resigned look. "I actually came here to see you today, Daisy. It's become obvious to me that Mark John is avoiding me and that he has no intention of talking about the diary."

It took you this long to figure it out? Daisy wondered, trying to keep her eyes from rolling.

"I'm afraid I can't speak for him, Brian. I found the diary fascinating."

Brian nodded and cleared his throat. "I thought so. That's why I brought along something else I thought you'd like to see," he said, sliding the package across her desk. It was wrapped in brown paper and tied with a red and white string.

"What is it?" Daisy asked, accepting the package and reaching into her desk drawer for scissors.

"It's called a dime novel. The Library of Congress has a huge collection of dime novels, probably the biggest collection in the world, and I know how fascinated you are with library collections. Being an anthropologist and all," he added.

"I know a little something about dime novels. They were popular around the turn of the twentieth century," Daisy said.

"I believe that's correct."

"And where did you find this one?" she asked.

"This one is on its way to the Library of Congress collection and I thought you might like to get a look at it first."

"Thank you. It was nice of you to think of me. I would love to read through it. When do you need it back?"

"Take your time. I'll make sure it gets to the proper place when you're done with it."

Daisy removed the string from the package and slid the book from its paper wrapping. One of the first things she noticed was the date on the cover of the novel—1910. Before touching it she reached into the desk drawer and drew out a pair of white gloves just like the ones at her apartment. Brian watched her curiously.

"These are so the oils from my skin don't get on the paper and degrade it," she explained, noting his questioning look. "I always keep a pair nearby just in case."

"Excellent idea," he said.

Daisy pulled on the gloves and gingerly touched the cover of the dime novel. It was orange with black print. It looked almost like newspaper print. There was a small pen and ink sketch on the front and several titles down the left side corresponding with page numbers on the right.

"Dime novels were the forerunners of today's paperbacks," she said.

She turned the cover to reveal the first page in the book. It was an advertisement for the company that published the book, Adams and Sons, a New York City firm that had been a popular publisher of dime novels.

"From what I understand, the paper the publishers used to print the books was very poor quality, so that's why relatively few dime novels exist today," she continued.

"This is the only one I've ever seen," Brian said.

"It's a shame they were printed on such lousy paper because more dime novels could have been preserved if the paper had been higher quality," Daisy said, rubbing her thumb across the print on the page. She picked up the book and smelled it.

"Why did you do that?" Brian asked.

"Just to see if I can detect a musty odor. If there is one, that means the book has been exposed to mold or mildew. In that case, I would tell you to take it over to the Library of Congress right away so they can start putting the book on microfilm before it's destroyed, but luckily I don't smell anything but paper. Old paper."

She continued sharing with Brian what little she knew about dime novels. "Of course, the appeal of the dime novels was that they were cheap—about a dime apiece, hence the name 'dime novels.' That's how the publishers were able to get them into the hands of so many readers, and particularly young women and the poor. That wouldn't have happened if the paper had been more expensive."

"I just thought you might find this interesting," Brian said, standing up. "Once you read it give me a call and tell me what you think of it." Daisy's mind was working furiously. Should she ask him about losing his job? About how he felt when he found out Walt had spilled his secret to the administration?

She opened her mouth to say something, but she couldn't bring herself to ask about it. Instead she said, "I will. Just don't expect a call too soon."

She watched Brian leave and noticed that he turned toward the main reception area instead of heading in the direction of Mark John's office. *Maybe Mark John is off the hook for now. What is wrong with me? Why can't I just confront him about what he did?*

Once Brian left Daisy was able to immerse herself in work again until she looked at the clock and was startled to see that it was after five. She stood up and was packing up her tote bag when Jude walked in.

"Don't you ever knock?" Daisy grumbled, half to herself. Jude appeared not to have heard her.

"I came in to see if you'd like to go out for dinner. Somewhere nearby," Jude said.

"Oh. Well, um," Daisy hesitated, frantically trying to come up with an excuse not to go anywhere with Jude. But she was flustered and couldn't come up with anything fast enough. "What restaurant did you have in mind?"

"There's a nice place not far from here called Tom Collins. It's a bar, but they have yummy food and a great happy hour. We could go there."

"All right," Daisy said, suppressing a sigh. She had replaced the paper cover on the dime novel and slid it into her bag between two notebooks. "Let's go."

The two women didn't say much as they walked to Tom Collins. Daisy couldn't imagine what had possessed Jude to want to go out after work. It wasn't like they were friends.

Tom Collins was dark inside. Polished wooden columns reached upward toward a high ceiling and several chandeliers giving off muted light hung far above the space. Dark wooden paneling, combined with oil paintings and slim wall sconces, lent a somber yet elegant tone to the room. People, mostly men, sat at small tables spaced a discreet distance from each other, speaking in hushed tones. "Classy place," Daisy whispered. *Didn't Jude ever go anywhere casual?*

Jude led the way to a marble-topped bar on the far side of the room. The bartender, a young man dressed in old-fashioned bartending garb, complete with black vest, black armbands, and a bow tie, greeted them. "What can I get you?" he asked.

"Ginger ale for me," Daisy said, shuddering when she recalled how much white wine she had consumed on Saturday.

"Napa Valley Cab, please," Jude said. When the man had brought their drinks, they looked around and found an empty table where they could sit down. Jude led the way and nodded to a table nearby set up with happy hour hors d'oeuvres. "Are you hungry?" she asked.

"Always," Daisy replied with a grin. "I'll check out the food and be right back."

She helped herself to a plate of roasted vegetables and horseradish dip as well as some cheese and crackers. She returned to the table, where she offered to share with Jude. Jude declined. Daisy hadn't expected her to share—she was so slim that Daisy figured Jude didn't eat too much.

"So what's up?" Daisy asked. It would be better to get right to the point of this outing, she figured, than stall all evening.

"I need your advice."

Daisy had been raising her glass to her lips and stopped in mid air. "You need *my* advice? What for?"

"It's Mark John. He's getting more serious and I don't know if I'm ready. You know him, so I wanted your opinion."

"I don't know if I can give an opinion about your relationship just because I work with Mark John. You work with him, too, and you know him far better than I do."

"I know, but you're so level-headed. I figured you have pretty good intuition when it comes to people."

"I'm not so sure about that, Jude," Daisy said, thinking about how long it took her to realize Jude and Mark John were dating.

"Just hear me out and tell me what you think. I won't hold you to anything, I promise."

"Isn't there someone, a close friend maybe, who could give you better advice than I can?"

Jude shook her head, looking over Daisy's shoulder as she spoke. "Not really."

Is it possible I am her best friend? Daisy wondered in amazement. *How could that be?*

CHAPTER 49

"All right. So tell me what's been going on between you and Mark John."

"He's not at all like the boss you know from the office. He's sweet and kind and funny. And of course it doesn't hurt that he's so good-looking, too," she said with a slight blush.

"Okay, sounds good so far," Daisy said, encouraging Jude to continue.

"He can cook and clean, too."

"I would hope so. He's a grown man living on his own."

"He and I like the same things. Classical music, books, romcoms. He even likes cuddling. Most men don't." Daisy winced. She was learning more about her boss than she really wanted to.

"It always amazes me that people who are talking about a serious relationship mention music and movies. Those aren't the really important things, as far as I'm concerned. I think the things to know are whether he wants kids, whether he's a saver or a spender, and where he likes to go on vacation. If you don't like the same music, you can always use headphones. If you don't like the same movies, you don't have to watch them together. But if one person wants children and the other one doesn't, that can create serious problems. Ditto with spending habits and the things you each like to do during your downtime. Are you two alike in those ways?"

"Well, I think I'd like children, but I'm not sure yet. Mark John doesn't, I know that. I bet I can change his mind, though, if I decide kids are in my future. I'm well aware that it will have to be sooner rather than later because I'm getting older every day. And we are both pretty conservative spenders except when it comes to clothes. And we both like to vacation at the beach. So I guess we like the same important things."

"That's a good sign," Daisy said. *Except the I-bet-I-can-change-his-mind part.*

"I just don't know if I'm ready for the next step."

"Which is?"

"Marriage. He's talking about it and I just don't know if I'm ready."

Daisy was dumbstruck. Marriage? Fiona was barely cold in her grave. Daisy didn't know what to say. She thought for a moment before responding.

"This is kind of soon, isn't it?"

"But you think we're compatible?" Jude asked, answering Daisy's question with one of her own.

Daisy wanted to say *You were practically made for each other,* but she decided on a more diplomatic response. "I think you're compatible based on everything you've told me and from what I know of both of you. But it's not just compatibility. Do you love him?"

"I think so."

"Then there's your answer: when you can definitively say 'yes,' then it's time to think about the next step. Until you know for sure whether you love him or not, maybe it's best to keep dating. Eventually you'll know the answer. And don't be afraid to slow things down," she cautioned. She couldn't believe Jude was even considering this step.

"But what do I tell him if he asks?" Jude seemed determined to ignore Daisy's warning.

"He hasn't actually asked you yet?"

"No. But he keeps talking about it."

"I would say if he asks and you're not ready to make a decision, tell him that. If he understands you and loves you, he'll wait until you're ready to decide. If he doesn't understand or refuses to wait, maybe he's not the one for you."

Jude nodded, twirling the stem of her wine glass, which was empty. "I need another glass. Want another soda?"

"Sure. Thanks."

Jude left to order the drinks and Daisy sat back in her chair, looking around the room. There was no accounting for the speed with which the relationship between Jude and Mark John was moving. Furthermore, she couldn't picture the Mark John Jude had described. He seemed like the dry documentary-type, not the rom-com-type. And as for being a cuddler, Daisy shuddered. She didn't even want to think about that. She glanced toward the bar where Jude was still waiting for their drinks. Was it possible Jude really didn't have any other friends? Daisy could imagine Jude being the type of person who had trouble making friends. She could be standoffish, but was that really a mask for shyness? She seemed judgmental, but was that possibly because Jude didn't know how to talk to people? Maybe Daisy didn't know Jude as well as she thought she did. Maybe getting to know the senior editor wouldn't be such a bad idea.

Jude returned with the beverages and sank into her chair. "Here's one thing that bothers me. Remember when I was sick? Mark John wanted to spend as much time as he could at work, except for when he was sick, of courses. He wasn't much of a nurse."

Daisy waved her hand dismissively. "Men are like that. They don't have that nurturing instinct that women have. I'll bet he just wanted to stay away from you so he wouldn't get sick."

"He said as much. Didn't work, though."

"I wouldn't read too much into that," Daisy said, smiling. "It's not unusual. In fact, it's probably the norm. How was he when he got sick?"

Jude rolled her eyes. "Like he was dying. He couldn't do anything for himself."

Daisy let out a laugh. "Also, not unusual. I knew someone like that once. Men are babies when it comes right down to it." She thought back to the last time Dean was sick. He had been in bed for three days, unable to get dressed, take a shower, or even work on his laptop. And as Daisy recalled, it had been nothing more than the common cold.

Talk turned to work assignments for a while, then the women left Tom Collins. They stood on the sidewalk out front of the bar, talking for a bit longer, before going their separate ways. Daisy made her way home along streets that were beginning to come alive with young people in the waning daylight. She couldn't help but feel sorry for Jude because the poor woman was so obviously torn over what to do about Mark John. And though Daisy now had a little more information than she needed about their relationship, she felt she had learned more about Jude in a couple hours than she had in the entire time she had worked at Global Human Rights Journal.

Daisy wondered how lonely Jude must have been before Mark John came along. She had probably been a workaholic.

That sounded familiar.

But *she* wasn't like Jude, Daisy thought with a little shake of her head. She had friends- good friends- and they did things together on the weekends and in the evenings sometimes. She wasn't avoiding people by hiding behind her work.

Was she?

When she got home Daisy thought about digging into the dime novel Brian had given her, but she was too tired to focus on the book. Instead she turned on the television and watched some mindless show for an hour before going to bed.

When she got to work the next day, Mark John was in a snit, barking out orders to everyone in the office. Daisy finally was able to learn from a whispered conversation with the receptionist that he had inadvertently missed a deadline at the printer and he was blaming anyone he could think of, including Daisy and Jude.

"Mark John, stop it," she overheard Jude saying to their boss. "You're acting like a child. Just man up, admit you made a mistake, and get on with your day. And let the rest of us get on with our days, too." Daisy smiled. She was glad to know that Jude wasn't going to let Mark John push people around and get away with acting like a spoiled brat.

But there are always consequences when the boss makes a mistake, and the incident with Mark John was no exception. He spent the rest of the day coming up with research and writing assignments for both Daisy and Jude, along with tight deadlines and big expectations. Daisy and Jude both knew that the next couple weeks would be a flurry of late nights, early mornings, and take-out meals.

It was later that same week when, after a long day of staff meetings and phone interviews with potential sources, that Daisy and Jude met in the conference room to share an order of sandwiches Daisy had picked up on a walk around the block. Mark John had left the office for a dinner meeting.

"I'm sorry Mark John has been such a jerk lately," Jude said, helping herself to one of the sandwiches.

"Why should you be sorry? It's Mark John who's been the difficult one," Daisy answered.

"I know, but I feel like I ought to be able to rein him in a bit."

"Because you're dating?"

"Yes. I should be able to talk to him, calm him down, get him off this dictator kick he's been on."

"Jude, Mark John is a grown man. He's also the editor-in-chief and he makes the decisions around here. The journal is his responsibility and he has to run it the way he sees fit. His attitude has nothing to do with you, so don't feel bad about it."

Jude didn't answer, but bit into her sandwich with a pensive look on her face.

"Tell me this," Daisy said. "Are things still good between you outside of work?"

"Yes."

"Then don't worry about it. This is the job that people in this office signed up for. There's no such thing as a job that doesn't have some difficult days. It's not your fault," Daisy repeated.

Jude's next words took Daisy by surprise.

"I don't think they're ever going to catch the person who killed Fiona."

"What makes you think that?" Daisy asked, her brow furrowing.

Jude shook her head. "It just grows colder and colder every day. Sometimes I wonder if Mark John will be able to get past it. What if they never find out who did it and he never moves on? I mean, I told you he's talked about getting married, but what if he's never really ready?"

"It's hard to imagine how he must feel," Daisy said. "When Dean died, I thought I would never get past it. But I did. That doesn't mean I don't think about him a lot, but I think about the happy stuff. I try not to think of how he died and what happened afterward. That's different from Mark John's situation because in this case someone really *did* kill Fiona, but I'm not sure it's that much different in terms of him being able to move on."

"Do you think he still loves her?" Jude blurted.

It was a question that required a careful answer. "I'm sure he holds a special place in his heart for her, but he also realizes that he needs to move on. There's nothing that says a widower can't find a second soul mate."

Jude seemed satisfied with the answer. "I just don't want to worry that he's always thinking of Fiona or wishing I were her."

Daisy scoffed at the idea. "Of course not. If Mark John weren't ready to date again, he wouldn't date. It's that simple."

"You make everything sound so neat and tidy. I wish I had your confidence," Jude said.

Confidence? That word wasn't what came to Daisy's mind when she thought of her own love life.

"I'm a pro when it comes to other people's relationships," Daisy said with a grin.

CHAPTER 50

*D*aisy didn't hear from Helena or Grover until Sunday that week, but she barely noticed because she was so busy with the assignments Mark John had given her. Helena finally called to invite Daisy to a concert with her and Bennett the following Friday evening and Grover called to talk late Sunday night.

"Any news?" Daisy asked.

"I just got off the phone with one of the detectives," he said. "He told me Melody had an alibi that checks out. They want to question me again. What do you think that means?"

That was bad news. "I wish I knew," Daisy replied. "So what's her alibi?"

"Her mother," Grover said with a snort. "What mother *wouldn't* provide an alibi if her child was suspected of murder?"

He made a good point.

"When are you going to talk to the detectives?" Daisy asked.

"Tomorrow morning."

"Are you taking a lawyer?" Daisy asked.

Silence. Daisy had her answer.

"Grover, you're making a big mistake," she warned, exasperated by his stubbornness.

"You have to let me do this my way," he said quietly.

"Then why did you call me?"

"Just for reassurance," Grover said.

Daisy winced, knowing she had provided anything but reassurance to him. She had probably only made matters worse, she thought.

"I'm sorry, Grover. I should be more supportive. Of course you need to do what you think is best. I just worry about you, that's all."

"I worry about me, too," he said. He chucked, but Daisy knew he was forcing himself.

"Do you want me to go with you?" Daisy asked.

"I would, but I know they won't let you into the interview. You should probably just go to work."

"All right, if you say so. But I'm available if you change your mind."

"Thanks, Daisy. I appreciate it. Anything going on with you?"

Daisy winced, remembering how she had acted trying to hide from him and Tish at the bakery. "It's been crazy at work. Mark John handed out an obscene number of assignments, all with a quick turnaround, and I've been working almost non-stop. Are you still retaining clients?"

"About half," he said. "Some have cancelled and been honest about it, you know, saying that because I'm involved in a murder investigation it would be best to cancel the contract. I don't blame them. But there are clients who are sticking by me. Summer party season is kicking into high gear, so I've been busy. I'm glad because it helps take my mind off things. Then when I'm not out doing a party, I'm in the office shoring up inventory and planning menus and all the other things I have to do to stay afloat."

"I'm sorry I haven't been able to help."

"That's all right. It sounds like you've been as busy as I have."

"There's a light at the end of the tunnel, though. Eventually the police are going to figure out who killed Walt and you'll be off the hook. Frankly, my money is still on Melody. Maybe the police will take another look at her alibi and she'll be arrested."

"I don't care who they arrest, as long as it's not me and I can get on with my life," Grover said. "Have you found out any more about Brian's test-cheating scandal?"

"No. Brian was actually in my office the other day and I just couldn't bring myself to ask him about it. It's kind of a sensitive subject."

"It must be," Grover agreed.

"Hang in there. I'm still trying to figure it all out."

"Thanks. You're the best," Grover said. His voice was warm, despite all the worries weighing on his mind.

Daisy hung up and stared at the phone thoughtfully. She needed to find a way to help him. He didn't deserve the damage to his reputation or the worries that accompanied his situation. It didn't help that she had been too timid to ask Brian about the scandal that cost him his job. Or that Melody's mother had provided her an alibi.

At least Grover hadn't mentioned Tish once. Thank goodness.

Daisy had thought more than once over the week, and usually with a twinge of guilt, that she hadn't taken a look at the dime novel Brian had given her. Once her deadlines had passed, she would need to settle down and read it. It wasn't fair to Brian that she hadn't even attempted to read the book, as she knew he was waiting for her to discuss it. And she knew the Library of Congress would be able to care for the book far better than she could; she wanted to get it back to Brian so he could donate it as soon as possible.

But she was too tired to take a look at it that night. All she wanted was to curl up in bed and drift off to sleep.

And that's exactly what happened, until a phone call jarred her from her dream in the middle of the night.

"Hello?" she answered, her voice groggy and slow.

A muffled sob erupted on the other end of the line, and Daisy stared at the phone in confusion. "Who is this?"

"It's Jude."

"What's wrong?" Daisy asked, immediately awake and alarmed. "What's happened?"

"I can't find Mark John. He isn't answering his phone and he said he would call me tonight."

Daisy let out an annoyed sigh. "Is that all? I'm sure it's nothing. He's had a tough week and he's under a lot of pressure at work right now. I wouldn't worry about it."

"But what if he's lying dead somewhere?" Jude asked, her voice breaking and the sobbing starting again.

"Jude, this is Washington. No one lies dead anywhere for long without someone finding the body." Daisy winced when she heard herself say such insensitive words. "I'm sorry. That was rude of me. But I really don't think you have anything to fret about. I'm sure he's fine."

"If he's fine, then why doesn't he answer my calls?" Jude asked, a hint of challenge in her voice.

"Maybe his phone died. Maybe he lost it. Maybe he left it at work. Maybe the ringer's off. There could be a thousand innocent reasons he's not answering his phone right now. You need to get some sleep."

"You really think he's all right?"

"I'm sure of it."

"I hope so."

Daisy had a hard time going back to sleep after Jude's phone call. Her heart was still beating fast and she had to admit it was odd that Mark John wasn't home in the middle of the night on a Sunday and not answering his phone.

She tossed and turned for an hour before deciding to get up and use her time for something other than being frustrated and increasingly angry at Jude for waking her up. She pulled on her white gloves and reached for the dime novel, which she had placed on her nightstand. She turned to the first page and began reading.

The Widower's Curse

By Harold Henderson

It was only a matter of time before this story would come to be told aloud. It has been whispered and bandied about among a discrete circle of persons for years and the public record must now be set straight.

The Widower Sheppard was a man of ugly disposition. Oh, he hadn't always been like that. He used to love and was loved in return, but certain family traits wormed their way into his mysterious heart and into his diseased mind as he grew older and he eventually became embittered and hateful. His father had been the same way, so it wasn't surprising that when the Widower Sheppard was finally laid to rest no one could be bothered to attend his funeral, save for the gravedigger and the widower's children, who were glad to see him buried, may the Lord forgive them.

Young Sheppard (who, at that time, was of course not yet a widower) began life with the promise of riches and success. He was born into a family of privilege and spent his youth in various pursuits common among the wealthy, such as traveling abroad, sailing, horse racing, attending the theater, and playing at cards.

One fateful day, Young Sheppard was at his supper club with a group of like-minded friends when he received sobering news. The valet of the club handed him a note, folded so no one else could read what was written there. Unfolding the note and holding it close to his chest in order to keep its contents private, Young Sheppard read the words that his father's valet had written and had delivered to the supper club. "Please make haste and return home, young sir, as your father has requested your presence with his lawyer."

Our young bachelor was inclined to ignore the note, as he considered his father's lawyer to be boorish and coarse, but he decided that he should behave as the dutiful son. Thus he returned to his home, albeit without the haste requested in the note. When he arrived, he found the household in a general state of bedlam, a condition far removed from the normal staid routine of the family.

Upon questioning his mother, he learned that his father's lawyer was awaiting him in the study. Once he was comfortably seated across from the lawyer and wondering where his father could be, the lawyer informed the young man for the reason behind his visit.

It seems the father had been visited by the local police and taken to a nearby police station for questioning in the murder of a young man who had lived in a neighborhood quite near the Sheppards' home. Young Sheppard was shocked to his very bones that his father was being accused of such abhorrent behavior, and he went, this time with haste, to the police station. He was accompanied by his father's lawyer, who spoke to his client there and was informed that the client was, indeed, being charged with murder.

When Young Sheppard had departed for his supper club earlier that evening, he could not have known that his life was about to take a drastic turn for the worse. The scandal which followed the arrest of his father and the subsequent trial that ended in his father's conviction for murder was enough to bring financial and social ruin to the family which had once held a privileged and enviable position in the city of New York.

In time, the Sheppard family ran out of funds and was forced to sell the mansion which they had always called home. With her husband in prison and no longer able to provide for the family, Mrs. Sheppard sadly found herself in a position of having to look for a job, something she had never dreamed of doing. With her own family deceased, she could not even turn to them in her grief and financial need. And since her husband had been branded a killer, she had a difficult time finding even the most meager employment.

She eventually found a job as a seamstress several miles from New York. It was a financial burden to find a way to the tailor's shop every day, but she managed. Her sons also found work, one at a printing shop, one as a baker's assistant, and one, Young Sheppard, as a carpenter's assistant. Mrs. Sheppard's daughters also found work, one as a nanny and one in a shoe factory making fancy shoes like those her mother could no longer afford.

With Mrs. Sheppard and all her children working, the family was finally able to buy a small home in a shabby neighborhood. The family was never again wealthy, except for Young Sheppard, but they were better off than some of New York City's poor. The two daughters eventually married and the sons, too, found wives. Mrs. Sheppard ended up living alone, but her children all lived nearby and they were able to help her as she grew older and more feeble in her later years.

As much as she was enjoying the story, Daisy's eyes began to close as she read and she leaned back against the pillow. The alarm woke her from a sound sleep Monday morning. When she got to work she found Jude pacing the hallway between her office and Mark John's office.

"Did you talk to Mark John?" Daisy asked.

"No. He's in his office now, talking on the phone. He's going to have some explaining to do when he finally hangs up and I can get in there. I'm going to wring his neck."

"Before you strangle him, remember there may be a perfectly reasonable explanation for him being off the grid last night," Daisy warned.

"I will," Jude said with a smirk. "I can't wait to hear his explanation."

Daisy went into her office and closed the door so she wouldn't have to hear the fireworks when Mark John got off the phone. She had too much work to do to worry about Mark John's whereabouts the night before, plus she was tired.

She hadn't been at the computer too long before Jude peeked her head around the door with a look of chagrin. "He had a migraine. He was asleep and turned off the ringer because the sound from the phone hurt his head."

Daisy smiled. "See? It was nothing for you to worry about. I hate to say I told you so, but—"

"I know, I know. You told me so. I'm just glad he's all right. His headache is better and he's in a better mood today. I think the stress of last week hit him hard."

Daisy had been thinking a lot about Mark John and Fiona since the last time she and Jude had spoken, in the conference room over sandwiches.

"Do you two ever talk about Fiona?" Daisy asked suddenly. Jude looked over her shoulder toward Mark John's office and slipped into Daisy's office, closing the door behind her with a soft *click*.

"We don't really talk too much about her," Jude said, sitting down across from Daisy. She picked at one of her fingernails as she spoke. "Mark John is very careful to keep the doors to his house locked all the time and he's always warning me not to go anywhere by myself, even in the middle of the day. I think the memory of Fiona's death is never far from his mind, at least in terms of staying safe and keeping me safe. But he never mentions her. Do you think I should say something to him?"

"It seems like talking about her would be the healthy thing to do, especially if you and Mark John are getting more serious," Daisy said, choosing her words carefully. It was amazing to her that the couple had hardly talked about Mark John's murdered former wife. Wouldn't that be the elephant in the room every time they were together? "So he never talks about what happened the night she was killed?"

Jude shook her head, her eyes downcast. "No. I've read about it online, of course, and in the newspapers at the time, but I've always figured that if he wants to talk about her, he will. And he hasn't, so he probably doesn't want to."

"Maybe he's waiting for you to ask."

"Maybe," Jude conceded, but she looked doubtful.

"Let me know how it goes if you two do talk about her," Daisy said, wondering if she should change careers to be a relationship counselor.

Jude took the hint and stood up to leave. "Thanks, Daisy," she said, opening the door and stepping into the hallway. "You give good advice." Her smile was genuine.

When Jude had shut the door behind her, Daisy tried getting back to work, but a horrible thought had struck her while Jude was talking.

Was it possible that Mark John and Jude had been romantically involved before Fiona's death? That Mark John had been cheating on his wife, as she had been cheating on him? That would explain why it seemed that Mark John was talking about marriage to Jude so quickly after Daisy thought they started dating. Maybe he hadn't mentioned it quickly at all. Maybe they had been together for a long time and marriage was just the next step.

Then an even more horrible thought occurred to Daisy. Was it possible that Fiona and Mark John were both involved in Fiona's murder so they could continue their relationship out in the open?

It was too horrible even to consider. Daisy shook her head as if to dislodge such a heinous idea and tried to focus on the document in front of her. But she couldn't concentrate. She needed to get out of the office for some fresh air, to clear her head so she would be able to get some work done. She grabbed her wallet and cell phone and headed downstairs and out into the steamy Washington morning. While she walked she phoned Helena. She hoped Helena would be able to talk some sense into her.

"Sorry to bother you at work," she said when Helena answered the phone.

"No problem. Is something wrong?"

"Not really. I want to run something by you so you can tell me how stupid it is."

"What?" The confusion in her voice was obvious. Daisy chuckled wryly.

"Just listen and you'll understand." Daisy recounted her conversation with Jude. She finished by taking a deep breath and asking Helena, "Do you think it's possible that Mark John and Jude somehow planned Fiona's murder so they could be together?"

"Whoa, slow down there. Daisy, you've had too much caffeine. You're making up wild stories that have no basis in fact. What would possess you to think you're working with a couple of murderers?"

"I don't know. It's just a thought that occurred to me. I knew it was far-fetched, so that's why I called you. So you could be the voice of reason." Thank God Helena was an engineer. She looked at everything logically. Well, most things.

"What you need is a nice cup of tea. Herbal tea, that is. Take a break from all the work for a while. Want to get together for lunch?"

"I really shouldn't. I've got so much work to do that I can't spare the time. Besides, I brought lunch with me to the office today. And if I'm going to be able to go to that concert with you and Bennett on Friday night, I can't be taking any more time away from my office."

"All right. Just make sure you don't let yourself get carried away with thoughts of murder and mayhem. I'll talk to you before Friday."

Daisy hung up with a feeling of relief. Of course Jude and Mark John hadn't planned Fiona's murder. She ducked into her favorite tea shop, which was just a block from her office, and ordered the herbal tea Helena had suggested. She let it cool while she walked back to work.

She was able to concentrate on her research and the afternoon sped by quickly, as did the next several days. Summoning the determination and focus she had cultivated in college and graduate school, she was able to push any thoughts of Jude, Mark John, and Fiona out of her head for the rest of the week. She and Helena spoke on the phone on Thursday night and the topic of murder didn't even come up. She was looking forward to the concert the following evening. Grover called next to ask if Daisy still wanted to help out at an event the following week. There was a graduation party scheduled for Wednesday evening and he could use the help. Daisy said she'd be happy to.

She finished two of her four assignments on Friday and was ready for an evening off. After work she changed her clothes, hurried to the Metro, and rode all the way out to suburban Virginia, where she was going to meet up with Helena and Bennett for the concert.

She saw them before they saw her outside the Metro station. They were laughing, leaning into each other, and looked perfectly at ease. Daisy felt a tiny twinge of jealousy, but pushed it aside and told herself firmly that this evening she wasn't going to have any negative thoughts. She smiled broadly at the happy couple as they approached and accepted a peck on the cheek from Bennett, as if they had known each other for years.

"Helena talks about you all the time," Bennett told her as they walked toward the park where the concert was being held. "I feel like I already know you even though we didn't get much of a chance to talk that night Dave and I met you."

Daisy felt her face flush at the memory of the double date, then repeated the evening's mantra to herself. *No negative thoughts. No negative thoughts.* She grinned at Bennett. "Helena can't possibly talk about me as much as she talks about you." Bennett and Helena exchanged glances and laughed.

Bennett had brought a big blanket and they purchased dinner from one of the food trucks set up around the big park. The atmosphere was bright and noisy and the promise of live jazz outdoors was just what Daisy needed after a long week at work. They settled on the blanket amid the crowd and waited for the music to start.

Daisy looked around absentmindedly at the crowd as more and more people gathered, setting up lawn chairs, hauling out coolers, and spreading picnics on the ground. She did a double-take when she saw Jude and Mark John sitting on a blanket about thirty feet in front of her. They were facing the stage and probably hadn't seen her. They were seated close together, Jude's hand resting lightly on Mark John's leg. They were talking animatedly about something, though neither one was smiling. It didn't look like a fight, just an intense conversation. Daisy eventually turned her attention back to Helena and Bennett, as it was more fun to pay attention to a conversation she could actually hear.

Before long the music started. The best thing about summer jazz festivals, Daisy thought, was the eclectic mix of fans. There were parents with young children, teens in groups, older couples, people on dates, and large groups of people of all ages. And everyone was there to enjoy the music and the atmosphere. She laid back on the blanket next to Helena and closed her eyes, listening to the music.

When she sat up to grab a bottle of water from her bag, she noticed Jude standing up. She stepped carefully over people in the crowd as she made her way to one of the port-a-potties along the perimeter of the park. Daisy idly watched Jude's movements for a moment, then turned her attention to where Mark John still sat on their blanket. She was startled to see a hooded look in his eyes and a sneer playing around the corners of his mouth as he, too, watched Jude weave her way through the crowd.

She thought back to her conversation with Jude, when Jude had mentioned that Mark John didn't like her going anywhere by herself out of concern for her safety. She wondered if Mark John hadn't wanted Jude to go the rest room by herself. But why wouldn't he just go with her?

Daisy reminded herself again that she was at the concert to enjoy herself and what happened between Mark John and Jude was really none of her business. Turning her attention back to the stage, she concentrated on being mindful of the music. It must have worked, because she didn't even notice when Jude returned to Mark John's side.

CHAPTER 51

*D*aisy dropped into bed that night, exhausted and happy. She had enjoyed the company of Helena and Bennett, and had been glad they kept their public displays of affection to a minimum. If she had to guess, she would say Helena had spoken to Bennett before the concert about Daisy's sorry lack of a love life and suggested that maybe they shouldn't flaunt their relationship.

Whether Helena had said something or not, Daisy was glad of it. She woke up Saturday morning feeling refreshed and ready to work, which was good because she spent every minute for the rest of the weekend working and was able to hand Mark John the files containing her completed assignments first thing Monday morning.

Mark John told her she had done a "nice job," which was high praise coming from him. She was glad when he suggested she get back to work on the articles about women's history she had set aside over two weeks previously. Before he could change his mind she took her laptop and tote bag and headed for the Library of Congress. This visit she took her time wandering through the Great Hall of the magnificent Jefferson

Building, admiring the artwork, the friezes, the mosaics on the ceilings, the floors, and the walls. Everywhere she turned she saw a sight more magnificent than the last. The murmuring of the tourists in the gallery subsided to a mere hush in her ears as she wandered around, trying to take it all in. She had seen the Great Hall before, of course, but it had been a long while since she had taken the time to enjoy it. She had worked so hard for Mark John over the past two weeks, she figured she deserved an hour-long break to sightsee in the library. She even stood in line to go up the stairs to the observation room where people without research passes could see into the Main Reading Room. She couldn't decide if she liked the view from above better than the view from the ground—they were both incredible.

When she had seen as much as her senses could handle for one day, she went back into the cool silence of the Main Reading Room to get back to work on the women's history research. She sat well away from any other people so she wouldn't bother them by typing on her laptop, then spent the rest of the day happily immersed in books, articles, and online resources for her research. It was toward the end of the after-noon when she checked the clock and thought for the first time that day about taking a look at the library's dime novel collec-tion. She hadn't gotten a chance to read any more of the novel about Widower Sheppard, and she intended to get back into it that evening after work. She first checked the Library of Congress website to learn more about their dime novel collec-tion and then went to the Rare Book Reading Room to inquire about them for herself.

It so happened that the librarian who greeted Daisy when she went to the Rare Book Reading Room was studying the library's dime novel collection. She was fascinated by Daisy's tale of the book Brian had lent her, and was excited to hear that Brian was planning to donate it to the library. With just a short time left before the library closed, the librarian offered to get one of the dime novels so Daisy could take a look at it. Daisy wanted to compare a dime novel from 1910, the year of the book she had at home, to one of the older editions.

When the librarian brought the book out, Daisy was mesmerized. She asked the librarian to turn the pages for her so she could take pictures with her cell phone, and the librarian kindly obliged. One of the things Daisy found most interesting about the dime novel was the advertising printed inside. It told the modern-day anthropologist what readers had been interested in learning at the turn of the twentieth century. Mostly the advertisements consisted of books and song lyrics. There were ads for books about managing pets and children, in that order, about making canoes, and about debating. There were ads for learning magic, playing cards, and becoming one's own doctor. Daisy was enthralled. She made a note of the librarian's name and promised to visit again soon.

Visiting the Rare Book Reading Room had rekindled Daisy's interest in getting back to the book Brian had lent her. She looked forward to spending the evening in her apartment with a glass of wine, her white gloves, and the story of the Widower Sheppard.

Following the death of the elderly Mrs. Sheppard, her sons and daughters eventually found more prosperous jobs. Unfortunately, one of the three sons moved far enough away, to the State of Maine, that he never did see his brothers or sisters again during his life on earth. Another son, our Young Sheppard, moved south, to the capital city of the United States. He had heard there were jobs for carpenters in the growing city and he went to make his mark. Sadly, his young wife perished on the trip, having been trampled by a horse who had been spooked. Our Young Sheppard had thus become a widower for the first time.

Young Sheppard mourned the death of his poor wife, naturally. But the time came when he chanced to meet another lovely young woman, one whose father owned a large number of buildings in the federal capital and who was quite wealthy. Of course Young Sheppard had known wealth growing up and he impressed the young woman's father with his knowledge of the pursuits of the affluent, such as racing, boating, and travel abroad. The father took a keen interest in Sheppard and eventually became the proud father-in-law of the young man. It was not long before Sheppard was the valuable assistant of his father-in-law and was prospering beyond what he had dared to hope following the imprisonment of his own father.

When the grandchildren were born the wife's mother and father could barely contain their glee. They showered the young children with love, with gifts, and with delightful experiences, such as riding along the Potomac River, vacationing in the mountains of Virginia, and visiting the seaside. You see, dear reader, the children's grandparents had never expected to be blessed with grandchildren and were grateful to be given by God the opportunity to shower love on their own grandchildren.

Thus it was with great sadness that the grandparents said good-bye to their daughter, their son-in-law, and their two beloved grandchildren when the time came for the small family of four to move west to take advantage of the building boom that was occurring with the westward expansion of the United States.

Mrs. Sheppard missed her parents dreadfully in the months after the family's departure from Washington, and though Mr. Sheppard tried his hand at farming, was exceedingly successful, and did his best to provide them with all the comforts of wealth and security, it was never enough for poor Mrs. Sheppard. She was lonely and despondent, even with the love of her children, and she eventually fell into an illness that only a return to her parents could cure.

When the children were still very young, Mrs. Sheppard disappeared one night, never to be heard from again. Though Mr. Sheppard assured the children their mother had returned to the bosom of her own family, he was not able to contact her or discern her whereabouts. Mr. Sheppard received letters from his wife's parents, meant for their daughter, which indicated they had no idea their daughter was missing and in fact believed she was still with her young family in the western territories of the United States. Mr. Sheppard promised the children he would do everything he could to locate his wife, but in the end he was forced to admit that she had probably died on the arduous trip east. The children were inconsolable.

Mr. Sheppard and his children could not stay in the town where they had settled, given the sadness that permeated every corner of their home. So again, Mr. Sheppard, who would end up changing the family's surname within a short time, uprooted the children and began the trek further west. He did not know where he was going, only that he would stop when he came to a town that needed a carpenter and where he could farm and raise his children in peace.

After what seemed like an endless trek over miles of undulating prairie, the small family with a new surname arrived in the Nebraska Territory (we, however, dear reader, shall at least temporarily continue to refer to them as the Sheppards).

Here Daisy stopped, a little surprised that her nighttime reading was again taking her to Nebraska. She lay awake for a long time, wondering how Mrs. Sheppard could have left her children and her husband behind to return to Washington and the comfort of her own family's home. How could any mother do such a thing?

It was almost beyond comprehension. But how badly must she have missed her parents to leave like that? It was heartbreaking to think about the millions of people who left cities in the east to make a better life for themselves out west over the course of the eighteenth and nineteenth centuries. So many of those families never saw their loved ones again. The mails were slow and unreliable, and often families moved again and again before their correspondence could catch up with them. But the book said letters were arriving for Mrs. Sheppard from her parents. How sad, Daisy thought. The Sheppard children would never know what happened to their mother. She wondered why Mister Sheppard had changed the family's name and whether mail from his wife's parents would continue to reach them.

Daisy flung her arm over her eyes so she wouldn't see the lamplight from the street outside reflected on her bedroom wall. *That's the problem with me,* she thought. *I get too caught up in the stories I read. I can't research all of them. And the story about Widower Sheppard is merely fiction.*

CHAPTER 52

*L*ater that week Daisy left work early to help Grover at the party he was working. She arrived at the lovely white mansion along one of the more affluent areas of Massachusetts Avenue well before the party was due to start, but after Grover and the rest of his staff had arrived.

She donned an apron she found in the back of the catering truck and went in search of Grover to ask where she should help. He gave her a tired smile when he saw her.

"Thanks for coming. I'm going to need all the help I can get tonight. Two of my staff called out sick and I'm short-handed. Can you start by setting the tables?"

Daisy headed for the truck to take a look at the diagram for the table set-up and found the florist unloading centerpieces from her van. Together the two women put a centerpiece on each table, then the florist left and Daisy began setting the tables. She thought back to her own high school graduation party, which had been a few friends and family on her parents' patio. And there was no time for a party when she had graduated from college and her postgraduate program—she had to start work right away. *Times have changed*, she thought. This party was going to make the society pages.

Like the other events where she had worked for Grover, this one kept Daisy running from the moment she arrived until long after the happy guests departed and the catering staff could begin putting away their supplies and cleaning up. She was walking back to the catering truck with an armload of serving utensils, ready to take a long swig of water and eat something, when she saw a man approach Tish, who was in the back of the truck, up to her elbows in soapy water.

"Hey," he said when he saw Tish.

"Hi there," she replied. She glanced at Daisy as she climbed into the van. "Daisy, this is my boyfriend Lewis. Lewis, meet Daisy. He came to help out so I could leave earlier."

Daisy shook hands with Lewis after depositing her utensils in the hot water, then helped herself to a bottle of water from the fridge. She sat on the grass in front of the truck pondering what she had just learned.

Tish has a boyfriend? What about Grover? Does he know? Daisy wanted answers. She couldn't bear the thought of Grover learning about Tish's boyfriend here at an event, so when she had finished her water she went back into the truck. Lewis was nowhere to be found and Tish was alone.

"Tish, could I ask you a quick question?"

"Sure. What is it?"

"It's about Lewis. I was just wondering if Grover knows about him."

"Oh, yeah. They've met lots of times."

"And does Grover know you and Lewis are dating?"

"Of course. What's this all about?"

Daisy gave Tish a sheepish look. "I thought you and Grover were dating, that's all. And since Grover is a friend of mine, I didn't want to see him get hurt if he didn't know about you and Lewis."

Tish tilted her head back and laughed. "You thought Grover and I were dating? That's funny. Whatever gave you that idea?"

"I don't know, really. I guess when I saw you that night in the bakery I just assumed you were an item."

"Gosh, no. We were going to be working on the books that night, so we were getting sandwiches. No point in working late if there's no food."

Daisy knew a flush had crept into her cheeks while Tish was talking. *It's amazing I didn't break my leg jumping to conclusions,* she thought with a grimace. Aloud she said, "I'm glad. I just didn't want Grover to get hurt, that's all."

"I wouldn't hurt Grover. He's a nice guy, plus he signs my paychecks," Tish answered with a wink.

Late that evening Grover dropped Daisy off at her apartment. "Everything all right?" he asked when she hadn't spoken for most of the drive.

"Yeah, everything's fine. Just tired," she answered. She hoped Tish wouldn't tell him about their conversation. She was embarrassed and didn't want Grover to get the wrong idea. But what *was* the wrong idea? She suppressed a sigh. She needed some sleep. This wasn't the time to be delving deep into her thoughts about Grover.

His next words took her by surprise. "I'm not busy tomorrow night. Want to meet for dinner?"

"Uh, sure. I'll be home around six. Want to meet around seven?"

"Yup. Text me where you want to eat and I'll meet you there." He pulled up in front of her apartment building. "Thanks for helping out tonight. I don't know what I would have done without you."

"You're welcome. Anytime," she said with a smile.

CHAPTER 53

The next day Brian phoned Daisy at work. "Hi, Daisy. Have you had a chance to look through that dime novel I lent you?"

"Oh, Brian, I have, but I'm not finished reading it yet. Can I hold onto it for a couple more days so I can get through all of it? I've been so busy with work that I've been too tired at night to read. But this week is easier, so I should be able to get through it."

"That's no problem," he answered. "Take whatever the time you need. Let me know when you've finished it and I'll come by to pick it up."

"Thanks."

She took a deep breath and was about to ask Brian if he had a minute to talk about the test-cheating scandal, but he didn't give her a chance.

"I've got to run, Daisy, I'm in a rush. Talk to you soon."

"Yeah. Okay, Brian." She would need to find another time to ask him about it. She made a mental note to get through as much of the book as possible that night, then remembered that she was meeting Grover for dinner. She would just have to eat quickly so she could get back to the book.

She texted Grover the name of a restaurant she knew they would both enjoy and he was waiting for her when she got there. They found a table outdoors and while they waited for their food she explained that she wouldn't be able to stay long because she had to get through Brian's book.

"That guy gives you a lot of stuff to read, doesn't he?" Grover asked.

"He does," Daisy agreed, "but it's interesting reading. And it's a privilege for me to be able to read something that's going to be donated to the Library of Congress, so I feel like I should get through it quickly. I need to return it to him."

"What's it about?"

Daisy told him as much of the story as she knew. "Sounds interesting, but why would he give it to you before he donates it?"

"Probably because he knows how much I love old things and reading old books and diaries and journals, in particular."

Grover sat back and fixed Daisy with an amused stare. "You really love your job, don't you?"

"You know I do. I love my job as much as you love yours,"

"Then we're both lucky," he answered. "There's nothing better than having a job you love. It's not like working at all."

"Easy there, tiger," Daisy said with a laugh. "I may love my work, but I don't love my boss. So it's not all fun all the time."

"You should come work for me."

"I love helping you, too, but then my anthropology degree would be wasted. When I get paid to work for Mark John and help you on the side, that's the best of both worlds."

He grinned. "Any time you want to help, you know my number."

They enjoyed their dinner and Daisy was sorry she had to get back to her apartment so quickly. She apologized again and left him standing on the sidewalk outside the restaurant. As she was walking away she glanced over her shoulder; Grover was watching her walk away, a smile on his lips.

Before long Daisy was in her pajamas, settled on her couch with a mug of herbal tea within easy reach and her white gloves donned and ready. She picked up the book and turned the pages gently to where she had left off.

Young Mr. Sheppard had found the place where he wanted to raise his children. The Nebraska Territory was wide open, with fertile land yearning to be planted and air that was sparkling clean. He found a room to rent in a small town while he looked for a homestead that would be suitable for him and his children. When he found land that would be perfect, he set about building a house for his family. His carpentry skills were such that he would be able to build a good, sturdy home quickly. The children were still quite young and each day they accompanied him to the home he was building outside the town.

It wasn't long before he caught the eye of a young woman, a pretty girl with freckles and hands that were rough from working. The children missed their mother grievously, and he missed having someone to talk to. The children needed someone to help mold their young minds, to teach them to read and write, to teach them right from wrong. They needed a mother. He loved them, but his affection simply wasn't enough. He found the young woman to be both intelligent and eager to help him with the children, and before a year had passed the two were married in a simple ceremony in a small church.

But shortly after his marriage to the young woman, he began to change. He would leave the house, with his children in the care of his new wife, and not come home for several days. He did not care to explain where he had been and it soon became apparent to the children, who were obviously growing older and more mature with each passing day, that his wife was too timid to demand to know of his whereabouts. He would become enraged over things that would not bother a reasonable man and his mood was inexplicably brooding.

Then came a very dark day. He had disappeared, again without explanation, and his wife had become frantic with worry about his behavior. When he finally returned home he sent the children out of the house and it was some time before he exited the house, too.

When the children were allowed to return to their home, the young wife was nowhere to be found. When they asked where their new mother had gone, their father refused to answer them. They were afraid that she had left because of something they had done, some misbehavior on their part.

Because they were afraid, they were unable to sleep that night. There was a crescent moon hanging low in the sky when the sister crept into her brother's bedroom to talk to him. They knew their father was downstairs reading a book. They were speaking in whispers about what they could have done to make their new mother like them more when they heard their father going outside. He had been quiet when he left, but the front door had a slight squeak and they knew when they heard the squeak that he had left.

They crept to the window of the boy's room and peered down, where they could see their father dragging a sack with something inside that appeared to be very heavy. They didn't know what it was or where it had come from. They watched as he loaded it onto the back of their wagon and drove west away from the homestead. They turned away from the window when Mr. Sheppard was out of sight. They continued speaking in whispers, though they didn't know why. There was no one else in the house. After a while the sister went back to her room and lay in the darkness, wondering what was going on and where her father had gone with the mysterious heavy sack. In his room, the brother was wondering the same things.

Both children were asleep when their father returned, and he was there to greet them in the morning when they awoke.

Daisy was amazed at how much this story sounded like the tale she had read in Trudy's diary entries. She ripped a piece of paper from a notebook and began jotting down all the similarities she could discern between Trudy's diary and the story told in the dime novel. There was a widower from Washington who had headed west with his two children, a homestead in Nebraska, a young new wife, and an unexplained disappearance. Daisy stared at her notes for a long while, trying to make sense of the two stories. It certainly seemed like they were connected somehow. She wondered if Brian knew whether the stories were related. But if he had, why wouldn't he have said something when she asked?

It was getting late and Daisy's head hurt from thinking so hard, trying to make connections without enough information to be sure of anything. She finished the last drops of tea and went straight to bed where she slept fitfully and woke several times, always thinking of Trudy and wondering if she met her end at the hands of her husband—and whether he put her body in a sack and dumped it somewhere.

The next morning she was in her office catching up on paperwork when Jude came in. Her eyes were puffy from crying and she held a crumpled tissue in her hand.

"Jude! What's wrong?" Daisy asked, getting up and closing the door when Jude sat down.

Twisting the tissue in her hand, Jude sniffled and hung her head. "Mark John and I are through," she said, taking two quick breaths.

"Jude, you need to calm down. Take a nice, slow, deep breath and tell me what happened."

Jude did as she was asked. "I think he's seeing someone else."

"What? What makes you think that?"

"We haven't been spending too much time together in the last week or so and he just doesn't seem to be interested in anything I say or do," she said miserably. "He took me to a concert last week and that was the last thing we did together."

Daisy recalled the look Mark John turned on Jude as he watched her walk away from him at the concert that night. *Jude might be right*, she thought to herself. *Maybe Mark John just isn't interested anymore. Would that really be the worst thing?* Then she chided herself for thinking that way. Jude was obviously very upset about the developments.

"Can you think of anything that made him mad recently?" Daisy asked.

Jude thought for a moment. "Not really. He hasn't been himself lately. I've been trying to get him to tell me what the problem is. Maybe that's what's making him mad."

"There's the death of his wife, too, don't forget. Has he actually said anything about breaking up?" Daisy asked.

"No."

"Then he probably isn't thinking in those terms."

"Maybe he's waiting for me to break up with him so he doesn't come off as the bad guy."

"You're overthinking this. Maybe he's got something personal on his mind that he's not ready to share yet. It happens, even to married couples, and God knows he's had a lot to deal with lately. I bet he'll tell you when he's ready."

"If it makes him this moody, I'm not sure I'm ready to find out. What do you think it could be?"

"I have no idea," Daisy answered. "I really don't know Mark John that well, despite the things you've told me about him. I suppose it could be anything. A job offer, a health problem. It could be lots of things. The most obvious possibility, of course, is Fiona's death. That's a traumatic event for anyone."

"I guess you're right. Should I keep trying to get him to tell me what it is?"

"I wouldn't. That approach hasn't worked well so far. I think you should just back off and take your cue from him. If he wants to talk, be ready to talk. If he wants some space, be prepared to give him that, too."

"I'll try," Jude said with a small sigh. "It's hard to do."

Daisy could remember what it was like being involved with a man who could be moody. "I know," she answered, "but you may both be happier in the long run if you just leave him alone for now."

"Thanks," Jude replied. After she left Daisy sat at her desk looking out at the Washington summer sun reflecting off the buildings across the street. This is why it's better to be single, she thought. No drama, no heartache, no worries about he loves me, he loves me not.

And no one to talk to while I'm getting ready for bed, no one to make me breakfast in the morning, no one to rub my back when I've had a nightmare. Which way is better?

CHAPTER 54

*D*aisy needed to get back to the Library of Congress. She simply *had* to find out what had happened to Trudy. Where to start? She went to the Rare Book Reading Room and found the librarian who had helped her the last time. The librarian recognized her right away.

"What can I do for you today?" she asked, coming up to Daisy in the roped-off area where the old card catalogs were kept.

"I'm looking for more stories by Harold Henderson," Daisy answered. "I'm fascinated by him and his writing."

"Let's see what we can find," the librarian suggested. She led the way to her computer and ran a search while Daisy stood on the other side of the gleaming wooden counter and watched the other researchers in the reading room. "Yes, he has written a few other stories. We have a couple on microfilm and a couple available to read in here. Which would you like to look at first?"

Daisy answered without hesitation. "The ones in here." The librarian made some notations on a piece of paper and asked Daisy to have a seat beyond the velvet rope in the reading room while she waited. Daisy sat down at a table by herself, looking around at the beautiful, calm room. The walls were a dusky rose color which tastefully complemented the ivory shades on the table lamps and the simple chandeliers that hung far above the readers' heads. Windsor-style chairs were set up at each table and in one corner of the spacious room there was a stack of special cribs for reading rare, old documents. The cribs were shaped so that a book could be studied in a slightly open position without needing to be held by a reader. This cut down on the number of times people had to touch the books.

The librarian returned ten minutes later with two more dime novels. They looked much like the one Daisy had been reading at home, and each cover listed a number of stories that could be found inside, along with the authors' names. Sure enough, Daisy noticed Harold Henderson's name on each volume.

The hours flew by while Daisy sat at the table in the Rare Book Reading Room, poring over the words Mister Henderson had written. The more she read, though, the more disappointed she became. There was nothing about a widower, anyone named Sheppard, or children left wondering what had become of their stepmother. There was no mention of Washington or the Nebraska Territory. Mister Henderson's tales were typical of others in the dime novel genre, including society romances and western adventures.

"These books don't have what I'm looking for," Daisy told the librarian at the end of the day.

"Don't forget about the microfilm," the librarian said. "I'll write down the call numbers of the other stories by this gentleman and if you can come back tomorrow I'm sure they can help you in the microfilm room."

Daisy accepted the piece of paper the librarian handed her a few minutes later and left the library just as it closed for the day. She was looking forward to going home and trying to finish the story Harold Henderson had written.

But she didn't get as far as her apartment before her cell phone rang. It was Jude and she was hysterical about something.

"Jude! Slow down! I can't understand a word you're saying," Daisy said.

"Mark John just called. He's at the police station. He wants me to come down and pick him up," Jude said, sniffling and breathless.

"Why is he there?"

"He didn't say."

"So why are you calling me? Get down there!"

"I'm on my way now. You're on speaker phone while I drive. What do you suppose the police want with Mark John?" she asked. Daisy figured Jude just wanted someone to talk to while she drove; Daisy couldn't blame her. She would want to talk to someone to keep her from becoming unglued, too. As she recalled, she had phoned her mother when she had been taken to the police station after Dean had died.

"Could be anything. Could be nothing," Daisy said, trying her best to soothe Jude's frayed nerves. "Maybe Mark John witnessed a car accident. Maybe he called them to report something and they have follow-up questions. I wouldn't worry about it until there's a good reason to worry."

She waited for Jude to process what she had said. "I wonder if he complained to the police about Brian following us that day," Jude pondered.

"I don't know. It seems like Mark John would have reported it right away if he was going to. And if the police had questions they would have asked him sooner than this. But you never know," Daisy said. She really didn't think that was why Mark John had been called to the police station, "Besides, would Mark John really call the police on his brother-in-law? He doesn't seem the type."

"You're right, he's not the type. He would talk to Brian

directly if he had to, but he wouldn't ask the police to do his dirty work for him."

"It's probably something else, then. Hopefully it's nothing. Maybe this is a good way for you two to get talking again," Daisy suggested.

"I hope so," Jude said. "Daisy, I've got to go. The traffic is terrible and I'm just too distracted right now."

"Let me know if you need anything," Daisy said, then hung up.

So Mark John was at the police station? She was dying to know what had happened. She rolled her eyes and scolded herself. *You've become such a gossip.* She walked the rest of the way to her apartment and made a beeline for the dime novel. She intended to finish the story that night.

Armed with her white gloves, a pillow, and a glass of iced tea a full arm's length away, she sat down on the sofa next to the lamp so she could see the print easily.

The children held a whispered conversation before going downstairs the next morning. They decided not to ask their father where he had gone the night before or what he had been dragging in that large sack. He had seemed angry lately and they didn't want to raise his ire toward them. They still wondered, though, what had become of their stepmother.

With the stepmother gone, the Widower Sheppard determined that it would be necessary to send the children to school. They did not want to go. Their stepmother had been teaching them to read and write and although their father did not believe they were learning quickly enough, they had a hard time keeping up with the studies their stepmother had assigned them. They did not look forward to attending school, where the school mistress might get angry with them for not being smart enough or quick enough. The girl was especially concerned.

But they did not have much time to brood over their father's decision because the following week they started school. They hoped their fears would be unfounded, but sadly, they discovered that the teacher did, indeed, believe they were slow learners who would have to work very hard to catch up to their schoolmates.

The sister had a particularly hard time in school. She found reading and writing much harder than when her stepmother had taught her, and the arithmetic was difficult, too. Before long the girl, who would leave the house every morning with her brother to make the long walk to the school house, had determined that she would no longer attend school. The brother would continue walking and the sister would leave off in a field nearby, hidden by tall grasses so the teacher would not see her. They continued in this way for more than two weeks, the brother allowing the Widower Sheppard to believe his daughter was attending school regularly and allowing the teacher to believe that Mr. Sheppard had elected to keep his daughter at home.

Then came the day when the boy had unsettling news for his sister. They had an agreed-upon signal that they used when the boy was getting close to the field where the sister spent her days. He would let out a long, low whistle and she would answer with an identical whistle. When she met up with him he was breathless from the news he carried.

"Teacher said people in town are talking about Father," he said.

"What are they saying?"

"That he's an outlaw."

"An outlaw?" his sister asked in a low voice. "What makes them say that?"

"They say he's been running from the law since he killed his first wife and that now he's killed his second wife."

"They must not know Mama was his second wife and our stepmother was his third."

The boy shook his head in response. Then he asked the question they had both been mulling over since the night they saw their father dragging the sack away from the house. "Do you think our stepmother was in that sack? Do you think he killed her?"

The sister nodded slowly. "Where else could she have gone? Even though we weren't her real children, she still would have said good-bye if she had left us."

"Not if she was afraid of Father. Not if she didn't want us to know so we couldn't be punished for not telling him where she was going." His sister hadn't thought of that.

"Why wouldn't she take us with her?" the sister asked.

"Because we're not her children, silly. She couldn't just take us from our own house and our own father."

The children were quiet for several long minutes, each lost in thought. Finally the boy spoke. "I'm beginning to forget Mama," he said, his face drawn and sad.

"So am I."

"I remember that she was lovely, but I don't remember what her face looked like," the brother said, a wistful smile on his face.

"She was lovely," the sister replied quietly, squeezing her brother's arm.

When the children arrived at home, the father was there to greet them. This was unusual, since he often worked until sundown.

"Where have you been?" he asked.

"School," the boy replied. His sister didn't answer.

"I see. And you were also in school?" he asked his daughter.

She looked at the floor and then at her brother, then she answered her father truthfully, as she had been taught always to do. "No, Father. I did not go to school."

"Why not?"

"Because the lessons are so very hard and I am behind and the teacher is hateful." She covered her mouth with her hand because it was so unkind to talk about her teacher that way.

Widower Sheppard gave her a hard glare. "I have heard in town that you were not attending school. Have you no respect for my authority?" His voice was steadily rising.

"I do, Father," the daughter replied in a small voice.

Then the father reached out and hit her in the face. He had never done anything like that before. The daughter brought her hand to her cheek, which burned with pain. She couldn't cry, so surprised was she by what her father had done.

The sister could see her brother from the corner of her eye. He clenched his fists. The father noticed. "Don't think I won't do that to you, boy," he said in a quieter voice. "You two are going to learn to obey me. I am your father."

"Yes, sir," the boy said.

"That's better," the father said. He turned his attention to his daughter. "Now go get something on the table. I'm hungry."

She scurried away into the kitchen and fixed plates for the small family. They ate in silence until the father announced, "I have decided that we are going to move."

"Again? I mean, where are we going?" asked the boy.

"New York City. I grew up there and I still have family there. They will help me take care of you two." The sister and brother exchanged glances. They were not sure how they felt about moving so far away.

"When will we leave?" the boy asked. The girl had said nothing since her father struck her.

"As soon as possible," the father answered. He pushed his chair back and stood up. "Neither of you has to go to school anymore. We'll enroll you in school in New York when we get there."

He left through the front door, letting it slam behind him.

The brother and the sister stood up slowly, clearing the dishes from the table.

"Why do you suppose we're moving?" the boy asked.

"You heard him. Because he has family in New York and he needs their help looking after us."

"No one looks after us here." The two children were silent for a long moment, then the brother spoke again. "He killed her, didn't he? That's why we're leaving."

His words hung in the air between them. "I think so," she finally said.

"Are you afraid?"

"A little. He's never hit me before."

"I wish he was dead."

"Don't say that," the sister cautioned in a whisper. "You never know when he might be listening. But I wish he was, too." The brother smiled a little bit at that.

"We'll have to pack our things," the brother said. "I'll start in my room now. It won't take me very long."

The girl packed her things that night, too, in a crate she found in the back room of the house. Neither child had any toys, so their possessions were minimal. When the father returned late that night the children pretended to be asleep.

The next morning they told him they had packed their belongings already.

"Good," he answered. "Because we'll be leaving tomorrow."

"So soon?" the boy blurted out. His sister shot him a look of reproach.

"Don't disrespect me, son," the father warned. He went to the back room and came back with two large crates. "Fill these," he instructed his children. "I am going to make sure the horse and wagon are ready to go."

"What if everything doesn't fit in those two crates?" the girl asked, knowing full well everything would not fit into the crates.

"We leave it behind," came the curt answer. Then the father left without another word to his children.

It was left to the boy and the girl to decide what to take and what to leave behind. There were a few small keepsakes that had belonged to their mother and a few belongings of their stepmother. They wondered if they should try to get her things to her family, but they knew there would be no time for that. They left their stepmother's things behind, hoping her family would eventually retrieve them.

The family did not own many books, but they all went into one of the crates. A large pot they had always used for cooking went, too, along with their plates and cups. Next into the crate went the locked box the father kept under his bed. He kept the family's money in there. Next the children packed the quilts and linens. None of the family's furniture would make the trip. Sleeping in the wagon would be uncomfortable, but they had done it before.

The next morning they were awake long before the sun was up. The father hurried the children into the cool summer morning and hopped up onto the wagon seat, leaving them to sit in the back. With a "Giddap!" the family was on its way.

They made haste leaving the town behind, then the father allowed the horse to slow down a bit and walk at a more leisurely pace as the small family made its way east.

It was a long trip to New York, made worse by the late summer storms that buffeted them as they traveled. It was a boring trip because the children did not speak much to their father and he almost nothing to them. They spoke to each other in low voices so as not to disturb their father, and never about the topics they yearned to discuss, such as the family's sudden early morning departure from the town in Nebraska or the townspeople's suspicion that their father had killed his young wife and the wife before her.

Upon arriving in New York several weeks later, the children

were met with yet another surprise. Their father said he no longer wanted to be known as Mr. Sheppard but instead wanted to be called Mr. Sweeney. They were also never again to discuss their stepmother.

"I don't understand," his daughter told him. "Is our last name Sweeney now, too?" she asked, indicating her brother with a wave of her hand.

"Yes. I have enrolled you both in school with the name Sweeney, so I expect you to use it from now on." He gave them a grave look. "Not only that, but I don't want to hear that you've ever again used the name Sheppard." Both children knew better than to ask why their father had made the decision to change their last name. They already knew.

It was getting harder and harder for them to be with their father, wondering about the things he had done. His status as an outlaw scared them, but they took some solace in knowing they would be hard to find with their new last name. They never spoke of it to anyone.

The children found that living in New York was exciting and interesting. They lived in a house that was much smaller than their home in Nebraska, but they did not mind having less room. Back in Nebraska they had enjoyed living on the plains with wide open spaces and fresh air; there was not as much space in New York, and far less fresh air.

But there were things New York had that Nebraska didn't: one was the number of playmates. There were children everywhere in New York. They came from families with different customs and even different languages. Another difference was the school. The children attended a large school where they were divided into grade levels. The teachers were not as mean as the teacher in Nebraska had been. And finally, there was family nearby and the children learned that they had cousins and aunts and uncles whom they had never known existed. It was exciting to learn about their new family.

One day the daughter was sweeping the parlor in their house. The father was nearby, reading a newspaper. Without thinking, the daughter recalled aloud an incident when her stepmother had taught her to read something by using a newspaper. It was the first time either child had mentioned the stepmother's name and the brother, who was reading a book near the fireplace, looked up sharply. The girl glanced at him and he gave her a warning look.

But he needn't have bothered. The father had heard his daughter's words. Very slowly, he laid aside his newspaper and rose.

"What did you say?" he asked his daughter, walking toward her with deliberate steps.

She stammered a response. "I— I was just remembering the time our stepmother taught us a word in the newspaper."

The father advanced a bit closer. "Have I not asked you never to mention her?"

"Yes, sir. I am very sorry, sir. I forgot."

The father had reached his daughter and stood staring down at her, his eyes gleaming in anger. He kept his voice low as he told her, "Hand me your broom."

She did as he had asked and stepped back. She knew what was going to happen. With one quick movement, he struck the side of her head with the broom handle. She fell to the floor, unconscious.

When she came to, she was still lying on the floor. Her brother was by her side, crying and begging her to wake up. His face wore a look of terror.

"What happened?" she asked, keeping her eyes closed because her head hurt.

"Don't you remember?" her brother asked. "Father hit you with the broom handle because you mentioned Trudy's name."

Daisy gasped. *Trudy*. That couldn't be a coincidence. Her suspicions had been correct--this was an account, written years later, of Trudy's story. It had to be. If it weren't, it would just be too much of a coincidence.

She finally had her answer. But how did this story in the dime novel come to be written? There were far more questions than answers. She kept reading, even as her mind reeled from her discovery.

Try as she might, the young girl could not recall what had happened in the seconds before her father hit her.

"We have to leave," the boy urged.

"We can't leave. Where will we go?"

"We'll think of something." The boy helped his sister to stand up and together they hobbled into the bedroom where the sister lay on her bed and quickly fell asleep.

She did not know how long she slept before she was awakened with a start by a noise next to her bed. Shrinking back in fear, she saw her father sitting beside the bed in a chair he must have dragged from the parlor. He was staring at her, his eyes red-rimmed. He was sniffling. She waited for him to speak because she did not know what to say to him.

"My darling daughter, I am so sorry. Please forgive my actions," he said, lowering his head into his hands and sobbing. "May God forgive the way I have treated you."

The young girl did not know how to respond to such a show of sorrow. She had never seen her father in this state. She searched her hazy mind for the appropriate words to say.

"I forgive you, Father."

The man sitting next to the bed cried harder at hearing these words. "Thank you, my child. It will never happen again."

And she believed him.

But alas, it did happen again and again over the months and

years that followed. As they grew older, the boy and the girl came to know when their father was in a violent mood and they would be very careful about the words they spoke in his presence, if, indeed, they spoke at all. The father never beat the boy, but he beat his daughter frequently. Try as they might, the two children never found a way to leave their father's house. They could not go to their relatives because they might tell the father where his children were. They could not leave to live on the streets because it was far too dangerous to face the violence out there. The violence they knew at home was preferable to the violence they had heard about on the New York streets.

Despite all that has been said, though, the story does have a happy ending.

The boy grew up and found a job as a carpenter, just as his father had before him. The girl became a schoolteacher and married a man who lifted her out of the sadness and violence of her home and brought her happiness and joy. The father died mercifully in his sleep one night after his children had moved away. His funeral was attended by three people—his children, who were there to assure themselves that their father was dead, and the man who had been hired to dig his grave.

A life of misery—creating it and living it—had finally ended.

The boy and girl, now a man and a woman, never found out what had happened to their stepmother, though in their hearts they knew. Their father had killed her as sure as he lived.

There are times when justice does not seem to visit those who are deserving of it, both the good and the evil. Justice was never afforded the stepmother, and the father never had to face its wrath. The man and woman who were his children contented themselves with the knowledge that the father would have received his justice in the hereafter.

CHAPTER 55

So it's over, Daisy thought. She closed the book carefully and sat staring at the cover for a long time, lost in thought. Mister Sheppard/Sweeney had killed his young wife-- probably two young wives--and gotten away with it. He never had to answer for his deeds. And not only that, he had abused his daughter, who had done nothing to incur such wrath.

Her musing was interrupted by the phone.

"Hello?"

"It's Jude. I'm at the police station waiting for Mark John."

"Did you find out why he was there?"

"They had more questions about Fiona's death. They received a tip and wanted to talk to him."

"How do you know?"

"The officer at the desk told me."

"What was the tip?"

"I don't know yet. I'll have to wait to ask Mark John. Wait, here he comes. I'll call you later." She hung up.

Daisy sat back on the couch, her thoughts torn between the story she had read and the one playing out in a suburban police station nearby. *What information could the police have gotten about*

Fiona's death? Not for the first time, Daisy wished she had known Fiona. She wondered what the woman had been like, what kind of a woman would marry Mark John and then cheat on him. She couldn't imagine the fear Fiona must have felt during her last moments of life, with a stranger or strangers in her home, meaning her harm. Daisy shuddered at the thought.

She poured herself a glass of wine and watched the news for a little while before going to bed. She drifted off accompanied by thoughts of Trudy and of the Sheppard/Sweeney family. She hadn't been asleep long when the phone rang. Jude again.

Daisy answered, her tone a bit testy because Jude had awakened her.

"Hello?"

"It's me, Jude." Daisy's tone softened immediately when she heard Jude crying softly. She sat up in bed.

"Jude, what's wrong?"

"Mark John is so angry about having to go down to the police station and I feel like he's taking it out on me." Another sob escaped her lips.

"Surely he knows you had nothing to do with it. Why is he mad at you?"

"Who knows? He's just angry at the world, I think. He wants this whole Fiona thing behind him and now he's been dragged back into it."

"So you just happen to be the closest person right now."

"Yeah, I guess so. He's not usually like this. I'm just not used to seeing his ugly side, that's all. I'm sorry I woke you."

"It's no problem. I'm sorry Mark John is being such a pill." That got a short laugh out of Jude.

"Ha! He's probably never been called that before. It describes his mood perfectly."

"So what did the police learn that made them want to question Mark John again?"

"They wouldn't tell him, but they asked questions about

where he was the night Fiona died. He was working late. You know, he does that when there's a big deadline coming up."

Daisy nodded to herself. "We've all been known to do that. Did they want to know anything else?"

"I don't think so. Mark John just mentioned that they asked about the time frame around when he got home from work."

"Well, hopefully the police got the answers they needed and they can leave Mark John alone after this."

"I hope so."

"I'll see you in the morning," Daisy said, then the women hung up. She was relieved to be able to get right back to sleep.

Daisy wasn't able to get back to the Library of Congress to view the dime novels in the microfilm room for several days because so much drama disrupted her routine at work. Jude swept into Daisy's office two days after Mark John's visit to the police station with tears streaming down her face.

"What's wrong?" Daisy asked with a quickening sense of alarm.

"I'll tell you what's wrong," Jude blubbered. "Mark John just told me he doesn't think we should see each other anymore!"

It came as a bit of a bombshell, since the two of them seemed so well-suited. However, Jude had mentioned that he seemed more aloof lately…

"Did he tell you why he feels that way?" Daisy asked.

Jude blew her nose loudly into a tissue she had decimated. "No, only that it's for my own good. What do you suppose he means by that? Do you think he's been seeing someone else?" She looked at Daisy in horror, as if having that thought for the first time, then started crying harder.

"Whoa, now wait a minute. You're jumping to some pretty big conclusions," Daisy cautioned. "There could be lots of reasons he wants to back off a bit."

Jude interrupted Daisy with a snort. "Back off? He wants

nothing to do with me! How am I ever going to continue working here?"

I suppose that's something you should have thought of before you started dating your boss, Daisy thought. Aloud she said, "It could be that he doesn't feel ready for another serious relationship right now. Maybe it's nothing more than a case of cold feet."

"But why didn't he say something when we first started to get serious?" Jude whined. "I could have dealt with it much better then."

"Maybe he didn't feel that way then. Maybe it's just hitting him now."

A knock at Daisy's door interrupted them. "May I come in?" It was Mark John. Jude stared at Daisy with a look of terror.

"Don't let him in!" she hissed. "I don't want him to see me like this."

"I can't keep him out," Daisy replied. "He's the boss. I'll go into the hall to see what he wants." She opened the door a crack and squeezed into the hallway, then shut the door behind her quickly.

"What's going on in there?" Mark John asked in a low, flat voice.

"Nothing. Why?"

"I'm not stupid, Daisy. I can hear her crying. Is she that upset?"

"Of course she's that upset!" Daisy replied in an urgent whisper, gesticulating toward her door. "And why wouldn't she be?"

"Just because I told her we need a break?" He sounded incredulous.

"Is that what you said? She said you didn't want to see her anymore."

"Sometimes she hears words that aren't there. I just think we need a break." He looked away, then back at Daisy. "Why am I telling you this, anyway?"

"Because you don't want me to meet my next deadline?" she

asked. "Because that's what's going to happen if I can't get any work done around here." He rolled his eyes in response.

"May I go in your office to talk to her?" he asked.

"Yes. But, Mark John, please don't upset her anymore. God only knows why you waited until the two of you were at work to spring this on her."

"I didn't mean to. It just slipped out."

"For an editor who prides himself on being a wordsmith, you sure picked the wrong words today," Daisy said over her shoulder as she stalked to the conference room. Her computer and files were in her office, so all she could do was sit in the conference room and read a magazine until she finally heard the door to her office open and close quietly. A moment later Jude and Mark John appeared in the conference room doorway. Jude cleared her throat. Her eyes were still red and a little puffy, but they were dry.

"Daisy, thanks for letting us use your office. We had a talk and I think we both feel better about things."

"You're welcome," Daisy replied. She wanted to know how their discussion had ended, but she didn't want to seem nosy. And frankly, she was getting a little sick of the whole thing. Besides, she was likely to hear from Jude about it at some point.

"Can we all get back to work now?" Mark John asked in exasperation. Daisy nodded and returned to her office immediately. If Jude wanted to talk, she was going to have to wait. Daisy had a deadline to meet the next day before the close of business and couldn't take any more time away from her writing and research to chit-chat.

But apparently Jude was of the opinion that once the workday ended, Daisy's deadline evaporated. Daisy's phone was ringing as she walked into her apartment after work that day. She answered it without checking the caller ID, but she had a good idea that it would be Jude.

"Hi. I called to let you know what happened between me and Mark John today."

"Okay. What happened?"

"He told me that he's been thinking a lot about Fiona's death and is unsure whether he's ready to move forward."

"And what did you say? How did you feel about that?"

Jude let out a long sigh. "I told him I'd like him to think about it for a while and not make any rash decisions. And I'm not really sure how I feel about his explanation. I think he's feeling this way because he was questioned again about Fiona's death and because there's still no one in custody for her murder. That weighs heavily on his mind, I know. I feel like if the police are able to figure out who killed Fiona, Mark John could rest easy and we could continue seeing each other."

"Maybe it's a good idea to do your own thinking while he's mulling things over in his own mind."

"I suppose you're right." Jude was silent for a long moment. "I should go. I'll see you at work tomorrow."

Daisy hung up, but then took the phone off the hook so she wouldn't be bothered for the rest of the evening as she worked. She shut off her cell phone, too. She worked until the wee hours of the morning and finally went to bed when she figured she could reasonably expect to finish the work before five the next day.

She kept her office door locked the entire day at work so no drama could barge in to interrupt her. At five o'clock she went into Mark John's office with a flash drive. "I present you the article on Middle Eastern schoolteachers you requested," she said, handing over the flash drive with a flourish.

"I knew you'd make the deadline, drama or no drama," he said dryly.

"Is it all right with you if I head over to the Library of Congress in the morning before I come to work?" she asked. "There's some research I need to work on."

"I suppose."

Daisy stopped at a bakery on the way home for a bear claw, one of her favorite ways to celebrate the meeting of a deadline. While she waited in line her cell phone rang. It was Grover.

"Hey, you're hard to get a hold of," he said in greeting.

"Oh, sorry. I had both my phones off last night because I had a deadline today. What's up?"

"I have another cancellation the day after tomorrow and I got two free tickets to a movie screening if you want to go. It's a thriller, but it's set in Egypt. I figured that would be right up your alley."

"I'm an anthropologist, not an archaeologist," she reminded him with a smile. "But I love thrillers. That sounds fun."

"Why don't we grab dinner first and then go to the screening," he suggested. "I'll meet you at Murphy's Pub at six and we'll head over to the screening at eight. The movie theater is right near Murphy's."

Daisy hung up the phone, paid for the bear claw, and walked the rest of the way to her apartment with a noticeable spring in her step.

CHAPTER 56

*D*aisy was at the Library of Congress the next morning when the doors to the Jefferson Building opened. She deposited her tote bag at the coat check, put all her belongings in a clear plastic bag, and headed for the microfilm room armed with the piece of paper containing the call numbers of Harold Henderson's other stories.

The librarians in the microfilm room were just as helpful as those in the Rare Book Reading Room. After an absence of only ten minutes, one of them returned to Daisy's side with two rolls of film. He made sure Daisy knew how to run a microfilm machine, which she had done many times in pursuit of her degrees, then left her alone to read.

The placement of Harold Henderson's stories in the front of the books suggested to Daisy that he might be a rather prolific writer. She wasn't sure, but Daisy assumed the more popular writers in the early twentieth century might have stories placed more prominently in the dime novels. Though it took a couple hours, Daisy read every word of the two stories.

She was disappointed when she found nothing to suggest a connection between the author and anyone in Nebraska, New

York, or anywhere else. The stories were well-written and fun, but dealt with topics of Victorian romance and coquetry. There was also a gruesome story about hereditary violence that read more like it came from the pen of Edgar Allan Poe than Harold Henderson. Daisy took notes while she read, but only out of habit. By lunchtime she returned the microfilm to the librarian who had assisted her earlier and thanked him for his help.

She called Helena to see if she wanted to meet for lunch and Helena agreed eagerly. She had news for Daisy. "We've made plans to go away together!" she squealed. Daisy smiled.

"First, I assume 'we' means you and Bennett. And second, I assume 'go away together' means you're going somewhere on vacation, not eloping."

Helena grinned. "Right on both counts. We're going to Aruba!"

"I hear that's nice this time of year," Daisy joked.

"I'd invite you and Grover along, but this is such a great chance for me and Bennett to get to know each other better," Helena said, her eyes twinkling.

"Me and Grover? Ha! What would you need with two platonic chaperones? I'm glad you two are getting away together," Daisy said with a smile.

Helena gave Daisy a knowing look. "I think you and Grover are perfect for each other."

"Oh, please. Not this again. We're both workaholics."

"Okay, okay. I won't harp on it," Helena said. She proceeded to tell Daisy all about the hotel where she and Bennett were planning to stay, along with the activities they had booked and the places she wanted to visit in Aruba. By the time Helena had to go back to work, Daisy felt like she could use a piña colada and a massage. Helena was a bundle of energy.

Daisy returned to her office, shut her door, and sat down at the computer.

Despite her vast knowledge of research methods and

sources, this time Daisy headed to Google to find the answers she sought. She typed in the name "Harold Henderson" and waited to see what would pop up. After just a couple seconds she had a several-pages-long list of possible clues to the identity of the person who wrote the dime novel Brian had given her.

But the list was disappointing. All the Google hits seemed to point toward living people; and in particular, sites offering to find the address, criminal background, and property value of every Harold Henderson in the United States. Daisy sat back and sighed. She erased that search and started another, this time typing in the words "dime novel" and "Henderson."

And there, at the top of the list of Google hits, was something about an author named H. Henderson and a connection to dime novels. Daisy clicked on the link and it took her to a page from a website belonging to a small private university in New York State. The page was one of several on the website that were apparently dedicated to the history of the dime novel and the writers who brought the popular stories to the masses around the turn of the twentieth century. Specifically, it focused on writers from New York who contributed to the phenomenon. The name of the person who had composed the list, Mary Browning, was on the bottom of the third page, next to a notation which indicated the list had been compiled two years previously.

Daisy kept that tab open on the computer and opened another tab for the university's home page. She found the main number for the campus library and before she had even formulated a list of questions, she called the number. When she was finally connected with a real person, she asked to speak to Ms. Browning. And there Daisy hit another snag.

"Ms. Browning retired last year," the librarian said.

"Can you give me her contact information?" Daisy asked, knowing that it was highly unlikely.

"No, I'm afraid I can't do that. Maybe I can help you?"

Daisy explained that she was looking for information about the author Harold Henderson. The librarian couldn't offer any guidance, but knew of the list Daisy had found online.

"Mary had a keen interest in dime novels," the librarian said. "I'll tell you what. Leave me your contact information and I'll get in touch with Mary. I'll give her your name and number and if she wants to, she can call you back."

"That would be great," Daisy replied, leaning forward in her desk chair. She gave the librarian her work phone, home phone, cell phone, and email address. She didn't want to take a chance that she might miss a call from Mary Browning. When she got off the phone, she tried to settle down to start work on a project Mark John had given her, but she found that her mind was spinning too fast to focus. She went for a walk to clear her head and returned to the office ready to sit down and get to work.

But she was waylaid by Jude as she walked past the conference room.

"Hi, Daisy," Jude called. Daisy peeked into the conference room, where Jude was sitting at her laptop.

"What are you doing in here? Why aren't you in your office?"

"My phone kept ringing and I needed to get some work done in peace. It's Mark John. I just can't talk to him right now."

"Why not? And why is he calling you? Isn't he in his office?"

"No, he stayed home today because he had to be home for a plumber or an electrician or someone."

"Oh. So why don't you answer the phone and tell him you're trying to work?"

"He's just been in such a bad mood lately. I don't want to make him angrier."

"Ignoring his calls may not be the best way to go about that."

Jude seemed to consider that, as if she hadn't thought of it before. "You're right. Maybe I should just answer the phone and tell him I'm busy."

"That's what I would do." Daisy turned around to leave, but Jude seemed to want to keep talking.

"I'm thinking maybe Mark John was right. Maybe we should take a break from seeing each other."

Daisy didn't really feel like being dragged into the middle of another of Jude's angst-ridden battles of indecision. "I guess that's something you'll have to decide," she said, then turned toward the door again.

"The thing is, I was so unhappy when he suggested it, but now that he's so miserable all the time, I'm thinking it might be the right thing to do."

"Maybe it is," Daisy said, pointedly looking at her watch.

"But what if he's depressed and unhappy and it's a secret cry for help? What if he needs me and this is just his way of showing me?"

Daisy shot Jude a dubious look, but Jude was staring intently at something off in the distance, out the conference room window. "Are you asking me what I think? Because I don't know what to think," Daisy said. "I don't know Mark John well enough to know if this is a cry for help or just a phase or something else. I wish I could help."

"You already did," Jude replied. "You made me see this from a different angle. I'm going back to my office and take his next call so we can talk. Thanks, Daisy." She closed her laptop with a swift *click* and stood up to leave, walking out of the room in front of Daisy. Daisy watched her go, bewildered, then shook her head. This office romance was too much of a distraction.

CHAPTER 57

*D*aisy spent the rest of the afternoon doing research into the issue of vaccine availability in a small corner of sub-Saharan Africa, quickly becoming engrossed in the plight of people who were dying of preventable diseases. When the receptionist finally buzzed Daisy's office to ask if Daisy wanted the front door locked for the evening, Daisy was surprised by how much time had passed. She gathered her belongings and went home.

Her phone rang while she was walking up the stairs to her apartment. She didn't recognize the caller ID, but answered the phone call in a tired voice, preparing to tell the telemarketer on the other end that she wasn't interested in buying solar panels or a new cable system or car insurance.

"This is Mary Browning," said a voice on the other end. Daisy snapped to attention.

"Oh, Ms. Browning, thank you for calling me back," she said, struggling to juggle the phone and her tote bag while she unlocked her door. "I don't know if the university librarian told you very much, but I'm interested in learning more about a certain dime novel author, a Harold Henderson."

"Yes, she told me that you wanted information about that particular author. It's interesting that you should ask about Harold Henderson, because that is one of the authors in whom I took a special interest."

"May I ask why?"

"Certainly. Harold Henderson was actually a woman." Daisy wrinkled her forehead. "It was common for women during that time to write stories that were included in dime novels, but for some reason Harold Henderson did not wish her identity to be known."

"Do you know the real identity of Harold Henderson?" Daisy asked. She realized she had been holding her breath while Mary spoke.

"I do. I went searching through my notes after the librarian called from the university and found Henderson's name. Or at least as much of it as I could find."

"What was it?"

Daisy could hear Mary leafing through papers during the pause that followed. "Harold Henderson's real name was A.S. Hightower."

"And A.S. Hightower, you're sure, was a woman?"

"Yes."

"How did you know that?"

"I found the information in old records belonging to the publishing company that released Henderson's work."

"What else did the old records contain?"

"They noted that Henderson was a *nom de plume*, so there was an instruction that the royalties for Harold Henderson were to be sent to A.S. Hightower in New York City."

"And what made you so interested in Henderson's work, say, as opposed to any of the other dime novel authors?"

"It wasn't just Henderson that I was interested in, but she was definitely one of my favorites. Her work seemed different from many of the other dime novels. It had an edge, a realism, to it that wasn't present in many of the more romanticized tales."

"I know exactly what you mean," Daisy said. "I often wondered if Henderson/Hightower was telling a personal tale."

"Then you see exactly what I mean," Mary replied. "I was interested in her work because there was more to it than just an amusing story."

Daisy and Mary chatted for a few more minutes, then Daisy hung up. She was excited to get back to the library to see what she could find about Harold Henderson, aka A.S. Hightower.

She was at the doors of the Library of Congress when they opened again the next morning. She headed straight toward the Main Reading Room, where she began her search in the extensive genealogy files. She went first to the birth records from New York State and searched across many years for A.S. Hightower. When that line of inquiry met with a dead end, she turned to birth records from the Nebraska Territory and searched those same years. Again, she didn't locate her quarry.

Daisy sat in the Main Reading Room, lost in thought. There were two problems with her searches: first, she didn't know the year of A.S. Hightower's birth, so she didn't know how far back to search in the birth records. It seemed reasonable to assume from the author's success that A.S. Hightower was an older adult, though probably not an elderly one, so that narrowed the search to, perhaps, a period of thirty to sixty years before the publication of the dime novel. But maybe Daisy would have to expand the date parameters. And second, she didn't know if A.S. Hightower had even been born in New York State. Or Nebraska. All this research could have been a wild goose chase. But Daisy wasn't ready to give up.

Since she didn't know A.S. Hightower's date of birth, she had another option. She could look through marriage records. She decided to start with marriages in New York State that had taken place within the forty years before the publication of the dime novel. She didn't know if Hightower was a maiden name or a married name, so she wasn't easily able to narrow her search. The library closed before she could get very far into her search of marriage records, so she vowed to return first thing in the morning.

She took the Metro home, preoccupied with questions about A.S. Hightower and the story she had written. Often Daisy tried to read on the train, but that evening she could only stare out the window, lost in thought. Normally she loved the thrill of looking for obscure information, the feeling of satisfaction when she found it. But this time it was different—this time her search for information about the author of the story in the dime novel had become an obsession.

Luckily she didn't have to spend too much time alone. She was looking forward to dinner and the movie with Grover. She was brushing her hair when the phone rang.

It was Jude. She was breathless. "You'll never believe what just happened!"

CHAPTER 58

"Slow down! What happened?"

"Mark John asked me to marry him." Daisy was stunned. She didn't speak for a long moment. "Daisy? Are you still there?"

"Yes, I'm here," Daisy said, shaking her head as if to clear away the fog of confusion. "Wow. That's unexpected. I guess congratulations are in order. Right?"

"I haven't given him an answer yet. I just can't believe it!" She let out a short squeal.

"Wow," Daisy said again. "How did this come about?" She wanted to be as happy and excited as Jude was, but something didn't feel right about this whole thing.

Maybe it was because Mark John had just suggested breaking up not forty-eight hours previously. And Jude had come to believe it wasn't such a bad idea.

Daisy wondered if Jude remembered that.

"You remember what happened in the office yesterday," Jude began. "I didn't want to take Mark John's calls because I was afraid of saying the wrong thing and making his mood worse.

He's been so agitated lately. Anyway, I ended up going to his house. Remember he was there to wait for someone? The electrician or the plumber or someone? Well, when I got there he was working at the kitchen table and whoever it was hadn't shown up yet. So I sat down with him and we talked for a long time." She paused.

"Go on," Daisy encouraged her.

"He told me that he's been very nervous about the prospect of taking the next step with me because his first marriage ended in such tragedy. He got so upset about it that he decided it would be better to take a break for a while than to have to worry about getting married."

"So then what?"

"Suddenly I knew he was the one and that I would wait for him. I took his hand in mine and told him that I didn't want him to worry about taking the next step because I would wait for him for as long as he needed. He said he was hoping that would be my response and our talk had convinced him that worrying about our future was a silly thing to do. Then he proposed! Isn't that exciting?"

"Yes, it's very exciting. So you haven't given him an answer yet? What are you waiting for?" Daisy hoped to hear Jude say that she wasn't sure this was the right thing to do, but Jude disappointed her.

"My mother always told me: never give a man an answer the first time they ask. Always wait until the second time. That makes him think that he's really, really lucky."

Daisy wanted to say *That's the dumbest thing I've ever heard and you're too smart to believe such dreck,* but she stayed silent.

"What do you think?" Jude asked, her excitement building again.

"I think it's incredible," Daisy said. She didn't want to lie and she didn't want to tell the truth, so she figured Jude would interpret that statement whichever way she chose. And as she suspected, Jude chose to interpret it as congratulatory.

"Thank you," she gushed.

"So when are you going to tell him?"

"The next time he asks me." Jude said, in a tone of voice which suggested she thought Daisy might not have been listening.

"So did he get down on one knee?"

"No, he just sat across from me and looked into my eyes. It was so romantic." *Humph. Doesn't sound all that romantic,* Daisy thought ungraciously.

"Aren't you glad the plumber or electrician or whoever wasn't there?" Daisy asked with a short laugh.

"Yeah. He never did show up. So we had the afternoon to ourselves. Of course Mark John took the rest of the day off. We went for a walk and had a celebratory late lunch and everything was just so perfect."

"Well, I'd better let you go so you can call everyone," Daisy said.

"I only have to call my parents," Jude answered. "But you're right. I should call them now. I just wanted to tell you first."

"Well, I'm honored. Thank you. Will you be at work tomorrow?"

Jude groaned. "Yes. I can't take another day off, especially if I'm going to be needing vacation days for a honeymoon."

"Just one more thing," Daisy said. "What does the ring look like?"

"He didn't give me a ring yet. He said we can pick it out together."

"Oh. Okay then. See you tomorrow."

When she got off the phone Daisy continued brushing her hair slowly and thoughtfully. She couldn't help feeling that this was not the right step for Jude and Mark John to take. It was a little before six o'clock when she put her hair in a ponytail and headed over to Murphy's Pub. When she arrived she found Grover waiting for her at a table inside. She sighed and sat down heavily.

"What gives?" he asked. "I thought you'd be excited to have dinner with *moi* and go see your thriller."

"I just have a lot on my mind."

"Like what? Care to share?" he asked as he handed her a menu.

Daisy told him all about the phone call from Jude, stopping only long enough for them to order wine and burgers.

"Do you think I'm wrong?" she asked at the conclusion of her story. Grover sat back and contemplated the tabletop.

"It definitely sounds like you're right, but you never know. What one person thinks is romantic and wonderful might be repulsive or at least questionable to someone else."

"That's true," Daisy conceded. "I just hate to see her making a mistake that's so life-changing."

"You've become pretty good friends with her, haven't you?"

Daisy grimaced. "Sometimes I feel like she thinks we're closer than I do. She went from being totally standoffish at work to fast friends really quickly. Sometimes I wonder if she's just grasping at the first person who came along and tried to see beyond her prickliness."

"She doesn't have any other friends?" Grover asked.

"Well, I guess there's Mark John. But when she called about their engagement, she said the only other people she needed to tell were her parents and she wanted me to know first."

"Sounds like a best friend to me."

"Me, too. But I feel a little weird because I don't feel the same way about her."

"You want to know what I think? I think you should stop worrying about it."

"You're probably right. Who knows? Maybe someday we'll be so close that I'll think of her as my sister," Daisy said, rolling her eyes and snorting a little laugh.

"So what else is going on?"

"Have you talked to Helena? She and her new boyfriend, Bennett, are going to Aruba together."

Grover raised his eyebrows. "That was quick. They haven't known each other that long, have they?"

"Not really," Daisy said, shaking her head. Then she laughed. "She thought it would be fun if you and I went, too, but then decided she and Bennett should just get to know each other better."

Grover smiled. "Aruba would be a fun trip. But I'm not sure I would want to go on vacation with Helena. Something tells me I'd never be able to relax, not with the way she's always on the go. It would be fun to go with you, though."

Daisy felt a not-uncomfortable warmth at his words. She glanced at him and then quickly looked away, gazing around the restaurant.

Grover cleared his throat. "Well, I can't be spending that kind of money, anyway. I've got to save all I can, especially with the party cancellations I've been getting."

"You've gotten more?" Daisy was disappointed to hear it. Why couldn't people mind their own business?

"A few. Let's talk about something a little more pleasant," he suggested.

"Fine by me," Daisy agreed.

"So," Grover said, a little too loudly, "are you looking forward to the movie? I haven't seen any of the reviews."

"I read a couple. I think it sounds really good." Talk remained on the safe topic of thriller movies until they finished dinner and left the restaurant. It was a warm evening and they had plenty of time to get to the movie theater.

They walked slowly, enjoying the sights and sounds of a Washington summer. The shadows were beginning to lengthen along the brownstone-lined streets when Daisy tripped on a crack in the sidewalk. Grover reached out to grab her arm, but he wasn't quick enough and she landed on her knees and the heels of her hands.

"Are you all right?" Grover asked, bending down to help her stand up.

"Yeah. Only my pride is really hurt, I think," she answered, grimacing. Grover held her elbow while she examined the scrapes on her hands, then she pulled up her pant legs and looked at her knees. There was a little bit of blood, but not much. She was more upset that she'd ripped her favorite linen pants.

She could feel her face redden from embarrassment and she looked up at Grover. He was looking at her with his lopsided smile, a sympathetic look in his eyes.

"What am I going to do with you?" he asked, pulling her close to him and giving her a little squeeze. He let her go and she fumbled with her purse, not knowing what else to do.

But she wished she could get another whiff of his cologne—up close.

They slowed their pace even more to get to the theater, with Daisy limping along and wincing every so often from the pain in her knees.

They both loved the movie and debated it the entire way back to Daisy's apartment. When they arrived in front of the coral-hued old house, Daisy invited Grover upstairs for a glass of wine.

"I'd better not," he said. "You should get your hands and knees taken care of and get some sleep. Maybe take some aspirin so it won't hurt so much in the morning."

"Okay," Daisy replied. She was surprised at how disappointed she was. "You sure?" she asked.

Grover smiled and nodded. "I don't think it's a good idea right now."

He turned and walked up the street, waving as he left. Daisy watched him leave, wondering what his cryptic words meant. Why wouldn't it be a good idea to have a glass of wine?

CHAPTER 59

*I*t wasn't until the middle of the following week that Mark John and Jude picked out an engagement ring. They went during their lunch hour and when they returned to work Jude was sporting a huge emerald-cut diamond nestled sturdily in a white gold setting.

Jude showed it to the receptionist and secretaries, then made a beeline for Daisy's office to show her the bauble.

"It's just beautiful, Jude," Daisy said. And she was being truthful—it was one of the most beautiful rings she had ever seen.

"Mark John said I could have any ring I wanted, and this is the kind I've always dreamed of," Jude gushed, turning her hand to and fro under the lights to see the sparkle from different angles.

"It's like something from a fairy tale," Daisy agreed.

"This weekend we're going to start planning the wedding and I might even start moving some of my stuff into his house. Mark John says he wants to have a hand in the preparations and it'll be so much easier if I'm living there. Isn't that wonderful? So many men just let the women take care of everything."

Jude's moving in already? Things are definitely speeding up around here.

"That's very nice of him," Daisy said, her voice a little bland.

"What's wrong, Daisy?" Jude asked.

Daisy couldn't tell Jude that there was something that just didn't make sense about her engagement. It seemed too soon after Mark John had suggested taking a break, and there had been that look he gave her at the jazz festival when she wasn't looking...

She glanced up at Jude. "Oh, it's nothing. I'm happy for you, Jude."

But am I? Is it possible that I'm actually jealous of her?

Jude seemed to accept Daisy's assurance. Smiling, she left, heading in the direction of Mark John's office.

Daisy tried to get back to work, but couldn't concentrate on her computer screen. She tried jotting notes in a notebook with a pencil to get herself to focus, but even that didn't help. Finally she picked up the phone and dialed Helena.

It was the wrong thing to do. Helena could only gush about her upcoming trip to Aruba with Bennett. Daisy was getting sick of hearing about everyone's successful relationships.

She listened to talk of Bennett's wonderfulness until she couldn't stand it another minute, then feigned a headache and told Helena she'd catch up with her later.

She sat at her desk looking out the window at the office building across the street. So many strangers over there, so many stories. Her mind began wandering, back to New York City and Dean.

Her world had stopped temporarily after Dean died and it had taken every bit of strength she could muster to get through the days, weeks, and months following his death. It had been horrible enough when he was killed. And then to become a suspect...it had nearly pushed Daisy over the edge. But now some time had passed and she was able to focus on the happy times.

But both his loss and the public suspicion of her still hurt. She was thankful to be away from Brooklyn, where there were still people who harbored doubts about her innocence, where there were still difficult memories.

And as for dating? She kept telling herself she wasn't ready. But was she scared to date, or was she haunted by memories? Or was it a bit of both?

One thing she knew for sure: she would never forget Dean. She had loved him with all her heart.

But hearts are capable of amazing things, and maybe the thought of sharing that love with another person was what really scared Daisy. Perhaps, she thought, she was worried about being disloyal to Dean.

Did she really want to be single forever?

This is ridiculous, she told herself sternly. *Get outside, go for a walk, then come back and get some work done.*

She followed her own advice and strode around the block twice before feeling calm enough to return to the office. When she entered the Global Human Rights suite the receptionist handed her a message scrawled on a small piece of paper.

"You just missed this call, Daisy," she said.

"Thanks," Daisy said, and she looked at the slip of paper. The message was from Mary Browning. *I wonder why she called.*

She closed the door and sat down at her desk before returning Mary's call. Mary answered on the first ring.

"Hi, Mary. It's Daisy Carruthers. I heard I just missed your call. How can I help you?"

"Oh, it wasn't a really big deal," Mary replied. "I so enjoyed talking to you recently about A.S. Hightower that I went back into my files to see if there was anything I missed. I got thinking about Ms. Hightower and her writing again, and I was reminded of how fascinating I found her."

"And did you find anything interesting?" Daisy asked. She wasn't sure where this conversation was heading.

"Just a little tidbit, nothing more than a footnote, really. I found out that the letters 'A.S.' stood for Adelaide Sweeney. It's been a long time since I read Hightower's stories, but I seem to remember the name Sweeney from one of them. I thought you might be interested in having that information."

Adelaide. Lady! Trudy's stepdaughter.

Daisy was speechless for a moment. Finally Mary spoke up. "Daisy, are you there?"

"Yes. Yes, sorry. Mary, you have no idea of the importance of that name to me. Thank you so much for letting me know!"

"Well, I'm glad I could help, even though I don't understand it," Mary said with a chuckle.

"Someday I hope to be able to tell you the whole story, but right now I'm not totally sure I understand it, either. I've got to run, Mary, but I'll be in touch. And thank you again!"

So Adelaide, the child who had hated school and had a difficult time learning to read and write, had become an author. And a popular one, apparently.

Daisy couldn't think of anything except the dime novel Brian had lent her. Was Adelaide's story fiction or nonfiction? Had it, perhaps, been her way of telling the world about her father's crimes against the women he married and even his children? Had it been a cathartic exercise, trying to rid herself of memories too painful to keep to herself?

She picked up the phone again and called Grover.

"You'll never guess," she began.

"What? Guess what?" he asked.

"You know the diary I've talked about for hours and hours? Remember there was a little girl in the diary who was Trudy's stepdaughter? And remember the dime novel I told you about that had a story that sounded just like the diary? Well, the little girl grew up to be the author of that story!" Daisy stopped speaking, breathless.

"You're kidding. What does that mean?" Grover asked.

"I'm not sure yet. It could mean that she was confessing to a murder on behalf of her father, or it could be a fictional account of what could have happened following the events in a child's memory."

"That's incredible. How are you going to figure out which it was?"

"I'm not sure I can. But it's so fascinating. I can't believe we figured out how the diary and the dime novel are tied together."

"We should celebrate," Grover suggested. "I have a small party to run tonight, but tomorrow I'm free until late afternoon. How about taking a drive somewhere?"

"Sounds good. Call me in the morning and I'll be ready. And thanks!"

Daisy hung up. She could feel the flush in her cheeks, her heart beating a little faster.

Were the flush and heartbeat the result of Mary's information about Adelaide? Or were they the result of Grover's invitation? Maybe both.

CHAPTER 60

On Saturday Grover surprised Daisy with reservations to a cocktail-making class at a local distillery in northern Virginia. He picked up Daisy in his car early Saturday morning and, after picking up bagels and fruit salad at a café near her apartment, they headed out of the city and toward the rolling hills of suburban Virginia.

The class was fun. Daisy and Grover hadn't known much about spirits before the class, but they left armed with knowledge of how to make two special Prohibition-era cocktails, the differences between flips and fizzes, and the history of the gimlet.

They ate lunch at the distillery with other cocktail classmates, talking animatedly with their new acquaintances about the weather, politics, their respective work, and living inside the Beltway. As they were driving back into Washington, Daisy's excitement hadn't waned.

"I didn't know you were so interested in politics," Daisy exclaimed, turning to look at Grover while he drove.

"Sure, I find politics fascinating. It just never comes up when we're together, I guess."

"Yeah, but how didn't I know that about you?" Daisy pressed.

Grover shrugged. "Maybe we should spend more time together," he suggested. Daisy didn't know whether he was teasing or serious.

"Maybe you're right. Who knows what else I might discover?" she replied.

Grover turned to look at her. "Who knows?" he asked with a wink.

Daisy didn't reply to that, but they talked the rest of the way back to Daisy's apartment of innocuous things, things that didn't require wondering or confusion. But Grover turned serious when he pulled up in front of the Daisy's coral brownstone. He turned off the car and unbuckled his seat belt, then turned to face her and took a deep breath.

"Daisy, I'm serious about maybe spending more time together."

She blinked and her heart started pounding faster. "What do you mean?" She was pretty sure she knew exactly what he meant.

"I mean, we're best friends. What could be better than best friends who become more than friends?"

For the second time in an hour, Daisy didn't know what to say. She looked into Grover's eyes, finding warmth...and something more.

Grover reached out and touched her hand. "What are you thinking?"

"I...I don't know, Grover. I'm not sure I'm ready. The thing is, I had a bad experience with Dean and I don't know if I'm the type of person who should be in a relationship."

"Have you been afraid to move on?" Grover asked. How could Helena and Grover always get so quickly straight to the heart of an issue?

Daisy nodded slightly. "I think so."

"Do you still love him?"

Daisy thought for a moment. "I'll always have a spot for Dean in my heart, but I'm not sure I'd call it 'love.' It used to be love, but I guess at this point it's just happy memories combined with an acceptance of what happened."

"I think I understand." Grover looked at her intently. "Would you be willing to try to move on? With me, I mean?" He smiled.

She returned his smile, suddenly shy around this man who had been one of her best friends since arriving in Washington. "Maybe," she said with a nervous laugh.

"I'll take it," he replied, touching her hand again.

"Call me later?" she asked, reaching for the door handle.

"You know it," he said, a broad smile on his face.

Daisy watched him drive away, knowing he was watching her through his rear-view mirror. She waved once and turned around to go inside.

One of her elderly neighbors, Mrs. Clement, was just coming outside. Daisy held the door for her.

"Has that young man finally made his move?" she asked with a wink.

Daisy threw her head back and laughed. "I think so."

"Took him long enough."

CHAPTER 61

Daisy cleaned her apartment that afternoon, walking around with an energy that surprised her, since she hated cleaning.

It wasn't until evening, when she had settled down on the couch with a good book, that the phone rang.

It was Jude.

"Hi, Jude. What's up?" Daisy asked.

"I just called to tell you about something weird that I found in Mark John's house. Well, two things, actually," she said in a low voice. Something in her tone suggested that all might not be well.

"What are they?" Daisy asked, her curiosity piqued.

"He ran out for a minute, so I thought I'd call you and ask your opinion."

"Okay. What are they?" Daisy repeated, the hair on her neck prickling.

"It looks like a family tree."

"That's not weird," Daisy said.

"I know, but it's annotated. Heavily. And there's an article stapled to it." Daisy could hear paper rustling.

Jude gasped. "It's...Mark John's back. Gotta run."

"Wait! What else did you find?" Daisy asked. But Jude had hung up.

Something's wrong, Daisy thought. A frightening thought was beginning to take shape in the back of her mind. She scrolled through her cell phone contacts and pushed the call button.

Brian answered right away.

"Hi, Daisy."

"Brian, I need to talk to you about that diary. I know you've been reluctant to tell me where you got it, but it's time. Right now."

She heard a sigh on the other end of the line.

"I really wanted to talk to you about the diary before we discussed its provenance," he said.

"Yeah, I know that. But we just haven't had a chance and I think it's going to have to wait."

"Tell me why you need to know right now where the diary came from."

"It's just a hunch I'm following. I'd rather not say."

"Fair enough. At least tell me what you thought of the diary and the dime novel, taken together."

"It seems obvious that they're connected," Daisy said, wondering if Brian knew of the Adelaide connection.

"It does."

"So please tell me where the diary came from."

He took a deep breath. "It came from Fiona."

"Fiona? Was it hers?" That wasn't the answer Daisy had expected, but she realized she didn't know what she had expected.

"It was not hers." *That makes more sense.*

"Whose was it?"

"It belonged to Mark John's mother. So did the dime novel."

"So how did Fiona end up with it?"

"It was in a big box of stuff Mark John's mother had left in his house before she passed away. Fiona was cleaning out the attic one day and found it. She asked Mark John if he wanted it. He didn't even know what was in the box, and he told her she could get rid of it."

"And then she gave it to you?" Daisy was confused.

"She gave me the diary and the dime novel along with a few other items. She thought I might be interested in reading them because I have such a keen interest in American history."

"And you read them and started to wonder why Mark John's mother would be in possession of such a strange diary," Daisy prompted.

"Exactly. There's something about Mark John that makes me uncomfortable, Daisy."

"So why did you ask him to read the diary?"

"I wanted to see what kind of a reaction he had to it. But he doesn't like to read things that aren't related to his job."

"So why did you ask me to read it?"

Another sigh. "Because you don't know Mark John that well and I wanted to see if you arrived at the same hunch that I did. And it looks like maybe you have."

"You mean that Mark John is somehow connected to Trudy and Adelaide," Daisy said.

"Yes."

"But what's the big deal about that?" She knew where this conversation was headed, but she wanted Brian to say it.

She could sense him hesitating. Finally he spoke. "The big deal is the other hunch I have."

"Which is?" she prompted.

"I think it's possible that Mark John murdered my sister." His voice was low and filled with pain.

Brian had just confirmed her suspicion.

He continued. "It's hard for me and my wife to imagine that Mark John could have killed Fiona, so I needed the opinion of someone who doesn't know Mark John very well. I needed to know if you arrived at the same conclusion that we did."

"I did," she said. "Now that I know where the diary came from, I'm sure that Mark John is related to Adelaide somehow. And we can be fairly certain that Adelaide's father, Thomas, was a murderer, as was her grandfather. And Mark John would, of course, be related to both of them."

"Have you ever heard of the warrior gene?" Brian asked.

Daisy remembered reading something about violence that ran in families, but wasn't otherwise familiar with the concept.

"That's a pop psychology name for it, of course, but it's a gene that can lead to violent behavior. Since it's a gene, that means it's hereditary and can obviously be passed down in families. There's plenty of evidence that generations of families can suffer from the same types of violence."

Then it hit Daisy. The gruesome story by Harold Henderson/A.S. Hightower about hereditary violence--that was a memoir and she hadn't realized it when she read the story.

"It makes total sense now," Daisy said, half to herself. Then she remembered Jude's words.

"Brian, Jude called me a while ago. She's moving some of her stuff into Mark John's house this weekend and she found something that she thought was a family tree in his house. She said it was weird because there were so many notations on it."

"Is she at his house now?" Brian asked, his voice taking on a new urgency.

"I think so. She had to hang up because Mark John had just come home."

"Whatever was on that piece of paper, she must not have wanted him to know she had seen it. We need to go over there," Brian said. "Can you meet me there? You probably know Jude better than I do, and she may need someone there for moral support."

"Sure. I'll meet you there." Daisy was already thrusting her feet into shoes by the front door. She hung up with Brian and used an app on her phone to call for a car, which arrived at her front door mere moments later.

She gave the driver Mark John's address and the car sped through the night as she sat in the backseat, staring grimly out the windows as the scenery became more suburban along the streets. There was no traffic.

She wondered how Jude would take the news.

She texted Jude to tell her to hide the family tree, that she would explain when she got to Mark John's house. When Jude hadn't replied a few minutes later, Daisy tried calling her. The phone went straight to voicemail.

It didn't take the driver long to get to Mark John's house. After he dropped her off, Daisy scanned the street; she didn't see Brian and there were no cars parked nearby. She shivered, though the night was warm and muggy.

A sound in a nearby yard spooked her and she ran lightly up the front walk to the door. She raised her hand to knock and the door swung open.

ark John stood next to the door. He wordlessly beckoned Daisy inside. His eyes, empty and bloodshot, looked her up and down.

"What are you doing here?" he asked.

Daisy was silent for a moment, listening. Where was Jude?

"I was worried about Jude," she said, her heart beginning to pound harder.

"Why would you be worried about her?"

Daisy had to think fast. "She called and sounded upset earlier. She said you had gone out and I thought I would come over and see if she was okay."

"She's fine. It's strange, because I've been here for a while. If you thought she was upset when I wasn't here, why did you wait so long before coming over?"

"I couldn't find your address," Daisy said lamely.

"Really." Mark John clearly wasn't buying it.

Mark John reached around Daisy's back and locked the front door. Daisy's blood ran cold.

"Follow me," Mark John directed.

"Where are we going?" Daisy asked, rooted to the spot. "Where's Jude?"

He didn't answer. Instead, he took Daisy by the elbow and maneuvered her toward the back of the house. When they came to the doorway of the den, Daisy took one look at the sight before her and whimpered.

Jude was on the floor, unconscious. At least Daisy hoped she was only unconscious. Blood pooled around her head and her face was bruised and swollen.

"Oh, my God! Jude!" Daisy cried, then took a step toward her friend. Mark John yanked her elbow to whip her back to her place next to him. She covered her mouth with her hands and closed her eyes to shut out the sight.

"Shut up!" Mark John bellowed. With lightning speed he reached out and hit Daisy across the face with his open hand. Tears of pain sprang to her eyes almost immediately and she stared at him for a brief moment, stunned.

"What's wrong, Mark John?" she asked, blinking furiously. She didn't want him to think he made her cry.

"Nothing!" he shouted.

"Mark John, there's something in your genes that's making you do this. Have you ever heard of the warrior gene?"

"Of course I've heard of it," he spat. "It's a curse!"

"But what it means is that you may not be fully responsible for your behavior. You can't help the way you are. We can get you help for this, Mark John, but you can't hurt Jude or me," Daisy said, holding perfectly still so he wouldn't wrench her elbow any further. "Please let go of me. You're hurting me."

"You don't understand anything, Daisy," Mark John said in a tired voice. "I know right from wrong. I know it's wrong to hurt people. But I just can't help it sometimes."

There was a knock at the front door. Mark John gripped Daisy's arm tighter and snarled, "Who's that?"

"It's Brian. He's here to help you."

"You're a liar!" Mark John yelled. His voice was so thunderous Daisy was sure Brian could hear him.

"Please, Mark John. Let us help you," Daisy said, glancing toward the door. She could see it from where she stood in the den and she wondered if she might be able to yank her arm from Mark John's grasp and reach the door before he could catch her.

"I told you to shut up!" he yelled again. His eyes flashed and his glance wavered toward the door for just a second. It was as if he knew what she was thinking. Before she had time to put her plan into action, he flung her to the floor with such force that when she hit her head on the corner of the couch, the room went black for several seconds. She could hear him muttering to himself, though, so she knew she wasn't fully unconscious.

When her vision cleared she looked over to where Jude lay on the floor, just a few feet away. Then she looked toward Mark John, who was sitting on the couch with his head in his hands, still talking to himself. Then she saw the briefest of movements outside the den window.

Brian! He had come around the house and was peering inside. She saw his eyes widen and he disappeared from view.

Daisy groaned inwardly. Where was he going? She tried pushing herself up onto her hands and knees, but they were still bruised and scabbed since she had fallen on them a few days earlier when she was walking to the movies with Grover. Besides, the room was spinning and she couldn't trust herself to move yet. She slumped back onto the floor. A noise escaped her lips and Mark John's head whipped around.

"Don't you ever give up?" he asked, getting to his feet.

"No," she croaked. He walked over to her and kicked her ribs with a vicious force. She could actually hear a cracking sound. She groaned in pain while her head lolled on the floor again. Mark John watched her for a moment, then apparently deciding she, like Jude, was unconscious, he returned to the couch.

Daisy had positioned herself so she could peer through mostly-closed eyelids and see both Jude and Mark John without him being able to see her. She hoped Mark John didn't hear her sharp intake of breath when she saw Jude moving.

Jude let out a whimper of pain and rolled over. Daisy could see her reach slowly and gingerly for the place where the blood was still seeping slowly from her head. Mark John glanced up from where he still sat on the couch.

"I'm sorry, Jude. I didn't mean to hurt you. It's just...it's just that...all of a sudden I felt this rage and I couldn't control it and...." He stopped talking. Jude wasn't responding. Daisy hoped with all her heart that Jude was smart enough to pretend to have fainted again.

Daisy opened her eye just a bit further and could see Mark John's shoulders shaking. *He's crying*, she thought. *Just like Thomas cried after hitting Adelaide.*

But then the shaking stopped and Mark John stood up again. He stalked over to Jude and lifted her by placing his hands under her armpits. He began to drag her toward the den doorway. Jude didn't move or make a sound. It was possible she had fainted again, or maybe she was pretending.

Mark John continued tugging Jude's body until he backed into the corner of a cabinet that stood near the doorway.

"Dammit!" he roared. Daisy squeezed her eyes shut again at the sound.

He let Jude slump to the floor while he shoved the cabinet with a force Daisy wouldn't have thought possible. His anger was palpable. The glass figurines and knick-knacks in the cabinet made tinkling sounds as they toppled over and broke inside the cabinet as it teetered for a moment, then settled back into its place. Mark John seemed oblivious to the sound of breaking glass. He turned to Jude and grabbed her by the arms, dragging her again, into the living room.

While he was busy with Jude, Daisy recognized her chance

to get out of the house. Very slowly, watching him out of the corner of her eye, she pushed herself, wincing, to a kneeling position. Mark John was so busy with Jude that he didn't notice her moving.

She took a deep breath and bolted toward the back door. At least she felt like she was bolting, but she didn't seem to be getting to the door very quickly.

This time Mark John noticed her movements. With a roar that didn't sound human, he lunged toward her as she reached the door, pulling it open and crashing onto the patio outside.

"Brian! Help!" she yelled. Her voice didn't sound very loud in her own ears.

Mark John was on top of her just a second later, pummeling her with his fists. She tried moving her head to dodge his blows, but he managed to make contact with her face several times. She could hear a voice screaming. Was that her?

She didn't realize what was happening when Mark John slumped over next to her on the patio. Daring to open her eyes and peer over Mark John's limp body, she could see Brian standing over his brother-in-law, a two-by-four in his hands.

He had, quite possibly, saved the lives of both Daisy and Jude.

"The police are on their way, Daisy," Brian said, kneeling down next to Mark John and peering at him in the dimness of the patio light. He still held his makeshift weapon. Then he turned to her. "Hang in there for just a couple minutes. Help will be here very soon.

"He's unconscious," he continued reassuringly. "If he wakes up before the police get here, I'll just hit him again if I have to," he continued.

"Jude?" Daisy asked hoarsely.

"I haven't been in to check on her yet. I don't want to leave you out here alone with him."

"I'll go check on her," Daisy offered, pushing herself slowly to her feet. But her body screamed in protest and she gently lowered herself back onto the patio. "Just give me a minute."

"I told the nine-one-one operator we'd need ambulances, too, so they'll be here any minute. You need to stay still right now," Brian said, keeping a wary eye on Mark John.

She closed her eyes again and tried to focus on something other than the pain, but it even hurt to breathe. She strained her ears and could, mercifully, hear sirens in the distance, getting steadily closer.

She took some shallow breaths and shifted her head to see if she could get a glimpse of Jude in the house. She could see her friend lying on the floor inside the living room doorway where Mark John had left her. A cold chill snaked up Daisy's skull.

Had Mark John succeeded in killing her?

She turned to look toward the gate in the backyard. The sirens had stopped, but she could see swirling lights reflecting off the neighbor's houses. The ambulances were in the driveway.

Brian gave a shout to direct the authorities to the backyard. Daisy knew he didn't want to take a chance that Mark John would come to and cause more pain if he woke up while Brian was showing the police and paramedics where the injured women lay.

A phalanx of officers and paramedics came into the backyard, moving cautiously at first, then building speed when they realized two people were lying on the ground. One of the officers barked an order for Brian to set the piece of wood on the ground and step away from Mark John.

Another officer approached Daisy and she lifted her head feebly.

"My friend is inside on the floor. Please, go check on her first."

The officer nodded and beckoned for a paramedic to join

him and the two of them went into the house as another officer and two paramedics walked swiftly to where Daisy lay.

While one paramedic tended to her and the other knelt by Mark John, a policeman asked questions about Mark John and Jude. Daisy could hear another officer asking similar questions of Brian just a few feet away. As they spoke Mark John began to move his legs. He groaned. One of the officers was by his side in an instant.

"Can you tell me what happened here, Mister Friole?" he asked.

Mark John shook his head limply from side to side.

"Did you attack this woman?" the officer asked, gesturing toward Daisy. Mark John nodded feebly.

In just a few minutes he was strapped to a stretcher. An officer was accompanying him to the hospital in the back of the ambulance.

Shortly thereafter Daisy was also strapped to a stretcher, being taken to another hospital. Brian asked if he could accompany her; the police and paramedic agreed he should ride in the back of the ambulance.

Jude went in a third ambulance to the hospital where Daisy was being sent. No one accompanied her except for the paramedic who rode in the back of the vehicle.

CHAPTER 63

The next morning Daisy woke up in the hospital. She looked around, blinking, wondering for a brief moment where she was. A nurse passed by her door and then Daisy had a dim recollection of the events of the previous evening.

That same nurse came into her room just a few minutes later, smiling brightly.

"How are you this morning?" she asked.

"I hurt all over, but I suppose it could be worse," Daisy said with a grimace. "Do you know how my friend is doing?"

"She was badly beaten, but she's going to be all right," the nurse informed her. "When you're feeling up to it I can take you to her room."

"I feel up to it now," Daisy answered quickly.

The nurse smiled kindly. "Try to eat some breakfast first, then we'll talk about it." She bustled around Daisy's bed, adjusting tubes and checking the dials on the machines surrounding her.

While the nurse was tending to Daisy another hospital employee came in bearing a breakfast tray. On it was an unappetizing array of runny scrambled eggs, cold toast, and congealing oatmeal, but Daisy ate it all hungrily. She found that she was starving, plus she wanted to prove to the nurse that she was well enough to visit Jude in her room.

"How'd I do?" Daisy asked as she sipped the bitter orange juice that was on the tray.

The nurse laughed. "You showed me, didn't you? All right, let's get you on your feet. If you're able to stand up, we'll go see your friend. She's just up the hall."

Daisy sat up with the help of the nurse's strong hands. She got out of bed gingerly, not expecting the pain to be as severe as it was. She winced.

"Take it nice and slow," the nurse cautioned. "Your body has been through a lot. You've suffered several broken ribs, facial fractures, bruises and lacerations, and probably a concussion. We'll be doing some tests in just a little while. You can't just get up and run." The nurse helped her ease into a wheelchair.

Together they made the trip to Jude's room, which was only three doors down but felt to Daisy like it was ten miles. Everything hurt. Even in the wheelchair, her bones felt like they were rattling around in her body and her head throbbed. She didn't mention it to the nurse.

And when she got her first look at Jude, hooked up to machines, her face swollen and bruised, and her head heavily bandaged, she knew her pain was nothing compared to Jude's.

The nurse wheeled Daisy close to Jude's bed and told Daisy she'd be back in a few minutes to help her get back to her own room.

"You have to get your rest and you have to let Jude rest, too," she said, then she slipped quietly from the room.

Daisy took one of Jude's hands in her own, noticing the bruising around the knuckles. "What did he do to you?" she breathed.

She bowed her head over Jude's hand, realizing suddenly

how lucky Jude was to be alive. Tears fell from her eyes, stinging the cuts in her face as they dripped onto the floor. "I'm so sorry, Jude," she whispered.

She felt the slightest pressure from Jude's hand. She looked up in surprise.

"Can you hear me, Jude?" she asked.

Almost imperceptibly, Jude nodded. Her eyelids fluttered, as if she were trying to open her eyes and couldn't, and Daisy squeezed her hand gently.

"Don't try to open your eyes. The nurse says you're going to be okay. I'm in the room right down the hall. I'm going to call your parents." Jude nodded again.

The nurse came back in to escort Daisy back to her room. Once she was settled in her own bed, Daisy reached for her cell phone and scrolled through her contacts. When she found the cell number of the Global Human Rights Journal office manager, she called the woman at home.

The woman was shocked to hear what had happened to Jude and Daisy. Daisy asked her to text her with the phone number of Jude's parents, as they would be listed as next-of-kin in Jude's employment files. They hung up and Daisy received the text just a few minutes later.

She dialed Jude's parents and introduced herself. Her parents were hysterical when they learned what had happened to their daughter and they promised to come to the hospital immediately.

Daisy then called Grover to tell him what had happened. He was shocked when she told him the story and promised to be at the hospital within a half hour.

And true to his word, he burst into her room twenty-five minutes later. "I called Helena and she's on her way, too," he explained breathlessly, then stood still, gazing at Daisy for a long moment. He reached out and smoothed her hair.

"I don't know what I would have done if this had been more

serious," he told her, then he bent down and kissed her on the forehead. "Are you sure you're all right?"

"Yes, I'm fine," she replied, tears springing to her eyes.

"Then why are you crying?" he asked, blinking back tears of his own.

"I'm just happy, I guess," she replied with a short laugh.

He grinned his wide, lopsided smile. "How can you be happy at a time like this?" he asked, shaking his head.

"Because you're here."

"I'll always be here for you," he said quietly, leaning over and kissing her lips gently.

"What's going on?" a voice asked from the doorway.

Grover moved aside so Helena could see her friend. "Oh, my God!" she cried. "Are you all right? And why was Grover kissing you on the lips?"

Daisy laughed, even though it hurt her ribs. "I'm fine and he kissed me on the lips because I wanted him to."

Helena let out a squeal. "I'm so happy! I mean, not just because you're going to be okay, but because you both finally came to your senses!"

Grover and Helena couldn't stay for long because Daisy's nurse was only letting visitors come for a few minutes at a time. When Daisy started tiring, the nurse sent Grover and Helena home with the promise that they could come back the following day, if Daisy was still a patient.

Daisy slept for much of that day, then spent one more night in the hospital for observation. Before she left the hospital the next morning, she limped into Jude's room. Jude's parents were there and Jude was sitting up in bed, her eyes open this time.

"Daisy," she said, her eyes welling up with tears. "I can't believe how stupid I was. I'm so sorry I brought you into this. I should have seen that Mark John was becoming more and more unstable."

"Jude, stop right there," Daisy scolded her. "You couldn't

have known what was going to happen. None of us realized what was happening. I'm just glad I was able to get to Mark John's house before he hurt you any worse." The silence hung in the air for a moment.

"I want to show you something," Jude said, shifting in her bed. "Mom, can you grab my pants from the plastic bag in the closet?"

Jude's mother stood up to retrieve the bag of the clothes and belongings Jude had had with her when she got to the hospital. She pulled a pair of jeans from the bag and handed them to Jude, then she and her husband left the room so Jude and Daisy could talk privately.

Jude reached slowly, painfully, into the back pocket and pulled out a folded stack of papers.

"This is the family tree I found. This is the one I was talking to you about on the phone when Mark John came home." She shuddered, then recovered herself. "I didn't get a chance to look at whatever's stapled to it." She paused. "Now I know why he didn't want children," she added quietly, looking down at her hands.

Daisy unfolded the papers. The family tree was on top, and there was a magazine article stapled to the top paper.

She glanced at the article's headline before looking at the family tree: "The Murder Gene: Nature vs. Nurture?"

So she and Brian weren't the only ones who knew about the murder gene. Someone had known enough about it to attach it to the Friole family tree.

She flipped the top page over without reading the article. The family tree was heavily annotated with scribbles.

Daisy set the paper on Jude's bedside table and ran her fingertip along the branches of the tree. Mark John's name was at the bottom. Above his name were those of his parents, then grandparents, then great-grandparents, then great-great-grandparents, then at the top of the tree, his great-great-great-grand-parents.

And there was the name "Thomas Sheppard/Sheri-dan/Sweeney," Mark John's great-great-great grandfather. The name "Adelaide Sheridan/Sweeney Hightower" was below Thomas's name and slightly to the left. And down through the generations to Mark John. Beside many of the men's names were curious notations.

Daisy looked closer at the paper. Beside the name of Mark John's father was scrawled, "Murder, imprisoned 1968." Beside Mark John's great-uncle was written, "Arson, imprisoned 1931." As Daisy examined the family tree, she realized with growing horror that she was looking at a record of the crimes committed by the members of Mark John's family—members who very likely shared the murder gene with him. She recalled learning from Adelaide's story, "The Widower's Curse," that Thomas Sheppard's father had killed someone, too. Who knew how many generations the murder gene went back? She thought briefly about all the parallels between Thomas's behavior and Mark John's behavior: the aloofness, the mood swings, the unkindness, the anger, the remorse after hurting a loved one.

Daisy leaned down to kiss Jude lightly on the cheek before she left, then she turned to leave. But a thought struck her as she was walking into the hospital corridor.

"Jude," she asked, turning to face her friend, "you mentioned you found something else at Mark John's house. What was it?"

"Walt's wallet."

"And one more thing--I'm not trying to upset you, only make sense of things. Were you and Mark John romantically involved before Fiona was killed?"

Jude nodded.

Somehow both answers were the ones Daisy had expected.

Grover was working at a party that afternoon and had been unable to find someone to work in his place. He had wanted to cancel the party, but Daisy insisted that he keep his commitment. Brian drove Daisy home from the hospital. On the way back to her apartment she told Brian all about the family tree and the other members of Mark John's family who had committed violent crimes.

"He's confessed to killing Fiona," Brian told her.

"How did he do it?" Daisy asked. "I thought he was at work that night."

"Apparently he took the service elevator, the one with no video feed, and went out the back of the building. He went home, killed Fiona, and went back to the office the same way he had left. Then he took the front elevators and exited the building through the front entrance much later."

He sighed. "I thought it would feel better knowing who killed my sister, but somehow it doesn't feel better at all. To think she died at the hands of her own husband..." His voice drifted off.

Daisy was quiet for a moment, then asked, "Why did he kill her? I mean, he didn't just kill her out of the blue, did he?"

Brian's eyes wore a faraway look. "Simple. She cheated on him. He couldn't take the embarrassment. And then he killed Walt, too, because Walt was The Other Man."

"I'm sorry, Brian."

"And then he has the audacity to start dating another woman almost immediately," he said bitterly.

"So you knew about that?" Daisy asked.

"Yes. I happened to see them together one day. They were holding hands and I couldn't believe he had the nerve to be seeing someone so soon after my sister's death." His voice caught. "I followed them to your neighborhood, actually. I was going to confront them, but they disappeared before I could say anything."

Daisy thought it best not to reveal to Brian just yet that Mark John and Jude had been having an affair during

Mark John's marriage to Fiona. Maybe she would never tell him.

Daisy shook her head. "I guess we don't really need to discuss Trudy's diary anymore, do we? Now that we know the ending of her story. And its aftermath."

"A very sad aftermath," Brian agreed.

"Brian, why were you waiting for me in front of that coffee shop across the street from Global Human Rights the day I found you in the office?"

He gave Daisy a look of shame. "I'm sorry if I alarmed you. I was debating about whether I should approach you and ask you your thoughts about working with Mark John, but I decided against it. When you told me you had the diary, I knew that would be a much better way to talk to you."

"You never dropped off books to Mark John that day--what were you doing in his office?" Jude asked.

"Looking for...I don't know, anything that would incriminate him."

"So why didn't you talk to me about it for so long? Why did you keep trying to talk to Mark John about it?"

"Because I wanted him to realize I was onto him. But it never happened." He shook his head. "And besides that, I needed time to think about it. So much had happened, and I wanted to make sure I wasn't making wild accusations that could ruin Mark John's life if he weren't guilty. But I did call in an anonymous tip to the police, advising them to talk to Mark John again about the night of Fiona's murder."

"That was you?" Daisy asked. Brian nodded grimly.

"You know, I thought maybe you had killed Fiona to keep her from telling the administration at your school about the cheating, and I thought you killed Walt for actually reporting you," she said.

This time the look Brian gave her was one of red-faced embarrassment.

"Helping those kids cheat was probably the stupidest thing I've ever done," he said. "I loved Fiona. I may have disagreed about her choices in partners, but she was my sister. I never would have raised a hand to her. The same goes for Walt. He did exactly what he should have done. I miss them both terribly."

"I also thought Melody might have killed both Fiona and Walt," Daisy said.

"She's been catatonic since finding out about the affair. She left her kids with her mother and has been under psychiatric care since then. She couldn't have killed them. But I didn't feel comfortable telling you about her breakdown."

He pulled up to the curb next to Daisy's apartment. He offered to help her upstairs, but she insisted on doing it herself. She watched Brian drive away, then she made her way slowly up the three flights of stairs to the third floor. She opened the door and the first thing she saw on the foyer table was a huge bouquet of white daisies.

She looked at the card that accompanied them.

For my Daisy. With love, Grover.

She smiled. She was feeling better already.

And when he knocked on her door that night bearing gifts of a teddy bear and a box of her favorite chocolates, she kissed him tenderly, with the knowledge that although she wasn't going to forget Dean, she was ready to move on.

CHAPTER 64

The offices of Global Human Rights Journal were closed for several days the next week, but it wasn't long before both Jude and Daisy were ready to get back to work, researching and writing about issues affecting the whole world despite their physical injuries.

Jude assumed the role of editor-in-chief and Daisy became senior editor, stepping into Jude's former position. There was no doubt that Mark John would never be returning to work at the journal.

Jude took Daisy out to lunch on their first day back in the office together. Future stories were on the agenda, but the two women couldn't talk about work after everything that had happened.

"How did you know to call me when you saw that family tree?" Daisy asked.

Jude shook her head. "I don't know. Something just told me I shouldn't keep it to myself. You were the only person I could think of to call."

It's time for Jude to make a few new friends, Daisy thought.

"I want to introduce you to a good friend of mine," Daisy

said. "Her name is Helena and you'll love her. She's smart and full of fun."

Jude smiled. "I'd like that. I could do with some other friends."

Daisy sat back in her chair and regarded Jude fondly. "You know, this is not where I envisioned us ending up when I first met you," she said.

"You and me both," Jude laughed. She held up her glass of sparkling water. "Cheers, Daisy. Here's to a beautiful friendship."

THE END

ABOUT THE AUTHOR

Amy M. Reade is a cook, chauffeur, household CEO, doctor, laundress, maid, psychiatrist, warden, seer, teacher, and pet whisperer. In other words, a wife, mother, and recovering attorney. But she is also the author of The Malice Series (*The House on Candlewick Lane, Highland Peril,* and *Murder in Thistlecross*) and three standalone books, *Secrets of Hallstead House, The Ghosts of Peppernell Manor,* and *House of the Hanging Jade.* She lives in southern New Jersey and loves to read, cook, and travel. You can find out more about her books at https://www.amymreade.com.

Made in the USA
Monee, IL
18 July 2023